THE BROADBELTERS

The
Broad-
belters

Maxine Schnall

M. EVANS
Lanham • New York • Boulder • Toronto • Plymouth, UK

M. Evans
An imprint of The Rowman & Littlefield Publishing Group, Inc.
4501 Forbes Boulevard, Suite 200, Lanham, Maryland 20706
http://www.rlpgtrade.com

10 Thornbury Road, Plymouth PL6 7PP, United Kingdom

Distributed by National Book Network

British Library Cataloguing in Publication Information Available

Library of Congress Cataloging-in-Publication Data Available

ISBN 13: 978-1-59077-392-5 pbk: alk. paper)

♾™ The paper used in this publication meets the minimum requirements of American National Standard for Information Sciences—Permanence of Paper for Printed Library Materials, ANSI/NISO Z39.48-1992.

Printed in the United States of America

CONTENTS

THE BROADBELTERS

Chapter 1 The Author

DISORDER BLOOMED in the Ehrlich penthouse that Sunday morning like a neglected garden. Cigarette ashes, gauzy as the ghosts of dandelions, dotted the ankle-deep rugs. Smeared caviar crunched underfoot like fallen berries. Half-eaten canapes lingered, mossy, in the crystal ashtrays. Liquor glasses, planted like trees atop the antique coffee tables, took root and pushed out rings. And in the fireplace that stood like a great abandoned barbeque pit an unconscious go-go girl lay entwined with a sodden musician in a post-orgasmic funk.

It was the sound of the maid knocking over the andirons as she attempted to rouse the stuporous couple that awakened Bonnie Ehrlich. She was enwombed with her husband Manny in their vast canopied bed, gently vibrating on the motorized mattress. Stirring, she rubbed at her eyes with her fists and pried open the false eyelashes she had forgotten to take off the night before. She writhed and stretched in a kind of agonized slow motion. Then her lips parted, and her voice revved up in her throat and roared out of her mouth like an outboard motor.

"Who's making that goddam noise?"

"I am, Mrs. Ehrlich," the maid's dulcet voice purred, stealing in on little intercom feet. "Good morning."

"Go to hell," Bonnie muttered.

Wearily her head sank back onto the pillow again. She lay there for a while, narcotized with drowsiness. But she couldn't sleep. A vague uneasiness tugged at her, a troubling sense that something was wrong.

And then she remembered. The subliminal message bubbled through her hangover-harried brain and surfaced to consciousness with a sick thrust: her press agents had bombed out.

For almost two years now, ever since they had come East and settled in Manhattan, she'd been shelling out a fortune to the biggest p.r. firm in New York—Pitchman, Flackery & Hocum—to get her into Society. They had tried everything: big donations to charity, masked balls, cocktail parties, clambakes, lunches, junkets, cruises. There had even been a Big Game Hunt in Africa where she had narrowly missed getting her ass shot off by some near-sighted *shvartze* with a rifle.

And now the party last night with that crazy rock-and-roll group, Lysergic Larry and the Hallucinogens, blasting out everyone's eardrums and stinking up the whole apartment with their marijuana cigarettes. But the worst of it was Hocum himself, with his sad fag's face, coming over to her on the last break and saying, "I'm sorry, Mrs. Ehrlich. It's no use. We notified all the society editors, but the only reporter who showed up is from the *Yonkers Gazette*."

"You *schmuck!*" she all but screamed. "Do you think I'm paying you five hundred bucks a week to get me in the *Yonkers Gazette?*"

Hocum, flushed, spoke with that clenched control of someone desperate to avoid a scene. "But it's not my fault, Mrs. Ehrlich. All we can do is ask the press to come; we can't force them. The truth of the matter is you're just not . . . not . . ."

"Not what?" she demanded.

"Not newsworthy."

"Don't give me that crap!" she said, angrily gulping down the drink in her hand. "The women's pages are loaded with pictures of horse-faced bitches no one ever heard of before."

"Yes," Hocum said in a tone of exasperation, "but they're people with *old* money. They were *born* into Society. With the New Rich, it's a different proposition."

Bonnie put down her empty glass and snatched another drink from a passing tray. "And what about that seventeen-year-old Cockney scarecrow who's on the cover of every magazine?"

"That's something else. The kid has talent. She's a model."

"Model, my ass. She hasn't got a tit to her name."

"But at least she *does* something," Hocum insisted. He gesticulated imploringly. "You've got to understand, Mrs. Ehrlich. Today you can't make it in Society any more just by having money. To be one of 'The Beautiful People' you've got to *achieve*. You've got to *do* something."

Bonnie drained her drink and glared at him. "Don't worry, Hocum. I'm gonna do something, all right." She put her face close to his and waggled a finger at him, a triumphant look in her eye. "You know what I'm gonna do?" she asked.

He waited.

"I'm gonna fire you, you shithead! Right now!" she shouted.

Hocum blanched and backed away. "But really, Mrs. Ehrlich . . . "

"No buts about it." She pointed imperiously ahead of her and ordered, "Now get the hell out of here and don't come back."

Hocum slumped in resignation. "All right, Mrs. Ehrlich, if that's your decision," he said quietly. He drew himself up, determined to have the last word. "But remember, you won't get anywhere in Society unless you do something to deserve it." Then he turned and left with all the dignified sorrow of a grey flannel mourner who has just buried a deceased account.

Bonnie sighed, remembering the fiasco last night, and arranged the pillows behind her as she sat up in bed. Damn that fool, Hocum. What did he know? She looked down at her full aging showgirl's figure and patted herself appreciatively. At forty-one she was still a good-looking broad: "strikingly attractive in a direct, sexual way," as one of Pitchman, Flackery & Hocum's better press releases had described her. She was in the prime of life, with connections and enough money to buy and sell The Beautiful People. There was no reason, no reason in the world, why she couldn't break in.

Disconsolately, Bonnie toyed with the Gibraltaresque diamond on her finger and picked up an issue of *Modern Screen* lying on her night table. She leafed through the magazine absent-mindedly, too disturbed to concentrate on its malicious complexities. It rankled her to think, as she glanced at the pictures of the stars, that twenty years ago she, too, in her own way had conquered Hollywood. And yet today all of these people were celebrities while she, still hungering after fame, was never more unknown.

But she remembered, her mind hurtling down the long staircase of the years, how little she had started with in Hollywood—and how incredibly far she had gone. And even then, there had always been the grim dissuaders, the practiced dealers in discouragement, telling her it couldn't be done.

The receptionist at the Barracuda Booking Agency glanced at Bonnie's application form, then tossed it into the wire basket on her cluttered desk. "I'm sorry, kid," she said brusquely. "We ain't got any openings for eighteen-year-old girls with no experience." She turned back to her typing. "If anything turns up, we'll call ya."

"Yeah, sure," Bonnie said bitterly. "That's what they all say."

The receptionist glanced up sharply. "Whaddya expect?" she snapped. "Every week a hundred new faces pour into Hollywood lookin' for work in the movies. There must be a thousand extras tryin' out for the same job." Her head bent back to her typewriter. "You're wastin' your time, kid," she said sourly. "Go to Woolworth's. Maybe they need a counter girl."

Dejected, Bonnie turned to leave when Tony Barracuda, a dark, wiry man with oily skin and a sharklike smile, appeared in the doorway of his inner office. He watched Bonnie's rounded buttocks, underscored by her clinging dress, jiggle as she walked to the door.

"Hey, wait a minute, kid," he called out.

Bonnie stopped and turned around. She looked questioningly at Barracuda while his eyes flicked over her sensuously pretty face, her bombular bustline, her shapely calves.

"You're in luck today, kid," he said, smiling. "I just got an emergency call for a job, and I think you could handle it pretty good."

He walked over to Bonnie and handed her a slip of paper with an address scrawled on it. "Get over there right away and ask for Gus Panders. Tell him Tony Barracuda sent you."

Bonnie stared at him, transfixed by his messianic presence. At first she was able to manage only small grateful noises. Then, mastering her voice, she bubbled effusively, "Oh, thanks, Mr. Barracuda. I'll never forget you for this."

Barracuda nodded mechanically. "It's okay, kid," he said, his mind already on other things. Quickly he wheeled around and returned to his office.

Bonnie watched him retreat. Then, clutching the scrap of paper in her hand, she floated to the door on a raft of elation. The smirk on her face as she turned and glanced at the receptionist's bent head was superbly eloquent.

It was obvious Barracuda had made a mistake. For a half hour Bonnie trudged up and down Lankershim Boulevard, searching in vain for the address the agent had given her. Down the road she had passed Universal's lot and Warner's.

But here, where the busdriver had insisted she get off because it was the end of the line, there was nothing but a desolate, hilly tract of short, coarse scrubgrass.

Bonnie was on the verge of tears. She was hot and thirsty in the afternoon sunlight, and her feet ached unbearably in her platform, high-heeled shoes. In desperation, she planted herself in the middle of the road and flagged down a car heading back in the direction of Warner Bros. There was a "Studio Executive" sign, she noticed, in the windshield of the car.

The driver stopped, and Bonnie shoved her scrap of paper with the address on it under his nose. "Please, mister," she begged, "can you tell me where this is?"

The man studied the piece of paper for a minute, then shook his head. "No, I'm sorry," he said politely. "I don't know where that would come in. Is it a studio lot you're looking for?"

Bonnie hesitated. "I . . . I don't know," she said. "But I'm supposed to get in touch with a Gus Panders there."

The man's face broke into a smile of recognition. "Oho," he said. "Why didn't you say you were looking for Gus?" He stared at Bonnie with a curious, almost leering expression on his face. "That Gus sure knows how to pick 'em," he said softly, more to himself than to Bonnie.

Bonnie was enormously relieved. "Then you know where it is?" she cried hopefully.

"Who doesn't?" the man countered. "Hop in and I'll give you a lift."

He leaned over and opened the door for Bonnie, and she climbed in, gushing gratitude.

The man reversed the car, then drove a few miles down the road to a secluded pathway so narrow and overgrown with brush it was barely visible from the highway. He turned onto the path and followed its winding course until they came to a big gate. Instead of the usual uniformed guard stationed at most studio entrances, they were met by a blowzy, broad-hipped redhead in a flowered dress who sat in a booth, idly filing her nails. As their car pulled up, she slid off her stool and lounged in the doorway, grinning lazily at the driver.

"Knockin' off a matinee today, Sam?" she asked.

The driver laughed. "No such luck, Gertie. I'm just delivering a new girl." He turned to Bonnie. "Well, miss, here you are."

Bonnie thanked the man and got out. As the car drove off, she stood in the driveway and looked around her in qualmish bewilderment. Certainly this was like no studio lot she had ever heard of before. To begin with, there was no billboard out in front announcing the name of the studio and the picture currently underway. And up ahead there were no signs of shooting anywhere—no trucks, no camera equipment, no big lights, no actors in costume. All she could see was a vast desert of black asphalt stretching away endlessly. Like a parking lot, the asphalt was dissected into spaces by white lines, and there was a metal meter of some kind in each space. On the opposite side of the road, mushrooming carelessly from the grass, stood a building that looked uncannily like an overgrown rooming house.

Bonnie turned to the woman at the gate and fought to control the uncertainty in her voice. "Where the hell am I?" she asked.

The woman threw back her head and laughed. "Don't you know, honey?" she asked. "You're at Gus Panders' Drive-in Brothel, the only one of its kind in L.A."

Bonnie clapped a hand to her forehead. Of course! The famous "Auto-Erotica," as they called it in the trade. The exclusive outdoor whorehouse that catered only to the highest ranking studio officials—directors, producers, and the like. Mother! If she landed a job here as a car hop, the possibilities were unlimited.

"Where can I find Mr. Panders?" she asked anxiously. "Tony Barracuda sent me."

The woman pointed to the large building. "He's over there in the dorms, auditioning."

Her strength replenished by hope, Bonnie walked the short distance to the house and found Panders in his ground floor office. He was a sallow-skinned, gap-toothed man with a thin mustache and a lean, athletic body.

He listened patiently to the story Bonnie told him, a story depressingly similar, despite certain minor differences, to the hundreds he had heard before. She had been born and raised on New York's Lower East Side. Her mother had died in her infancy, and her father, a peddler, had been so poor he was reduced to renting his empty pushcart out for illegal assignations. She had gone to work on the pushcart as soon as she was old enough, but the lack of space had been ruinous and the business failed. She had seen her father die a penniless and broken old man, unaware he would some day be hailed as the founder of the modern motel. Badly shaken by the old man's death, she had been goaded into leaving New York by ambition and the local police force. She had come to Los Angeles to get into the movies, having crossed the country by befriending a series of railroad conductors and promising them unlimited access to her free lower berth.

"So you see," Bonnie concluded confidently, "I've had lots of experience in moving vehicles."

Panders leaned back in his chair. "Sounds good," he said laconically, "but you'll have to take our aptitude test." He pointed to an adjoining room. "Go in there and get undressed."

Bonnie found the room bare to the point of institutional drabness. It contained only a sequestered double bed and a big sign on the wall that bore the legend, "Curb Your Sex Drive at Auto-Erotica." The starkness of her surroundings intimidated Bonnie, but she gamely took off her clothes and lay down on the bed, assuming a carefully conceived erotic pose.

When Panders walked in he slowly circled the bed a few times, mentally checking out Bonnie's parts like a garage mechanic inspecting a car. Then he abruptly pulled down his trousers and got into bed with her.

She was concerned that her anxiety might impair her performance—after all, she had never had so much at stake before. But her fears were groundless. Panders was pleased, so unequivocally pleased in fact, that he told her she was hired on the spot. Cosseted into a rare mood of conviviality, he even stayed in bed with her for a little while, smoking a cigarette and talking. He told her about the wife who had left him years ago, about the children he had but never saw, about how he had buried himself in his work, hoping some day to break into the movies himself as a director.

When he ran out of words they fell into an awkward silence, staring absently at the only adornment in the room, the sign on the wall. Panders pointed to it casually. "How do you like our new slogan?" he asked.

"It's very clever," Bonnie said. Hoping to further ingratiate herself with a compliment, she asked, "Did you think it up?"

"Nah," Panders said somewhat reluctantly. "It's by some guy in our publicity department—Manny Ehrlich. He's from New York, too." He patted her playfully on the thigh and grinned. "They sure got a lot of talent in New York, don't they?"

Bonnie smiled. She thought she was going to like working at "Auto-Erotica" very much.

It wasn't until a year had passed that dissatisfaction began to burrow wormily into Bonnie's mind. Hard-working and aggressive, she had built up an enviable popularity. But taking stock at the year's end, she saw that except for a handful of worthless promises, she was still no closer to moviedom.

Then one hot summer night, when activity at the drive-in was even steamier than usual, the great Greek producer,

Hercules Fokis, pulled up in his black Rolls-Royce. Flushed with success and *ouzo*, he had come straight from a party celebrating the completion of his brilliant sex farce, *Tit for Tat*, in which Errol Flynn's portrayal of Tat was certain to win an Academy Award nomination.

Lowering the window, Fokis reached for the intercom speaker alongside the car and gave his order. "I want a nice young boy, about fifteen, sixteen years old," he said.

Minutes later the management regretfully informed Fokis that it was unable to fill his request. Infuriated, he roared off in a blind rage, gesturing obscenely with his hands and filling the air with strange-sounding Greek curses.

At that very moment Bonnie emerged, smiling, from a neighboring customer's car. The departing Rolls rushed at her malevolently, a black fury that struck her down and hooked her wide leather belt on the rear bumper. Her cries for help were drowned out by the noises of passion around her, and she found herself being helplessly dragged along in the wake of the speeding car.

It was not until he was halfway to Beverly Hills that Fokis sensed something was wrong. With growing irritability he realized his Rolls was not living up to its usual standards of excellence. "You can't trust these goddam foreign jobs," he muttered as he swerved off the road and stopped.

Disgusted, Fokis climbed out and lumbered around to the rear of the car which, through the mists of intoxication, he recognized as the source of the trouble. He stumbled over Bonnie's battered form with a shriek of startled horror.

"My God, lady!" he cried. "Who the hell are you?"

Dazed and bleeding, Bonnie murmured weakly, "A car hop." Then she lapsed into unconsciousness.

Alarmed, Fokis disengaged her from the fender and scooped her up in his arms. He looked down at her and shook his head in amazement. "What some broads'll do to meet a producer," he mumbled to himself.

He opened the door of the car and carefully set Bonnie down on the back seat. Then he got in front and sped away to a private clinic not far from his rented home on South McCarty Drive.

The sleepy-eyed doctor, roused from his bed, stood in the doorway, gaping. "Good Lord, Hercules!" he exclaimed. "What got into you?"

"I didn't touch her," Fokis snapped. "I just ran over her with my car."

Carrying Bonnie as if she were some nameless pestilence, Fokis stepped into the darkened hallway and followed the doctor as he led the way to his treatment room. Briskly, the doctor snapped on the lights and helped deposit Bonnie on the examining table.

While Fokis hovered squeamishly in the background, the doctor worked over Bonnie with grim efficiency. Finally, he straightened and faced Fokis squarely. His tone was grave but self-assured. "Well, I think we can save her. She must be made of iron."

Fokis looked relieved. "Whew!" he sighed. "That was a close one." He approached the table cautiously and peeked down at Bonnie's inert body. He winced. "Can you do anything about those skid marks, Doc?"

"Leave it to me," the doctor said.

Fokis grabbed his hand and pumped it gratefully. Vulnerability danced in his eyes for an instant before callousness chased it away. "Add her to my bill, Doc," he said gruffly as he turned to leave. "And when she's fully recovered, send her over to the studio."

Several weeks later Bonnie sauntered into Fokis' private office, good as new. Except for the faint odor of iodoform which still clung to her, every trace of the accident had disappeared.

She stood in the room, overawed by the fantastic opulence

that surrounded her on every side: the luxuriously plush car-
pet, the blinding chandelier, the stuffed heads of deceased
superstars mounted on the walls. Only in her most surrealistic
moments had she envisioned such magnificence.

Fokis, seated behind the felled redwood tree that served
as his desk, was enthroned on a dais several feet above floor
level. He pushed a button, and Bonnie felt the ground beneath her rise, lifting her in space until she stood opposite
Fokis, eyeball to eyeball.

He stared at her appreciatively for a moment, marveling at
her recovery. Then he casually plunged a hand inside her
blouse. "Feeling better, sweetie?" he inquired.

Bonnie nodded yes.

"That's good," he said. "You look wonderful. First rate."
He lifted his hand out of her blouse and continued to stare at
her thoughtfully. "Now I want to ask you a couple of questions," he said. "But I want the truth." He pounded on the
desk with his fist. "The truth! Is that clear?"

Bonnie, cowed and spastically nervous, nodded again.

"Fine," he said. "First of all, what I want to know is, can
you act?"

"No," Bonnie said in a small voice.

"Can you sing?"

"No."

"Can you dance?"

"No."

"Do you have any talent?"

"No."

The questions stopped. There was a long pause during
which Bonnie steeled herself for disaster. Then, to her astonishment, she saw Fokis' face break into a broad, rippling
grin. "Congratulations, sweetie," he said. "I think you got
what it takes to be a star."

He stopped smiling and suddenly slipped his hand under
her skirt. "But I have to make sure," he said, rummaging
around inside her panties.

After a while, a flush of pleasure spread across his face. He shook his head affirmatively a few times, each time with increasing conviction. Then came the pronouncement. "Sweetie, you're another Wanda Wunder."

Bonnie felt an icy shiver run through her. It was excitement and Fokis' platinum watchband pressing against her thigh.

To be another WW. A famous star, an idol, a legend. Fokis had discovered Wanda when she was an obscure stunt girl, grueling herself for a living. Attracted by her body bruises, he gave her a starring role in *Outhouse*, his shocking exposé of rural plumbing conditions. The script originally called for a sultry torch singer as the lead, but after seeing the first rushes Fokis insisted the character be changed to a deaf mute. It was a divine inspiration, traceable in part to the chance remark of his co-producer who said, "That broad acts like a deaf mute."

The picture catapulted Wanda into overnight fame, bringing her fifty-seven starring roles in three years. And in not one of them had she ever spoken a word. That Fokis was predicting a similar future for Bonnie seemed incredible. It was beyond any expectation she had dared harbor.

"Okay, sweetie," Fokis said, removing his hand from her panties. "As soon as the right part comes along, you'll hear from me. It may take a little while, but we don't want to waste someone of your caliber on any piece of junk. Meantime," he said, "there's an opening in the commissary for a waitress. Report for work on Monday."

He scribbled something on a piece of paper and handed it to her. She opened her mouth to speak but he had already pushed the down button, and Bonnie, weightless and lightheaded, was overpowered by a sinking feeling.

Bonnie lifted the heavy tray of dirty dishes and staggered under its weight. As she looked down at the nauseous *mélange* of ashes floating in coffee, lipstick-coated glasses, congealed fat, and soggy bread, wings of rage and frustration beat inside her. She was furious. Already a year had gone by, and Fokis was still stringing her along—climbing all over her at night and ignoring her in the daytime. She was sick of the filthy pig and his cruel, empty promises.

With a sigh, Bonnie put down the tray and picked up a fresh one. As she wove through the crowded lunchtime traffic, she caught sight of a man with a disturbingly familiar face. It was Manny Ehrlich. He had come to the studio for a promotion tie-in between "Auto-Erotica" and a new movie about Henry Ford's private life: *Back Seat*.

Manny felt Bonnie staring at him as she passed his table, and curiosity impelled him to stare back. When their eyes met, he was stunned by the impact. There was something about her that made his heart leap inside his chest and a rosy warmth kindle in his loins until it grew into a fiery red flame.

"Hey," he said to Bonnie, "you're spilling the borscht on my fly."

"Lay off, creep," Bonnie said. And in a sudden generic fury against all men, she emptied the soup bowl on his head.

Manny found her totally irresistible. Spitting out shredded beets, he was moved to produce one of his strikingly original turns of phrase. "Say, baby," he said, "don't I know you from somewhere?"

Bonnie eyed him warily. What was this joker up to? Was he another wise guy feeding her a smooth line just so he could get inside her pants? No, she didn't think so. He seemed strangely sincere, and he *did* look familiar. She could see that, even through the waterfall of borscht cascading down his face.

"Where're you from?" she asked, handing him a napkin.

"I'm with Gus Panders, in the publicity department."

Auto-Erotica! That's where she'd seen him before. He was the little guy who was always running around thinking up slogans.

The mere mention of her former employer brought nostalgic tears to Bonnie's eyes. "How . . . how're things at the drive-in?" she asked. "I used to work there, you know." "I thought I seen you before!" Manny cried. He finished wiping his face and stood up. Then he took the tray out of Bonnie's hands and invited her to sit down with him.

Bonnie hesitated at first. She had been burned once too often before. But as she looked at Manny she sensed a kindness in him, a genuine warmth that came through and won her over.

She sat down, and her defenses crumbled like an army in rout. Sobbing quietly and dabbing at her eyes with a napkin, she poured out her story to Manny. In halting phrases she told of Fokis' criminal negligence and of his cavalier treatment of her after the accident.

Manny was shocked and indignant. He couldn't bear to think of another man besides himself taking advantage of a woman.

"That dirty Greek bastard," he said when Bonnie had finished. "He'll have you slingin' hash 'til you're ninety."

Bonnie stared ahead forlornly as Manny lapsed into a thoughtful silence. Unaccountably, he felt a curious kinship with this girl. He felt bound to her in some mysterious manner as though they had been born under the same sign of the Zodiac, their destinies linked and intertwined, so that her future would be his legacy as well. He had to help her.

"There's gotta be an angle somewhere," he said softly. "If you know where to look, you can always find an angle." And he stared hard at the deep V neck of her uniform.

Suddenly he lifted his head and shouted above the clatter of dishes and the tintinnabulation of forks and spoons, "Jesus! I got it! Can't you see it, baby?" He hurled the words at her. "We'll sue!"

Bonnie looked at him with suspicions of lunacy. "Oh, sure," she said sarcastically. "Very funny. What are we gonna use for a lawyer?"

Manny smiled at her. "Dead Eye Deever," he said triumphantly.

"Are you nuts?" she laughed. "What makes you think he'd take the case?"

Manny looked smug. "Because I know Dead Eye, that's why. He goes in for this kind of thing." He saw the look of acid doubt in her eye, and he lowered his voice to a sly whisper. "Dead Eye's a steady customer at the drive-in, and I'm on real good terms with him."

"Even so," Bonnie said, her doubt softening a little, "how could we ever afford a guy like that?" Unconsciously, she had acknowledged Manny as a co-defendant.

"Don't worry. If Dead Eye smells big money," he assured her, "he'll work on a straight percentage. The sonofabitch may be crazy, but he knows how to make a dollar."

It was true. According to all the newspaper accounts, Dead Eye Deever was the richest, most famous lawyer around, as flamboyant outside the courtroom as he was in. He had descended full-blown on California from his native Texas, and he still dressed for the ranch: ten gallon hat, cowhide boots, bugged shoestring tie. Around his hips hung a brace of pistols, which he was known to shoot off almost as recklessly as his mouth. In demand all over the country, he flew to his appointments in his private custom-made plane, equipped with a well-stocked bar, five naked court stenographers, and a skywriting device that spelled out T-R-I-A-L as the heroic lawman winged his way through the air like a vulture.

Feared by people in high places, Deever was beloved by the common criminal. Murderers, thieves, pimps, rapists—they were all crazy about Dead Eye. He played to win; and as long as the stakes were high enough, no case, no matter how bad the stench, was offensive to him. As Deever himself once put it with an epigrammatic flair that was to immortalize him in the legal Hall of Fame: "Pay me a fat fee, baby, and I'll get you justice."

But money was by no means the only thing that mattered to Deever. He also thrived on scandal. All it took was a simple homespun theme of incest, sodomy, adultery, or fornication, to keep Dead Eye happy. Like an innocent child playing in the mud, he liked to wallow in slime simply for the pure, uninhibited joy it gave him, confident that sooner or later he could convert it into pay dirt.

"When he hears the facts, Deever'll take this case with bells on," Manny said.

Bonnie was beginning to believe him. Like a blind woman approaching a faith healer, she reached for his hands and held them. There was no bitterness in her voice now, only fervent hope. "God," she whispered, "if you can only pull this off, we'll be made for the rest of our lives."

Manny leaned forward and kissed her on the check. "You got nothin' to worry about, baby. I'll come through," he promised.

And Manny was as good as his promise. Some weeks later, on a quiet night at the drive-in, he watched Dead Eye's plane land at its special clearing place. While Dead Eye was busy, Manny slipped inside the plane unnoticed and waited in the front of the cabin. At a propitious moment he threw himself at the great man's feet and begged for his help. Dead Eye kicked him a few times with the pointed toe of his finely tooled leather boot while he considered the more salacious aspects of the case. "All right, son," he said finally. "You got yourself a lawyer."

On the day of the trial, the courthouse was a carnival scene. Public sentiment had been roused to a feverish pitch by the drama of the poor working girl battling for her life against the despotic tycoon. Dead Eye Deever was always a big draw, and with an inflammatory press solidly behind him, crowding out the national and local headlines for weeks with biased news of the trial, the turnout broke all records.

The mob, surging behind velvet ropes strung up outside the courtroom door, spilled down the courthouse steps and onto the sidewalk where many encamped, hoping for a seat after the noon recess. They had come prepared with sandwiches, Thermos bottles, and collapsible chairs, and they were looking forward to an entertainment that promised to be as emotionally titillating as any weekly soap opera.

Speculation on the outcome ran high. Bookmakers were offering odds on the verdict based on the amount of damages. Dead Eye was going for a million dollars plus a controlling interest in the studio, and while everyone hoped he would get it, the smart money said he would not.

The reason was Loophole Levin, counsel for the defense. Fokis had hired the one man capable of defeating Dead Eye. Reputed to be invincible, Levin had a record of acquittals that attested to his redoubtable chicanery and skill. An urbane, sophisticated Easterner in contrast to the more folksy Dead Eye, he was considered a master strategist. His favorite tactic was to bombard the courtroom with so much braggadocio about his own knowledge of the law that no juror would dare vote against him for fear of being thought a blockhead. To immutably establish his image as a legal giant, Levin had authored two sensational best-sellers tracing his career, *My Life as a Genius* and *The World's Greatest Living Lawyer.* No man in his own lifetime had ever been accorded a more impressive eulogy.

It was small wonder, then, that Loophole's arrival in the courtroom was greeted with a respectful, almost reverent silence. Scarcely a word was spoken as, with ramrod dignity, he took his place beside Fokis at the defense table and promptly began to comb his hair and apply his pancake makeup in preparation for the photographers.

Next to arrive was Bonnie, leaning heavily on Manny's arm and pitifully dragging a leg according to Dead Eye's instructions. Her customary decolletage was demurely covered by the collar of her white middy blouse and a five-inch neck brace.

Then the door flew open like a lava blast and in strode Dead Eye Deever, blazing away with both his pistols. Awestruck, the spectators gasped aloud in astonishment. As they sat watching the room fill with gunsmoke, a woman suddenly screamed and fell to the floor where she lay clutching her head.

"Dead Eye! Dead Eye!" shouted a bailiff, springing forward. "You've shot a lady's ear off!"

Dead Eye brushed him aside. "Don't bother me, son," he said. "Ain't you ever heard of a little thing called 'assumed risk'? I ain't liable." And to emphasize his point, he reached down and pinched the rump of the court stenographer, now fully clothed, trotting along beside him.

The earless woman was removed to a hospital for treatment, and matters settled down quickly. Solemnly ordering everyone to rise, the head bailiff called the court into session. The black-robed judge loped in from a side door and took his place behind his high desk. He called for the jury—eleven Mexican wetbacks and a cretin—and they filed in and sat down. Then the judge ritualistically banged his gavel, and the trial began.

It moved along swiftly until the climactic moment when Bonnie came forward and took the stand. She looked chastely pretty, her neck brace lending her the aura of a bruised flower. Her voice was tremulous and breathy, and she recounted her testimony in heart-rending, well-coached fashion. When she stepped down, pity hung in the room like a fog.

But Loophole counterattacked brilliantly. Keeping his best profile on view to the jury at all times, he hammered away at the plaintiff's case piece by piece like an expert chiseler, an epithet often applied to him. His oratorical outburst at the end of his cross-examination held the court spellbound. "I submit that these two people," he declaimed, carefully shooting his cuffs and pointing a stern finger at Bonnie and Manny, "are nothing but a pair of unprincipled opportunists, unconscionable scoundrels who have concocted this preposterous scheme solely for the purpose of defrauding my client, an innocent victim whose noble humanitarianism, creative genius, and steadfast dedication to his craft, are unparalleled save by my own."

Loophole took a deep breath and continued, "For a striking analogy to the circumstances at hand, I refer you to the famous case of Sunshine Village v. Bilker, which I describe in fascinating detail in my latest book, now on sale at all bookstores for only $5.95. In the chapter entitled 'How to Avoid Probation,' I have recounted in lucid and sparkling prose one of the most thrilling courtroom dramas of modern times, demonstrating how my skillful obfuscation of the issues resulted in a complete dismissal of all claims against Mortimer A. Bilker, a financial wizard accused of swindling thousands of aged and infirm senior citizens out of their life's savings. Not content to let the matter rest, I then instituted and won a remarkable countersuit for libel, clearing Mr. Bilker's name of any stigma and allowing him to expand his business operations unchecked."

Before concluding, Loophole turned and glowered at the jurors like a backwoods preacher evoking brimstone. "And if there is anyone in this room," he shouted, "who does not now understand why I am called 'The World's Greatest Living Lawyer,' which, incidentally, is the title of my new book, currently number one on every best-seller list in the nation, then that person is *ipso facto* totally lacking in any knowledge or understanding of legal principles, and his setting foot in a court of law is tantamount to a trespass."

Vaingloriously, Loophole returned to his seat at the defense table and Fokis flung his arms around him, pressing his tear-stained cheek against the lawyer's chest. Loophole disengaged him gently. "Please Hercules," he said, "you're wetting my silk and mohair hand-stitched lapel."

Shaken by Loophole's rhetoric, Bonnie glanced at Dead Eye Deever for reassurance. She was relieved to see how slyly confident he looked, like a poker player with a full house watching his opponent triumphantly set down three aces. It was obvious he had a card up his sleeve, and he was merely waiting for the right moment to show it.

The moment came. It was time for Deever's summation, and he rose and slowly approached the jury, whom he had carefully selected from over three hundred candidates. Observing that several of them were softly snoring on the back row, he cleared his throat like an alarum. With a dramatic flourish he loosened his shoestring tie, freeing his Adam's apple of the bugging device, and stretched out his arms in a gesture of supplication. Tears glistened in his eyes, and when he spoke his voice rang out with the clear, vibrant resonance of unbridled authority and passion.

"Ladies and gentlemen of the jury," he cried, "my client has been screwed!"

And he took his seat.

For a long moment the courtroom sat in stunned silence. Then, as one man, the crowd was on its feet, thundering an ovation. They shouted and whistled; they stamped their feet and they wept. For in Dead Eye's plea, so brief yet so eloquent, the people had recognized the age-old cry of wounded innocence. They had heard in its ringing tones their own outcry against the abuses of power, against the malevolent system that at one time or another had tricked and defeated them.

And they sensed, too, that in just five simple words Dead Eye had given them a legal masterpiece. It was the shortest summation on record—and the most accurate.

As Bonnie, flanked by Manny and Dead Eye, made her way out of the courtroom, the mob swarmed over her, pressing against her to offer congratulations and shake her hand. People thrust papers at her for her autograph, and a tearful woman pressed a bouquet of roses into her hands. The photographers shouted her name again and again, begging her to smile. The crowd was paying its homage, and Bonnie rejoiced and reveled in it, deeply savoring that first heady, addictive draft of fame.

The next day the newspapers bannered the verdict in headlines an inch tall:

HEAD OF UNITED MISALLIANCE OUSTED
Fokis Loses Control of Studio and $1 Million

For Bonnie and Manny the victory was mind-boggling. After settling with Dead Eye, who contented himself with a cool half million, they still had $500,000 in cash and a controlling interest in the studio worth God knew how many millions. They were, as Bonnie had envisioned, set for life; and it was hard to believe that only a few short years ago they had been at bedrock, clawing their way into the sunshine with nothing to go on except their own wellspring of guts and venality.

When Manny asked Bonnie to marry him, the tenderness of her answer brought tears to his eyes. She said, "I want a mink coat with horizontal stripes, a villa on the Riviera, a penthouse apartment in New York, a chauffeur-driven Cadillac, a private plane, a yacht, forty-five in help, and no children." If ever Manny had heard a protestation of love, this was it.

Even by Hollywood standards, the wedding was a spectacularly lavish affair. Over two thousand guests attended. They were all extras hired by Manny at $1.10 an hour, exquisitely gowned and outfitted by the wardrobe department. Champagne flowed freely from magnificently carved fountains marked "imported" and "domestic." The ballroom bloomed with a profusion of fresh flowers and exotic plants, some of them rumored to be man-eating. Overhead flew hundreds of gold-dipped pheasants that were later caught, melted down, and served under glass for dinner. Nelson Eddy and Jeannette McDonald sang a medley of love songs, accompanied by the

London Philharmonic Orchestra, specially flown in for the occasion.

At the first strains of the Wedding March, the bridesmaids, twelve strippers in delicate pink ostrich feathers, began advancing down the aisle as if it were a runway.

Then, as the orchestra reached a booming crescendo, the room darkened and a spotlight heralded the arrival of the bride and groom: Bonnie and Manny seated in regal splendor atop a live Afghan camel. Never before had there been anything to approach it—an authentic double hump ceremony!

Bonnie closed her copy of *Modern Screen* and put it back on her night table. With a wistful little sigh, she dismissed the glories of the past. What did they matter now? She had to face the truth. And the truth was that for all their apparent success, for all their money and connections, the Ehrlichs had never achieved the status of celebrities.

Not that Manny hadn't tried. He damn near bankrupted the company trying to make her a star. All those goddam movies she made—and every one of them a box office bomb. It was the critics, the bastards. She still remembered the things they said about her: "the acting style of a sequoia"; "excrementious performance."

She'd never admit it, but it was a relief when the other executives paid Manny off to stay the hell out of the studio. Who cared if it was a slap in the face? A little more money never hurt, and ten years of traveling to the best resorts hadn't been so hard to take either.

Besides, Manny hadn't lost anything, really. He'd been smart enough to hold onto his stock in the company even if he couldn't work there. That Manny! You had to hand it to him, the little genius. Everything he touched turned to money. Like *Satyr*, that girlie magazine he'd invested in with Sydney Crotchnick turning out to be a goldmine, and all that real estate he owned.

But what was the good of having so much money if you

were still a nobody? If no one knew you were alive? God damn it! She was sick of reading about all those socialites, and not one lousy word about her. She was as good as any of them. She didn't need their finishing schools and the rest of that phony bullshit. It was all a cover-up, anyway.

Well, they could ignore her all they wanted. She'd make it in spite of everyone. But how? For two years she'd been rotting away in New York, and all she heard from that turd Hocum was "do something." Do what, she wanted to know. Do what?

She turned and looked at Manny sleeping peacefully at her side, the embroidered ME on his silk pajamas staring up at her with childlike simplicity. He was a sturdy Volkswagen of a man whose rich bronze patina spoke of endless sunnings in Miami Beach and Palm Springs and whose eyes, a pair of round brown headlights, and softly curving nose hung low over a bumper of shiny chromium teeth. He was not much to look at, but to Bonnie, no matter how much she abused him, he was everything. They were so much alike that sometimes it must have seemed to her they were emotional Siamese twins, fused at some focal point in their central nervous systems, with the personality of one constantly flowing into that of the other. She loved him with a love they both knew was beyond the corrosion of time and change. Oh, there had been other men since Manny, and she would probably go on having them. But that was only sexual curiosity. The others were mere dalliances, random threads in the fabric of her life; Manny was the fiber itself. He was her mainstay, her support, her unassailable buttress. And no other man, however young or beautiful, could do for her what Manny did, be for her what he was.

She reached over and gently butted him in the groin with her knee. "Come on, Manny," she prodded. "Wake up."

He awoke with a startled grunt. "Jesus, Bonnie, that don't tickle," he said gruffly. His voice was sleep-roughened, and his speech ungrammatical.

"Listen, we've got to do something," she said urgently.

He groaned. "Oh, God, Bonnie! Not so early in the morning."

"No, no. That's not what I mean. I'm too upset to even think of sex now."

For Bonnie that was a critical statement. Manny sat up in alarm. "What is it?"

"I fired Hocum last night. It's ridiculous. We've been pouring money down the drain and not getting anywhere."

"Oh, that's all," he said in relief. "So what's the big deal? We'll hire another p.r. firm tomorrow."

"It won't help," she said despondently. "The trouble is, Hocum's right. Nobody gives a damn about you unless you're important. And the only way I can be important is to do something big, something dramatic."

"Like what?" he asked.

"That's just it," she wailed, her hands pressed to her forehead. "I can't think of a goddam thing."

Manny looked at her and sighed. Why the hell couldn't she be happy? Nothing he gave her was ever enough. She was always pushing, always reaching for the brass ring. She wouldn't be satisfied until the whole world loved her.

"Well," he said reasonably, "there's gotta be an angle. If you know where to . . ."

"I know, I know," she said impatiently. "If you know where to look, you can always find an angle. But where?" she demanded.

The expression on her face was so comically beseeching that Manny laughed. He shook his head in wry amusement. "You're such a nut, Bonnie," he said. "Honest to God, someone oughta write a book about you."

Bonnie stared at him. Her eyes widened until they seemed almost to usurp her face. "Did you say a book?" she asked breathlessly.

He nodded.

"That's the smartest thing I ever heard!" she cried. "Why

didn't I think of it myself?" She clapped her hands together excitedly. "A book's the answer, all right. But not a book *about* me. That's not it. What we want," she exclaimed in triumph, "is a book *by* me—a best-seller."

He looked at her in amazement. "Are you nuts?"

"Not as nuts as you think," she answered with a sly smile. "What's so hard about writing a book? It's not like acting, where they all watch you work and they know right away if you don't have it. But with a book . . ." she grinned impishly ". . . who knows what? You can always hire a ghost-writer to do it for you."

Manny's amazement metamorphosed into mild interest. "And supposin' you hire someone," he asked cautiously. "What would you write about?"

She frowned for a moment, and then her face broke into a bright smile. "What could be better?" she asked. "I'll write about the broads I used to know out in Hollywood."

He shook his head. "No good," he said. "Polly Adler done that bit years ago."

Bonnie laughed. "Not those broads, stupid. I mean actresses I knew when they were starting out. The ones who made it big."

"That's different." He mulled the idea over in his mind. "There's always a market for that kind of stuff," he admitted, "but how do we know it'll be a best-seller?"

"We make it one," she answered emphatically. "We go to a publisher and we offer to kick in a little money for advertising and promotion. We make sure he gives it a big push coast to coast. We pull out all the stops. And if it's dirty enough, it can't miss."

"How do you know the publisher'll go along with you? Most of those phonies are too arty-farty for business deals."

"For money you can always get," she answered axiomatically. "Ask your friend Sydney Crotchnick. He knows a lot of people in publishing."

"You think Sydney's so easy to get ahold of? He's a big shot nowadays."

"Big shots have phones. Give him a call," she said impatiently. Manny's resistance was beginning to annoy her. "Look, what is it with you? Don't you think the book is a good idea?"

"I don't know," Manny said doubtfully. "First we gotta hire a ghostwriter. Then we gotta help pay for advertising and promotion. Plus whatever else the publisher sticks us for." He wrinkled his brow. "This thing could cost a fortune."

Bonnie's face contorted in anger. "I don't give a damn how much it costs," she yelled. "I want it. It wouldn't cost more than another diamond necklace, and I'm tired of diamond necklaces. I want *this!*"

Manny saw that intransigent look in her eye he knew only too well. He felt his will come unglued with an inner twinge, and he knew he would give in. Why fight it? What difference did it make really? A villa, a yacht, a piece of jewelry, a best-seller—they were all the same. As long as it kept her quiet.

His voice sagged with resignation. "Okay, Bonnie. You win. If it's a bestseller you want, you'll have it."

"Oh, Manny," she burbled, her face melting into a golden smile. Joyfully, she threw her arms around his neck and rewarded him with a syrupy, voluptuous kiss.

As he lowered the straps of her nightgown, Manny observed with delight that the dollar sign on Bonnie's left breast, that charming little birthmark of hers which had so endeared her to him when he first saw it, was all aglow like the sunlight.

Chapter 2 The Publisher

MANNY WHISTLED admiringly under his breath. Enthralled, he and Bonnie stood on the sidewalk at 74th Street and Lexington Avenue and gazed up at the towering skyscraper. Their eyes dwelled on an outsized marquee which proclaimed:

SHMEER BUILDING
THE HOME OF BEST-SELLERS

"Crotchnick sure knew what he was talkin' about," Manny said approvingly. "This guy's got some setup."

"I'll say!" Bonnie agreed. "It's another Radio City Music Hall."

In a rush of expectancy, they approached the glassy entrance and spun through the revolving doors. The interior lived up to the promise of the façade: vast, ultramodern, pretentious, gaudy, and garish. "Gorgeous," Bonnie murmured as her eye swept over the splashing fountain, set like a jewel in a mounting of plastic shrubbery and metallic futurist sculpture.

In the plush anteroom to Shmeer's private office they were greeted by the receptionist, a curvaceous blonde in an upper-thigh-length dress, who offered them seats and said throatily, "Mr. Shmeer will be with you in a minute."

They waited, flipping through magazines and lost in private speculation. Bonnie's mind was filled with wild conjectures about publishing requirements, and Manny's about whether the receptionist wore anything under her dress.

A voice cut into their thoughts. "Mr. Shmeer will see you now," the receptionist throbbed.

They jumped up and followed her—Manny as closely as possible—down a long corridor to a room identified as the "Executive Office." The receptionist opened the door, and out flew the tail end of Mr. Shmeer's telephone conversation:

". . . full of crap as far as I'm concerned, and you can tell the goddam bastard to go screw himself!"

Manny winked at Bonnie. "How do you like that?" he whispered. "This guy speaks our language."

Shmeer banged the phone into its cradle. He looked up as the receptionist drew the Ehrlichs into the room, announced them, and quickly retreated. Smiling affably at Bonnie and Manny, Shmeer pushed back his chair and came out from behind his desk. Short, chunky, and balding, with a brisk manner and a pair of dangerously shrewd eyes, he looked like a fat, hairless fox.

"How d'ya do," he said, extending his hand to each of them. "I'm Dave Shmeer." He motioned them into chairs and retreated behind his mammoth desk once more. Clasping his hands in front of himself judiciously, he asked, "Now what can I do for you?"

Manny glanced at Bonnie, then spoke up. "It's like this, Mr. Shmeer. My wife wants to write a book, a best-seller. But she . . . uh, well . . . she ain't exactly a writer." He smiled awkwardly. "So we need someone that maybe we could work a deal with."

"I see," Shmeer said, nodding. He studied Bonnie's chinchilla coat and hat, her Dior suit, her alligator bag and shoes, her Elizabeth Arden glamour, and her arsenal of jewelry. "Something tells me you came to the right place."

"Oh, that's wonderful!" Bonnie exclaimed happily. There was a look of inordinate relief on her face. "I was so afraid,

Mr. Shmeer," she confided shyly in a voice soft with respect, "that you only took people who could write."

Shmeer laughed. "Why would I want to do that?" he said. "Those literary types are murder—prima donnas who fight with you over every comma." He shook his head. "No. In my firm, we only take people who *can't* write. That way, they do what we tell them and they never give us a hard time."

Bonnie smiled. "You don't have to worry about that with me, Mr. Shmeer. I'm very cooperative." Her smile broadened. "You might even say I'm a pushover."

"That's what I thought," Shmeer said agreeably. He cleared his throat. "Well, now that we have your qualifications, tell me, what is it you want to write about?"

"Hollywood," Bonnie answered quickly. "I'd like to do an inside story on some of the people I knew out there in the forties." She averted her eyes modestly. "I used to be an actress, you know. And my husband was a studio executive."

"Hmmmm," Shmeer said, thinking. "A show biz story. I guess you want to do an exposé type thing on their private lives—tell all about their sex habits, alcoholism, drug addiction—stuff like that?"

"That's the idea!" Bonnie cried excitedly. "How did you know?"

Shmeer smiled indulgently. "I have a sixth sense in these things." Sobering, he said, "There's one big trouble with this kind of book that we have to watch out for. I take it these people you want to write about are still living. Are any of them famous personalities today, easily recognizable to everyone?"

Bonnie's face fell. She hadn't even thought about libel laws.

"Well?" Shmeer persisted. "Are they famous?"

"Y-yes," Bonnie stammered. "I'm afraid they all are."

"Wonderful!" shouted Shmeer. "We only want dirt about Big Names. We can't sell scandal unless it's about a public figure. Who wants to read about the *yenta* next door? Besides," he added slyly, "using real celebrities saves us the trouble of making the characters up."

"But won't they sue?" Manny asked.

"You must be kidding," Shmeer said. "They're grateful as hell. Where else could they get publicity like that for nothing?" He gave a reassuring smile. "Anyway, to be on the safe side we always change the names and issue a disclaimer."

Bonnie was surprised. "Is that all you have to do?"

"Well, it's a little more complicated than that," Shmeer said, "but we'll get to that part later." He smiled knowingly. "First things first."

With the deftness and dramatic flair of a surgeon making the first incision, Shmeer opened his desk drawer and took out a notebook. "Right now the question is," he said gravely, "if we have room for you on our list."

"It must be a helluva long one," Manny ventured.

"No, that's just the point," Shmeer said. "We only put out five books a year. But we give each one the big build-up. Our motto is 'Every Book a Blockbuster.' You see," he explained, "we have it down to a science. We avoid anything highbrow, no matter how good it is; and we stick to the surefire stuff like religion and sex. This year," he added, "we're dropping religion."

While Bonnie and Manny waited breathlessly, Shmeer consulted his notebook. "Let's see. First we have *In Bed With the Boston Strangler—An Intimate Autobiography* by his ex-wife. Then we have *Oui, Oui*, the memoirs of a bisexual French courtesan. Then we have *The Life and Times of Marilyn Monroe* as told by her gynecologist. Then we have *A Comprehensive Guide to Successful Adultery* by a team of anonymous contributors. And then we have . . ." He stopped. "No, that seems to be it. Well," he said with the air of a lifeboat captain addressing a shipwreck survivor, "it looks like we have room for you."

Bonnie was ecstatic. "Oh, that's marvelous!" she cried. "What do we do now?"

"Now," said Shmeer, "we discuss terms." He took a brochure from his notebook and slid it across the desk to Bonnie and Manny. "As you can see," he said, pointing to the brochure, "we have three classes of blockbusters: first class, known as 'runaway'; second class, or 'sensational'; and third class, called 'hit.' With the first class, or 'runaway,' you get a guaranteed minimum of forty-eight weeks on the Best-Seller List with at least 50 per cent of that time as Number One. You get the full-scale . . ."

"Wait a minute," Manny cut in sharply. "You mean the Best-Seller List is fixed?"

Shmeer looked up, faintly annoyed at the interruption. He picked his words carefully. "No, I wouldn't say it's 'fixed,' exactly. We just manipulate it a little, that's all." There was a crafty look in his eye. "We're very friendly with some of the bookstore personnel who do the reporting. Then, too, our advertising program is pretty persuasive in some quarters." He lowered his voice. "As a last resort," he confided, "we get the book on the list by hiring people to buy it."

Shmeer turned back to his brochure and picked up without skipping a syllable . . . "publicity and promotion treatment with interviews on every TV and radio talk show in the country having over twenty-five listeners. You get ads, reviews, or write-ups in every major newspaper in the nation and a hundred and two magazines including *Life, Time, True Detective, Feed Age, Good Housekeeping, McCall's, Ladies' Home Journal, Soybean Digest, Soil and Water Magazine, Look, Newsweek, The New Yorker, Lawn Equipment Journal, Saturday Review, Saturday Evening Post, The Medical Missionary, The* . . ."

"Okay, okay," Manny said with a wave of his hand. "You convinced me. We always like to go first class anyway." An apprehensive look crossed his face. "But give it to me straight, Shmeer. How much is all this gonna cost me?"

Shmeer stared at him, a look of indignant surprise on his face. "Why, it won't cost you a penny," he declared huffily. "We're not a vanity house. We're a reputable publisher."

Manny was incredulous. "Are you sayin' you'll pay for everything—all that advertising and stuff—all by yourself? You don't expect me to contribute?"

Shmeer smiled disarmingly. "Not one red cent. We take care of the whole works. We pay the printing costs. We pay for the book's campaign, usually around $70,000. And we pay the author," he nodded magnanimously toward Bonnie, "a $20,000 advance."

Manny gaped at him open-mouthed. His voice squeaked with disbelief. "You mean to tell me you're gonna pay us $20,000, and we don't have to give you nothin'?"

"That's right," Shmeer laughed. "Nothing except the book, of course." He paused for a moment and added, "And one other thing."

"Aha!" Manny cried triumphantly. "I knew there was a catch." He eyed Shmeer warily. "Okay, what is it?"

The words were an ultimatum. "A guarantee of a movie sale for one million dollars. We split it fifty-fifty."

Manny slapped his forehead. "You're outta your head!" he exclaimed. "What movie studio in their right mind would shell out a million bucks just for screen rights?"

Shmeer's gaze was penetrating. "Yours," he said levelly. His fox eyes narrowed. "I understand from our mutual friend, Sydney Crotchnick, that you own fifty-one per cent of the stock in United Misalliance. That means the board of directors is virtually under your thumb." He smiled cagily. "If you want to buy a property, who's to say no?"

"Yeah, but they'll get suspicious," Manny protested. "I haven't been active in the company for years."

"So this year you'll be active."

"But a deal like this could hurt the studio," Manny insisted.

"So you'll take a tax loss." Shmeer grinned. "With me you'll make money coming and going."

"Well, it sounds good," Manny admitted, "but . . ."

"Good?" Shmeer thundered. "It's fabulous! There's nothing to think about." He leaned forward and adopted a tone of pure reasonableness. "Look, let me explain how we operate here. We don't want to make a few dollars on a book—we want the author and publisher to get rich. So we go after the big dough, the sale of the subsidiary rights. And we split the income down the middle." He turned a few pages of the brochure in front of them and pointed to a chart. "Now with your wife's book, there'll be enough notoriety in it to bring close to $500,000 for paperback rights, $250,000 a piece. Unfortunately, it'll be too dirty to sell to the book clubs because they cater to the family trade." Shmeer shrugged indifferently. "But who cares about that," he asked, a slow smile spreading across his face, "when we've got a guaranteed movie sale of a million each?"

Manny smiled back. "I think you got a winner here, Shmeer."

"You know I do," Shmeer said. He rubbed his hands together vigorously. "Now let's see," he murmured, jotting down figures on a note pad. "We'll put out a first printing of 300,000. Then we'll . . ."

"A first printing of three hundred thousand?" Manny was amazed. "How will you get that many books into the stores?"

"It's easy when you have an aggressive sales force like ours," Shmeer said proudly. "Our men are highly trained in all the latest marketing techniques. We even have a couple of karate experts on the team." He grinned. "You may not believe this, but one of our district managers is a Black Belt man."

"Jesus," Manny said.

Shmeer turned to Bonnie. There was an expression of self-reproach on his face. "You know, we haven't even touched on what *you'll* get out of this proposition," he said, "and that's the most important thing of all. For you this book will be only a means to an end. It's the vehicle we'll use to shove you on the public as an exciting new personality." He pointed at her dramatically. "By the time we finish, you'll be a topflight star in your own right. You'll be in demand all over the country for paid personal appearances and speaking engagements. You'll be asked to cut records, write beauty columns, endorse . . ." he gave her a swift appraisal . . . "brassieres and other commercial products."

Bonnie was staring at him, her lips slightly parted, a look of unendurable yearning in her eyes. "Oh, God, Mr. Shmeer," she blurted. "That's what I've been dreaming of all my life. You don't know what it would mean if you could do that for me."

Shmeer reached over and patted her hand encouragingly. "Of course we'll do it for you. That's all part of the package." He flashed a confident smile. "And we'll groom you for the part perfectly. The minute you sign our contract, you'll be enrolled in TRAP, our Television, Radio, and Personal Appearance course. You'll be coached and drilled on every phase of appearing in public by a staff of experts. And you can take my word for it," he said convincingly, "we know our stuff around here. Look what we did for the Swinging Nun."

Bonnie's eyes popped. "You mean you helped *her?*"

"Whaddya mean 'helped' her," he laughed. "We *made* her." He leaned back in his chair, remembering. "When she came to me she was still Sister Mary Margaret Vermicelli, a little nothing nun, a complete nobody. She was teaching in a convent school, and I don't think she had two rosary beads to click together. But the funny thing was," Shmeer recalled with amusement, "she loved to dance. I mean *really* dance. One day she confiscated a kid's transistor radio and taught herself the twist, the frug, the jerk, the monkey, and the Watusi in six minutes flat."

"Not bad," Bonnie allowed.

"When the Church got wind of it," Shmeer continued, "they sent her down to Greenwich Village to dance in the coffee houses. They figured she'd bring religion to the Beats and the Hippies. But instead," Shmeer chuckled, "she got turned on. She couldn't stop dancing to save her soul. It got so bad, the other sisters at the convent began calling her 'Our Lady of Perpetual Motion.' "

"That's a good one," Manny guffawed.

"Anyway," Shmeer said, "somebody told me about her, and I smelled a good thing so I took her out to lunch at Twenty-One. She embarrassed the hell out of me by getting up and frugging between courses, but I got her to agree to write her story for us—our way."

"Wasn't that *God Is My Hang Up?*" Bonnie asked.

"That's right," Shmeer replied, flattered by her recognition. "I don't have to tell you what a big one that was. But it was nothing short of a miracle how we took that pale, skinny Vermicelli dame and turned her into one of the hottest properties in show business today." He removed a *Variety* clipping from his notebook and handed it to them. "Look at the rave reviews she got when she played the Copa. They called her the 'slickest act since J.C. Walked on Water.'

"And look at this shot of her when she played the Palace," Shmeer said, sliding a glossy photograph toward them. "Her two-week run broke all attendance records. And her finale— God, you never saw anything like it. It brought the house down every night." He closed his eyes and dropped his voice to a husky, theatrical whisper, recreating the scene for them:

"A drum rolls, the lights go down, and a single spotlight beams on the center of the stage. She stands there, all alone, her pale skin gleaming whitely around her sequined Cross-shaped pasties. The house is hushed, waiting. Then the orchestra leads into a folk-rock version of 'Nearer, My God, to

Thee.' She begins to belt the lyrics. Her voice is pure and clear as a trumpet, and the words pour out of her, reaching down into the audience. 'Though like the wanderer . . . hey, hey, hey . . . The sun gone down . . .'

"Then the chorus slowly files onto the stage—twelve former Mister Universes in black tights, their St. Christopher medals shining on their bare chests. A huge wooden cross sways in their arms as they chant a low, rhythmic accompaniment. Solemnly, they lift the Swinging Nun onto the cross and nail her to it. But her voice keeps throbbing out the words, strong and clear as ever—'Darkness be over me . . . My rest a stone.'

"They start to carry her off the stage in a somber processional. The orchestra swells to a crescendo. But her voice reaches out over it, leaping, climbing, soaring to a big finish— 'Yet in my dreams I'd be . . . Nearer, my God, to Thee . . . Nearer to Thee.'

"The stage is bare. It's very still for a moment. Then the house explodes with cheers, louder than peals of thunder. The crowd keeps calling 'Sister! Sister!' But the spotlight is off. The house lights come up. The show is over."

Shmeer opened his eyes and slowly shook his head, a visionary clearing his mind. "Lord, she was beautiful," he said.

"Never mind the raves and the pictures," Manny said, his eye fastened on the *Variety* article. "Look what it says about her income: 'From her TV series, record royalties, club dates, and movie lucre, the Swinging Nun earned over $6,000,000 last annum.' " Manny returned the clipping to Shmeer and said, "Give me your contract. I wanta sign it right away. I'll call the studio in the morning and tell 'em we just acquired the rights to a great new book."

"Now you're talking," Shmeer said. He produced the papers, and Bonnie and Manny signed them while Shmeer beamed. "Smartest move you people ever made," he said. "You'll never regret it."

As they shook hands all around, Bonnie's smile congealed

on her face, and her eyes rolled in panic. "Oh, my God," she gasped in the throes of a sudden realization. "How will I ever write this frigging thing?"

"Now, now," Shmeer clucked reprovingly. "You're such a worrywort." He pulled a pamphlet out of his notebook and handed it to her. The title of the pamphlet was *Basic Formulas of Blockbuster Writing*.

"To be honest with you," Shmeer said, "it really doesn't matter what's inside the book or even whether the people read it or not. As long as we get enough of them talking about it, we'll be okay." He smiled at Bonnie and pointed to the pamphlet. "Anyway, if you follow the instructions under 'Runaway: Nonfiction-disguised-as-fiction,' you'll have no trouble. After you get started, just mail us in the required amount every two weeks."

"Will it be all right," Bonnie asked, "if I get someone to help me?"

"By all means," Shmeer replied. "It makes it a lot easier for us if the sentences are grammatical." He raised a warning finger. "But stay away from established writers—they'll charge you an arm and a leg. What you need is one of those 'literary specialists' who advertise in the newspaper. Those poor *schnooks* are so hard up for money, they'll write anything."

"That sounds like a good bet," Manny said.

"But in any case," Shmeer informed Bonnie, "you have nothing to worry about. No matter how miserable your material is, we can always whip it into salable shape. Our editorial staff is the finest in the country—absolutely crackerjack." He snapped his fingers. "Tell you what," he said. "We're all through here, so how about coming down with me and meeting our editorial department before you go?"

"Oh, I'd love to," Bonnie said with honest enthusiasm. She was growing tired of Shmeer's showmanship and wheeler-dealerism, so reminiscent of all the Hollywood sharpies and slick businessmen she had known in her lifetime, and she was anxious to meet a more cultivated prototype of the publishing world.

Shmeer sprinted from behind his desk and ushered the two of them out of his office, down the long corridor, and into a waiting elevator. They got off at floor "E," the firm's designation for Editorial.

"Follow me," Shmeer said as he led the way down another long corridor to a door marked "Private—Personnel Only." With an exaggerated flourish he opened the door, and they all stepped inside.

The room was awesomely white, sterile, and devoid of any sign of humanity.

"For God's sake!" Bonnie exclaimed. "There's nothing in here but machines!"

"That's right," Shmeer said proudly. Like a field marshal inspecting the troops, he surveyed the monolithic row of machinery, whirring and clicking with computerized precision. "We're the only publisher in the world with a fully IBM editorial system," he announced. "You won't find another one like it anywhere."

Shmeer walked up to one of his gigantic machines and stroked it lovingly. "This one handles all our 'historicals.' " He pointed to its next-door neighbor. "That one does all our 'contemporaries.' " For a moment it looked as if he might put his arms around the machines and hug them. "You have no idea the headaches and aggravation these babies save me," he said gratefully. "No hair splitting, no indecision, no margin for error. All you have to do is tell them what you want, feed them your material, and out comes a blockbuster every time."

Shmeer reached for a phone on the wall and said, "Send Reynolds down here right away. I want him to meet some new clients." Turning to Bonnie and Manny, he explained, "Reynolds is our chief programmer in charge of data processing. He's the one who'll be handling your book."

Within minutes a tall, owlish looking young man, slightly

stoop-shouldered, walked into the room. He wore thick, horn-rimmed glasses and carried a clipboard.

"Hello, Mr. Shmeer," he said deferentially.

"Reynolds," Shmeer said, "meet Bonnie and Manny Ehrlich. Mrs. Ehrlich is going to do a 'contemporary' for us on the Hollywood scene. She'll have her first assignment ready by the end of next month."

"That's fine," Reynolds said with a bob of his head and a smile that was so quick it was almost a grimace.

"Now that you're here, Reynolds," Shmeer said, "how's *In Bed With the Boston Strangler* going?"

"Moving along well, sir." Reynolds referred to his clipboard. "Chapter Seven is just about finished. We have only another 1,653 words to go, approximately 431 of which will be four-letter Anglo-Saxon."

"Good, good," Shmeer said. "All right, Reynolds. That'll be it for now. You can go."

"Thank you, sir." Reynolds turned to Bonnie and Manny and gave them another fractional smile. "Nice meeting you. 'Bye now," he said, already backing out of the room.

After Reynolds had left, Shmeer encircled Bonnie and Manny in his arms and beamed at them with paternal benevolence. "Well, folks, how do you like 'the house that Shmeer built'? Not bad, eh?"

Manny's voice brimmed with respect. "I gotta hand it to ya, pal. You sure run a tight ship."

"Thanks," Shmeer said. He dropped his arms and began walking them to the door. "Now you two run along and enjoy yourselves. It's been a big day." He took Bonnie's hand and pressed it warmly. "After all, my dear," he said, his face spreading into a creasy grin, "you just became an author."

Chapter 3 The Collaborator

THIS IS IT, Bonnie said to herself when she saw the ad in the Sunday *Times:*

PROFESSIONAL WRITER, accepts assignments, fiction or nonfict. Expert ghost writer, any topic. Reasonable. Percy Bysshe Hack, 359 W 57th St., CO 5-5884.

She called the number immediately, and a young man answered on the first ring. In a voice that spoke precise diction and sounded painfully eager to please, he agreed to come out that very afternoon to discuss Bonnie's book project.

In person he was exactly what she had expected: a gangly post-graduate type, mid-twentyish, attractive in a seedy intellectual way. He wore a faded corduroy jacket, smelled of ink and pipe tobacco, and had the pale, faintly befuddled look of a thinker.

"Thank you, sir," he said as he perched himself on the edge of a plush Louis Quatorze chair and gratefully accepted the drink Manny thrust into his hands. His eyes were busily darting about the room, plainly bedazzled by the rich appointments.

Retreating to the sofa, Manny sat down beside Bonnie and together they ogled Hack with undisguised curiosity.

"Now supposin' you tell us something about yourself, kid," Manny suggested.

"Yessir," he answered obligingly. Balancing his battered attaché case on the table of his knees, he launched into a catechistic recital of his credentials. "I received my B.A. in English from N.Y.U. in 1964 and my Master's degree in eighteenth-century Japanese literature in '66. I spent the year of 1965 in Japan on a foundation grant studying haiku at Kyoto University."

"Studying what?" Manny asked.

"Haiku." He waited for a sign of recognition. "The Japanese verse form," he prompted. He looked anxiously from one blank face to the other and coaxed, "You know, those little three-line poems Hirohito writes?"

They nodded uncertainly.

Hack plunged on helplessly, the way he sometimes did when he was having one of his more garrulous sessions with his psychiatrist. "My thesis entitled *Eastern Literature: A Study in Wordlessness* was put out by Bleak House last year, and I'm currently working on a volume of original haiku poetry with a contemporary outlook." He sipped his drink nervously. "I haven't been able to interest a publisher in it yet, but I'm quite optimistic."

"That's good," Bonnie said. "You don't get anywhere without confidence." She studied his frayed shirt collar and in the loose threads, like tea leaves, she read the letters l-o-s-e-r.

"When you're not workin' on this Jap poetry," Manny asked, taking up the cudgel, "what do you do for a living?"

Hack lingered uncomfortably over his drink for a while before answering. "I'm employed by Won-Ton Food Products in their fortune cookie department," he said finally. He went on hurriedly, "But it's only a temporary job until I get established as a poet. I'm afraid the opportunities for someone of my inclinations are rather limited."

"Well, no one starts at the top," Bonnie said encouragingly. "We all have to put in our time somewhere."

Hack repaid her with a shy smile. "You're very understanding," he murmured. He put down his drink and opened his worn attaché case, removing a bundle of papers. "Would you like to see some samples of my work? Of course, this is only a smattering, but it'll give you an idea of the kind of thing I do."

He handed the papers to them, explaining, "You'll notice I write my poetry under the pen name Nona. Actually, that's just my fortune cookie name—Anon—spelled backwards. It's not authentic, but it does sound rather oriental, don't you think?"

"It sure beats Percy Bysshe Hack," Manny said, taking the papers and shoving them under Bonnie's nose. "How did you ever get a moniker like that?"

"It's my mother's fault," Hack said, retreating to his chair. "She wanted her children to be writers, so she named us after famous poets to inspire us." He gave a rueful little laugh. "I've got a sister named Edna St. Vincent Lieberman."

"Is she a poet, too?" Bonnie asked.

"No, but she was a top copywriter for a big advertising agency. She's the one who wrote "Burn My End" for Brite-Lite Candles." He smiled. "Now she's married to an accountant in Bensonhurst, and she's president of her Great Books group."

"I see," Bonnie said, swallowing her rising gorge with a gulp of her drink. She glanced down at the first page of Hack's material, her eye skimming over the lines:

Moonlight waterfowl
    Glides across the still river . . .
    Condemned: pollution.
             * *
Withered yellow leaf
    Floating in a rain puddle . . .
    Alas! Clogged drainpipe.
             * *
Giant silver crane
    Carves a jagged line of sound
    Hark! Con Edison.

* *

Shimmering snowflake
When I see you dance outside . . .
Chills and a virus.

* *

Expect a big boost from someone close to you in a public
vehicle.
Your fear of high places will be conquered in a fall.
Guard your important secret until the wedding.
Get the lead out.

"I like the last one," Bonnie said smiling. "It comes right to
the point." She put the papers aside and looked at Hack,
twisting her lips in thought. She spoke hesitantly, the effort at
delicacy taking its toll. "Your work has . . . style . . . and all
that, but to be honest with you, I'm not sure you're the right
one for the job. You see, the kind of book I'm doing is . . .
well . . . it's . . ."

"It's one of them big sexy shockers about Hollywood,"
Manny cut in. "Plenty of dirt and four-letter words and all
that crap. You don't do that kind of stuff, do you, kid?"

Hack, embarrassed, peered into his drink as if something
had drowned there. "I don't normally tackle that kind of
thing," he said slowly. "It's not the sort of work I particularly
relish. In fact, you might even say it goes against my grain."
He looked at Manny soberly. "But I'm sure I could do it if I
applied myself. How much does the job pay?"

"Ten thousand bucks."

"I'll apply myself!" Hack exclaimed, bolting up in his seat
like a projectile. "Ten thousand dollars! My God!" He closed
his eyes for a moment and dreamily pictured a hundred
chubby little green-faced Ben Franklins fighting and shoving
their way into his wallet. He thought of the bills he could pay,
the luxuries he could afford, the joy of quitting his job with
Won-Ton. He opened his eyes and looked at them implor-

ingly. "This assignment is right up my alley. I know I can handle it beautifully. You have no idea what a perfectionist I am, even in things I dislike."

Bonnie glanced at Manny and tried to read his expression, but his face was impassive. "Well, I don't know . . ." she said doubtfully.

Desperation goaded Hack into instant salesmanship. "Look, I've got an idea," he said. Frantically seizing on familiar snatches of mail order language, he made his pitch. "Why don't you let me do a sample chapter for you free of charge? If you're not completely satisfied with it after looking it over, you'll be under no obligation to hire me."

Bonnie thought it over. "That sounds fair to me," she said, nodding. She turned to Manny. "What do you think?"

"Go ahead," he shrugged. "Give it a whirl. What have you got to lose?"

"Oh, thank you!" Hack cried. He whewed his breath out in a thick gust of relief. "Please forgive me if I sound overanxious," he said contritely, "but at the moment I'm going through a terrible financial crisis." He pressed a hand to his forehead. "If only I could discuss it with my psychiatrist."

"Why don't you?" Bonnie asked.

"Because he won't see me any more," Hack said glumly. "I owe him too much money." He looked despondent. "The ironic thing is, it was my analysis that threw me into debt in the first place."

Manny smiled. "Then you're better off not seein' him for a while," he said. "It'll give you a chance to get back on your feet."

"Yes, I suppose you're right," Hack replied vaguely. He finished his drink and abruptly composed himself, assuming a brisk, businesslike manner. "Now about this book you're doing, Mrs. Ehrlich. Do you have an outline or any specific plan in mind?"

Bonnie smiled. "Mr. Shmeer, my publisher, thinks of everything. He gave me a little pamphlet that tells you exactly how to write the whole book step by step."

"He did?" Hack's eyes bugged in astonishment. "I've never heard of that before. It sounds incredible."

"No, it isn't," Bonnie assured him. "I've got the pamphlet right here." She pointed to it lying on the cocktail table in front of her. "Do you want to take a look at it?"

"Yes, I'd love to." He got up and came over to the sofa, approaching the pamphlet cautiously. "Have you read it yet?" he asked Bonnie.

"No," she said. "I thought it would be best if we all studied it together. That way, you could explain it to us." She patted the sofa beside her. "Here, have a seat."

Obediently, Hack deposited himself next to Bonnie and watched her affix a pair of granny glasses incongruously on her nose. Then she centered the pamphlet between them, and Hack leaned over her left shoulder while Manny leaned over her right. Like moons colliding, their three heads knit into a tight ball of concentration as they bent to study *Basic Formulas of Blockbuster Writing*, looming up at them apocalyptically from the cocktail table.

Hack was the first to finish the Introduction. He was unable to control his amazement. "Fantastic!" he exclaimed. "This is a whole new concept in fiction writing. The Pre-fab Novel. It's like those oil paintings you do by coloring in the numbered sections."

Bonnie stopped reading and looked up. "You mean paint-by-numbers?" she asked.

"Exactly! Only this is 'write-by-numbers.' Actually," Hack said, reconsidering, "it's more like those kiddies' puzzles where you connect the numbers to make a picture. The numbers are the scenes, and the connecting line is the narrative." He shook his head in disbelief. "I've never seen anything like it."

"Well, now that you're seein' it," Manny said, "where do

we go from here? We're doin' a 'Runaway,' 'Nonfiction-disguised-as-fiction,' ya know."

Hack, fascinated, turned to the appropriate section. Like an English teacher conducting a subrosa seminar, he proceeded to read aloud:

HOW TO WRITE THE NONFICTION-DISGUISED-AS-FICTION BOOK

This is perhaps the easiest genre to master since it requires virtually no gift for invention on the part of the author. The only skills needed are an ability to mishandle facts and a knack for passing hearsay off as the truth.

The following are the three simple steps to this technique:

1. *Select the right characters and events.* You must always start with *factual* characters and events that are well-known to millions of people, hopefully most of them potential readers.

Try to pick subjects whose fame is *tainted* in some way, preferably by unwholesome sex practices, crime, or depravity. Remember: *mess attracts mass.*

Some examples of successful subjects are:

A famous female singer whose emotional instability (alcoholism, drug-dependence, overeating) has made her private life a shambles

An eccentric millionaire industrialist and movie producer whose involvement with Hollywood beauties and life as a recluse have made him a national enigma

A Latin American diplomat and lover whose political dealings and marriage to the world's wealthiest woman have made him a romantic figure

The actress daughter of a middle-aged leading man who achieved stardom by posing for nude film scenes and magazine centerfolds

A study conducted by a team of sex researchers whose findings shocked the country

2. *Distort your characters and events slightly.* It is essential to make deliberate errors occasionally in the biographical and historical facts. These "little white lies" will give your work a twist of originality and, more important, they will enable you to escape suit for libel.

Remember, a party can't sue if the book is *not* about him.

Some practical examples are:

If the subject's second husband was a movie director, change him to a dress designer (*Over the Rainbow* was not about Judy Garland)

If the subject lived in the Dominican Republic, change the locale to South America (*The Conquistadors* was *not* about Porfirio Rubirosa)

If the subject conducted his sex research at Indiana University, change it to a college in Wisconsin (*The Latham Report* was *not* about the Kinsey researchers)

(Note: Always mention the name of the subject you are *really* writing about somewhere in the book.)

3. *Spice your characters and events with gossip.* You must make common rumors come alive by giving detailed fictional versions of them. It is immaterial whether there is any credence to the rumors or not—*you* must make the reader believe them.

Some helpful examples:

If a character purportedly spent some time in a

sanitarium, give a harrowing account of the character receiving hydrotherapy in a mental institution

If a character is an heiress rumored to have
bought her husbands for their sexual prowess, create
a "dowry" scene in which her fiancé bargains with
her lawyers by revealing a gift from the heiress in-
scribed with a testimonial to his studmanship

When writing about a tycoon who supposedly
transacts business deals in hotel lavatories, create a
men's room scene in which millions of dollars ride
on a bargainer's ability to overshoot the next urinal

This, in essence, is the Nonfiction-disguised-as-fiction
technique. Simply bear in mind the fundamental approach—"blur the facts and blow up the rumors"—and
success will be yours.

Hack paused and glanced, in turn, at Bonnie and Manny.
"Well, is all that sufficiently clear?" he asked.

They nodded a dual assent.

"All right, then," said Hack. "We're ready for Basic Formula Number One. Here it is." And he read:

$$R = PS^3$$

Manny looked up, puzzled. "That's Greek to me. What
does it mean?"

Hack scanned the glossary in the back and explained, "It
means you get a runaway by promoting a sensational sex story
that has a *shtick*." He turned quickly to the back of the book
again. "I'm afraid I can't find what a *shtick* is," he said in a
troubled voice.

"That's easy," Manny laughed. "Who don't know what a
shtick is? It's a gimmick, a trick. Something about a guy that
makes him different."

Hack nodded slowly. "I get it. In other words, it's a piece of
business." He thought for a moment. "Like in *Caine Mutiny*,

for example, Captain Queeg's *shtick* was rubbing the two steel balls together all the time."

Manny chuckled. "Sonny, if that guy had steel balls . . ."

"Oh, shut up," Bonnie said irritably, poking an elbow into Manny's ribs. "We're getting off the track." She was all business now, a chromeplated lady executive. Frowning at Formula One, she said, "Now let's break this thing down." She held up a finger. "The promotion's Shmeer's job, so we don't have to worry about that." She held up a second finger. "The sensational thing'll be the way we give the inside dope on the Hollywood stars. Sex," she smiled, "that's no problem." She threw all her fingers up in the air. "But the *shtick* —what'll we do for that?"

Hack pursed his lips. "As I see it," he said thoughtfully, "the *shtick* ought to be some hang-up the stars have in common, some abnormality they secretly indulge in . . ." he stabbed at the air ". . . like kleptomania, maybe."

"Like what?" Manny asked.

Hack broke it down into syllables. "Klep-to-ma-ni-a—you know, compulsive stealing."

Manny shrugged. "What's so unusual about that?" he asked. "Everyone steals."

"Yeah," Bonnie said. "That's no good. It's gotta be something sexier."

"Sexier, eh?" Hack stroked his chin. "Well, it shouldn't be too hard to come up with a decent sexual aberration. Let's see," he said, professorially ticking them off on his fingers, "you've got voyeurism, transvesticism, masochism, flagellation . . ." He stopped. "Flagellation!" he cried excitedly. "That ought to be great!"

"Flaja who?" Manny asked. "Talk English, kid. We don't understand them fancy terms."

Hack took a deep breath. "Flagellation," he explained patiently, "is the practice, in abnormal eroticism, of beating someone to produce sexual excitement."

Manny looked perplexed. Then his face broke into a knowing smile and he said, "Oh, you mean them *meshuggenehs* with the whips."

Hack nodded. "That's the idea. We'll make the main characters a bunch of showgirls who love being slapped around in bed."

Bonnie stiffened and sat up, a pointer sniffing game. In a state of quivering equipoise, she cocked her head and then began to nod it vigorously. "I like it!" she cried. "It's exciting, sophisticated!" She searched for the right word. "It's got class."

Hack was delighted. "I was hoping you'd go for it," he said happily. "You see, I was looking ahead to Formula Two, here." He pointed to the pamphlet and read:

$$C = 2BS + N$$

A *c*hapter equals two *b*edroom *s*cenes plus *n*arrative. He smiled broadly. "The flagellation *shtick*'ll give us great bedroom scenes—real knock 'em down, drag 'em out affairs."

Bonnie nodded her head emphatically. "I love it," she said. "It's marvelous. The kind of thing the public'll eat up with a spoon." She hesitated. "I'm just wondering, though. What do you think we ought to call it?"

Hack seemed taken aback. "Gosh, I don't know." He thumbed through the pamphlet. "I don't think they cover titles in here."

The question plunged the three of them into deep thought. Minutes crept by inexorably, the clock-ticking silence finally shattered by Manny's eager shout, "I got it! I got it!" He looked at them intently. "How about *If You Can't Melt 'Em, Belt 'Em*"?

Bonnie made a sour face. "No, that's awful," she said in disgust. "It's too long."

Another silence ensued, this time broken by Hack. "*Whiplash*"? he suggested.

"Terrible," Manny said. "They'll think it's about insurance claims."

"*Carry a Big Stick*"? Bonnie offered.

"Too political," vetoed Hack.

Bonnie tried again. "How about *Beaten Babes*"?

Hack looked up sharply. "I think you're on the right track now. You've got the feeling we want, but it has to be a little more dramatic. More important sounding. Something like . . . *The Babe Beaters*." He shook his head negatively. "No, that's not it either."

In the spurt of meditative silence that followed, Hack turned to Manny. "Didn't you say something about a belt before?"

Manny nodded.

"Belt's good," Hack said. "It gives the idea of flagellation. Now, let's go back. We had 'Babe' . . . *The Babe Belters* . . . no, no, almost, but not quite . . . um, ah, . . . not the 'Babe' but the . . . *The* . . . *The* . . ." The words pressed against his teeth, pushing, straining, struggling, until they burst through his lips with urgent natal force ". . . *The* . . . *The* . . . *The Broadbelters*."

There was a moment of terrible quiet.

Then Bonnie was crying ecstatically, "Oh, that's it! That's it! It's perfect! It's the absolute end!" She beamed at Hack. "Percy, you're a genius!"

"It ain't bad," Manny admitted. He rolled the name out luxuriously. "*The Broadbelters*." He nodded slowly. "It has a nice sound to it, like a geography term or somethin'."

"I'm glad you like it." Hack smiled, flattered in spite of himself. He seemed relieved, flecked with a light froth of confidence. "This book's going to be a lot easier than I'd imagined. The pamphlet's a Godsend." He gave Bonnie and Manny a back-slapping look. "We've already got the basics settled. From here on in it ought to be a cinch."

"Maybe it's a cinch for you," Bonnie laughed, "but me, I still wouldn't know where to begin."

Hack riffled through the pamphlet, pausing to consult the glossary for the meaning of such terms as DWC (dirty word count) and SPA (semisensational piece of action). He put the pamphlet down and smiled at Bonnie reassuringly. "There's really nothing to it," he said. "Just decide who the main characters will be—I guess three or four will be plenty —and then jot down everything you know about them."

Bonnie smacked her lips hungrily. "Everything?"

"Right. Everything—how they looked, talked, their fights, their love affairs, the things they did to get to the top—the works." He spread his arms wide. "I'll need all the incidents and anecdotes you can remember."

Bonnie leaned her head back. "You mean, like the time Kim Howard . . ." She stopped and laughed. "Kim Howard," she said sarcastically. "When I knew her, her name was Alma Gluckhaus." She resumed. "Anyway, like the time Kim's husband came home unexpectedly and caught her in bed screwing Eddie Can . . ."

"No, no, not now," Hack put in hastily, blanching a little. "It's important that you take your time so you don't forget anything. Spend a few weeks, a month if you have to, and jot down all the facts for me."

Bonnie looked worried. "If I have to write it," she said, "it may take forever."

"Well, tape record it then. That ought to be easy enough. Then mail the tape to me at my home, and I'll take it from there."

"Good. I'll get it to you right away," Bonnie said. She looked at Hack anxiously. "How fast can you do the first chapter?"

"I don't know. It all depends on how long it is. Why? Do you have a deadline?"

Bonnie nodded, worried. "I promised Shmeer I'd get my first installment in by the end of next month. He's got to feed it to his machines."

Hack gulped. "His machines?"

"Yeah, you should see 'em," Manny said. "He's got these great big computers instead of editors. It's fantastic!"

Hack looked stunned. "I'll bet," he said weakly. He shook off his daze and pulled himself together. "I'll put a rush on it then, but I can't work too fast. After all, I've got to do a good job."

"Just make it dirty enough," Manny said, "and it'll be A-1."

"I'll do my best," Hack said earnestly. He picked up the *Blockbuster* pamphlet. "Do you mind if I take this home with me? I'd like to read it over and prepare myself."

"Sure," Bonnie said. "You're the one who'll be needing it."

Hack rose to leave, carefully tucking the pamphlet inside his attaché case. "I suppose I might as well be going," he said. "There's nothing more we can do today, it seems to me."

"Nah, I guess not," Manny said, getting to his feet. He fished a fifty dollar bill out of his pocket and slipped it inside Hack's palm as he shook hands with him. "Here, you better take a little expense money." He grinned conspiratorially. "In case you wanna do some research for the book."

"Oh, thank you, Mr. Ehrlich," Hack said. "That's most generous of you, really."

Bonnie, too, stood up to say goodbye. She grasped Hack's hand in both of hers and flashed him a warm smile. "Good luck, Percy."

He smiled back at her, wordlessly nodding a reply. Then he turned to leave and Bonnie, in a sudden and rare display of coyness, reached up and brushed his cheek with a demure, motherly kiss.

Chapter 4 The Beginning

"You're right on time," Bonnie said as she opened the door for Hack and led him into the apartment. She looked wickedly chic in swirling hostess pajamas that were so diaphanous it was impossible to tell where the pajamas ended and the hostess began. And whenever she moved, her heavily perfumed body seemed to stir up unseen clouds of fragrance.

Hack sniffed uncontrollably as she glided past him. "I didn't want to keep you waiting," he said. "I knew you'd be anxious to see the material."

"You bet I am! I've been on pins and needles all day." She smiled at him. "This is worse than having an affair."

Hack laughed nervously, a short loud noise that sounded like a seal's bark. He followed Bonnie into the living room and settled himself on the sofa while she poured drinks.

"How's Mr. Ehrlich?" he asked politely.

"Oh, he's fine. He's almost as excited as I am." She brought the drinks over and sat down beside Hack, peering at him intently. "Now tell me, was my tape all right? How did you make out?"

"Great. I think you'll be very pleased," he said, taking a sheaf of typewritten pages out of a manilla envelope and setting them before him. He gave her a congratulatory smile. "Your tape was amazingly complete. If I were you, I'd destroy it as soon as the book is finished."

Bonnie laughed. "You'd be surprised what you can remember when you set your mind to it." Eying the typewritten pages, she asked, her voice hushed with awe, "Was it hard?"

"Oh, no. It was really quite simple. After my initial revulsion wore off, I even enjoyed it in a feeble-minded sort of way."

"Did you have any problems?"

"Well, I was a little worried at first about not having a style, but I followed the pamphlet's advice—I stole one from a leading best-seller writer. I guess that does make the book rather derivative," he added ruefully, "but I didn't have much choice under the circumstances."

Bonnie leaned forward and patted his shoulder. "I'm sure you did a swell job."

"I hope so," Hack said, catching a giddying glimpse of her breasts as she bent over him. He hurried on. "I've got about twenty pages here. Do you want to hear them?"

"I'm dying to!"

"Okay. But before I begin, let me explain the general scheme of things. The way I plan to do it, the book will be divided into sections dealing with your three main characters, whom I've called Phyllis, Carol, and Tina. All the chapters in a section will have the date at the top." He grinned mischievously. "That's a little trick the pamphlet suggested to cut out a lot of boring exposition."

Bonnie nodded, rigid with anticipation.

"Here we go," said Hack. He cleared his throat, picked up the papers, and began.

O N E : *October,* 1946   Phyllis

The lush flanks of Los Angeles opened up beneath the descending plane like a woman's legs. Phyllis Benson peered out the window at the purple hilltops turning blood rose in the falling sun. She watched the day die just as her marriage had died on the white Nevada desert at Reno.

As the plane dropped, Phyllis tightened the seat belt across her firm, flat belly. A deep sigh escaped her, lifting the jetting rocks that were her breasts. She dreaded having to face the horde of reporters and photographers lying in wait for her below. But somehow she'd manage to smile and wisecrack and hide the tears that blurred in her eyes behind her dark glasses. That's what you had to do when you were Phyllis Benson, the biggest star in Hollywood. The distant, unattainable Goddess.

The plane touched down, and Phyllis felt the jolt in her gut that meant home. Home. A forty-room mansion in Beverly Hills with every room empty. So different from the small cottage in Malibu where it all started. The night she came off the set of Windfall. Only three years ago.

It was after ten that night when Michael Dalton, Windfall's director, wearily dismissed the cast and crew. In the dressing room with the other extras, Phyllis took off her bit-part costume and slipped into a sweater and a pair of slacks.

Outside, in the cool night air she broke her long-legged stride at the studio gate. She dipped into her handbag for a cigarette and put it between her lips.

The rasp of a match came from behind her and a flame sliced the darkness. "Here, let me light that for you," a man's voice said.

The man held the flame close to Phyllis's face, illuminating the honey blond hair, the high brow, the green eyes that glowed beneath their ice.

Phyllis caught the man's hand and held it. His warmth surged through her fingers. "Thanks," she said. She stared into his face across the flickering light. Her eyes widened, but she said nothing. She blew out the match and waited.

He took the cigarette from her and dragged deeply on it.

The smoke burned into his lungs. "I've got my car here," he said. "I'll drive you home."

He gave the cigarette back to her and took her arm. Again she could feel the warmth of his hand pouring into her through her thin wool sweater.

Silently she followed him out to the car. They climbed into the big convertible and he threw it into gear.

"Malibu," she said softly.

The car gobbled up the miles to the beach house. He pulled up at the cottage and cut the motor. His voice was a harsh, urgent whisper in the night. "Let's take a swim."

They got out of the car and walked down to the beach. It was a clear Pacific night. The moon hung in the black fur sky and the surf pounded wildly against the shore.

He watched while she shed her clothes with a fluid motion and stood naked before him, her golden body luminous in the dark. He cupped his hands around her breasts, and the nipples burst into his palms. Then, all at once, she leapt on him like a catamount, clinging, moaning, and writhing, her legs fastened around his, her tongue searching his mouth, her frantic fingers ripping off his trousers to clutch at his core.

"I think I'm a Lesbian," she said.

"No," he answered. "You're just shy."

Gently he lowered her onto the sand. She clung to him and pulled him down on top of her. She drew him inside her voraciously. He felt her body begin to move beneath him in a wild, frenzied rhythm of its own, rising and falling, rising and falling. Deeper and deeper she dragged him into her white-hot furnace until, with shuddering sighs, they were both consumed.

She lay in his arms, spent, exhausted, and he stroked the cool, soft flesh of her shoulder. His lips pressed against her cheek. "Don't worry," he said. "It'll be better next time. You have to learn to let yourself go."

"I know," she said. She turned her head toward him and her eyes met his. "How did you know about me?" "I saw you yesterday, sitting at the soda fountain in Schwab's. I knew you were the one." "The one," she repeated. Her eyes grew large. "Who are you, anyway?" He took a card from somewhere inside his shorts and handed it to her. She looked at it in the moonlight. It was an expensive card with a name engraved on it—Bryan Young. And in the left-hand corner there were the words: Talent Executive, International Pictures.

TWO : December, 1943

When Bryan walked into the board meeting the next day, the gloom was so thick you could cut it with a knife. Max Segal, president of the studio, had called the emergency meeting because Windfall was in trouble—serious trouble—and so was the studio.

Segal sat slumped at the end of the long mahogany table, his pudgy fingers clamped around a cigar. "I knew that Carol Gordon CHOLERYEH would be poison," he was moaning, "but what else could we do? She fixed herself up with a three-year contract, so she had us by the BAITZIM."

Dalton, the director, sounded desperate. "But how can we go on like this? You said yourself, every day she stays out on a drunk it costs us thirty-five thousand. And when she come in, she's so bombed out on pills, it takes fifteen retakes to get one scene."

"You think I don't know it?" Segal shouted. "You think

it's not eating out my NESHUMEH?" Angrily he slammed his fist on the table. "Already the production schedule's a month behind. A hundred and forty grand I'm pissing away in stand-by salaries alone while that fat SHIKKER is laying home with ice packs on her KOPF."

He chewed on his cigar savagely and punched the papers in front of him with his finger. "Her last two pictures were box office smashes, GOLDENNEH GLICKEN, and we lost a million bucks on each one."

Crawley, the treasurer, took off his thick glasses and rubbed his eyes. "If we junk the script now," he said morosely, "we'll have to pay a half million in costs to Warner's alone. The stockholders'll never stand for it."

A door opened, and a thin, tight-lipped man came in. He returned to his empty seat and sagged into it.

Segal scowled at him. "Well?"

The man shook his head negatively. "Nothing doing. MGM can't give us Hayworth. They've got her scheduled for something themselves."

"What about Barbara Stanwyck?"

"I just hung up on her. She says she wouldn't touch the part with a ten-foot pole. Not enough prestige."

"Prestige the UMGLICH wants!" Segal screamed. He smashed his cigar into an ashtray and buried his head in his hands. "OY VAY ISS MER. We're dead," he wailed.

"No we're not," a voice said calmly. It was Bryan's, the first time he'd spoken since the meeting began. He was leaning back in his chair with a peculiar smile on his face.

Segal lifted his head from his hands and glared at him. Smart aleck GOY. What did that SCHNORRER know besides screwing COORVEHS all night on the beach? "So NU, genius, talk," Segal snapped.

Bryan put a cigarette in his mouth and lit it. He dragged deeply. "It's very simple," he said. "We suspend Carol, and we put in an unknown for one-tenth her price."

"*This you're telling me?*" *Segal glowered.* "SCHMUCK! *Unknowns I don't need. It's box office we got to worry about.*"

"*You'll still have box office,*" *Bryan said.* "*Remember, we've got Rod Talbot playing the male lead. With a little rewriting, we can build his part up and play Carol's down so anyone can handle it.*"

Segal was beginning to look interested. Maybe the SHLEMIEL *wasn't so dumb after all. They were paying Talbot good enough money. Let the* GONIF *earn it for a change. He peered at Bryan intently.* "*So tell me,* GANSE MACHER, *you got somebody in mind maybe for Carol's part?*"

Bryan inhaled on his cigarette and let the smoke come out slowly. "*There's a bit player we could try—Phyllis Benson.*"

"*I know the one,*" *the director said.* "*The tall blond with the big tits.*"

Bryan nodded.

"*She's a good looker, all right,*" *Dalton said,* "*but can we take a chance on a complete unknown?*"

The secret smile came back to Bryan's lips. "*I guarantee she'll be great. I've already tested her.*"

"*Where,* K-KNOCKER," *Segal threw in,* "*on the beach?*"

A wave of laughter rippled through the room, cracking the tension in half.

Segal took a fresh cigar from the humidor and put it between his lips. He leaned back in his chair and stared at the wall for a moment. Then he sat up abruptly. "*So get your asses moving already,*" *he shouted.* "*Send for the writers to change the script. Start shooting the exteriors. Get out the releases on this Benson* NAFKA. *And send a wire to Carol telling her not to report. That's it.* FARTIG."

Segal watched them all scurry out like mice. He struck a match, held it to his cigar until it lit, then threw the match in the ashtray. He reached for the telephone and picked it up. "*Get me Harry Cohn at Columbia.*"

He drummed his fingers on the table, waiting for the click.

"Hello, Herschel? I got good news for you. We can loan you Carol Gordon until April. I'll let you have her for a hundred and seventy-five grand . . . what? . . . a hundred and fifty, then . . . Oh, all right, a hundred and a quarter, final. Believe me, you MOMSER, it's a steal."

THREE : *April*, 1944

Phyllis walked across the giant sound stage into the camera and Dalton shouted "Cut! Wrap it up!" Windfall was finished.

Instantly the stage turned into a madhouse, with everyone applauding, laughing, and talking at once. Champagne flowed, sandwiches were brought in, and a band began to play. The mood was festive, and the air crackled with an unmistakable electricity, the lightning flash that signals the birth of a star.

Phyllis stood back and took it all in. She watched the mob milling around Dalton, fawning over the director so he would remember to use them on his next picture. She smiled at the way Lila Reed, the pert brunette who'd inherited Phyllis's bit-part, wriggled her way through the crowd and planted a kiss on Dalton's cheek.

Phyllis turned her head, aware that someone was staring at her from across the room. It was Rod Talbot, her co-star. Phyllis felt a warm flush creep up her neck as his eyes bored into hers. Slowly he raised his fingers to his lips and blew her a kiss. Then he disappeared into the crowd.

A sudden wave of dizziness rolled over Phyllis. She put out a hand to steady herself, and Max Segal rushed up and pumped it excitedly. "Phyllis, SHAINELEH, you were wonderful! Marvelous! We'll gross ten million if we make a penny."

*Phyllis managed a thin smile. "I'm very happy, Mr. Segal,"
she said politely.*

Then someone pulled Segal aside, and Phyllis felt Bryan's
firm, slim fingers on her shoulder, his warm breath whispering
in her ear. *"You were fabulous, baby. Your scenes with Talbot
were dynamite. I'm proud of you."*

*She stared up at him and a rush of happiness flowed through
her. "Thanks, darling," she said quietly.*

*His eyes met hers. "I've got to stay for the party here, but
you look tired. Why don't you go home and rest awhile and
I'll pick you up later?"*

*Relief flooded into her eyes. "Good," she said. "I'm really
beat."*

*She turned to leave, but Bryan's hand bit into her shoulder
and held her. "By the way," he said, "Segal's giving you a five-
year contract. You start your next picture with Talbot in three
weeks."*

*"Oh, Brian," Phyllis said huskily. She bent forward and
kissed his forehead. Hot, grateful tears scorched her eyes, and
her lips were trembling so hard she could scarcely speak.*

When Phyllis stepped out of her bath, she felt her old vitality flowing back into her again. The hour's nap she'd taken
when she came home had done wonders, and in the bathtub
all the weariness had washed out of her into the warm soapy
water.

She picked up a towel and wrapped it around her expertly,
a deep sigh of contentment running through her body. Bryan
would be there soon, and already she could feel his strong arms
closing around her, taste his lips crushing against her mouth.

She opened the bathroom door and walked into the darkened bedroom. She stopped, and her breath caught in her
throat. Rod Talbot was sitting in her armchair, naked to the
waist, his shirt and jacket slung over the back of the chair.

Phyllis felt a tight knot of panic coil inside her. She was

afraid of Talbot. There was a terrifying maleness about him, a brutal sexuality that had come to light during their long months of shooting love scenes.

She tried to keep the fear out of her voice. "What are you doing here?"

"What do you think?" he said softly. "Waiting for you."

She pointed to his bare tanned chest that sloped like a grassy mountainside toward his flat, hard stomach. "Like that?"

"I'll let you take off the rest," he said, smiling. He rose and walked toward her. His muscles rippled startlingly under his skin.

Phyllis glared at him angrily. "What's the matter with you? Everyone knows I'm Bryan Young's girl."

"I don't," he spat at her. He was close to her now and there was a wildness in his eyes she had never seen before. "You've been leading me on for weeks," he said hoarsely, "but I'm through playing games."

She backed away from him. "Are you crazy?" she said. "That was for the camera. We were working. It was all make believe."

"Was it?" he asked. Suddenly he reached out and pulled her toward him. The towel slid down between them. His mouth closed over hers, then moved down her throat and across her breasts.

"Stop it!" she gasped. She wrenched away, and the towel slid to the floor.

He stared at her heaving breasts, the fires raging inside him. He grabbed her to him again and buried his face in her neck. He could feel her pulse beating wildly beneath his lips.

She writhed away. "No!" she begged. "Please! Bryan will be here any minute."

"Forget Bryan," he hissed. He seized her arm and pulled her back to him. His hand caught her hair and held her head back. "You're nothing to Bryan but a monument to his own power," he breathed into her upturned face.

"That isn't true," she gasped hoarsely. "You're jealous." She beat at his chest with her fists and sank her teeth into his shoulder.

"Bitch!" he yelled. He seized her fists with one hand and slapped her viciously across the face. The blow knocked her onto the bed.

"Bastard!" she said as he fell on top of her and pinned her down. Her nails clawed a bloody trail across his chest.

"Whore!" he yelled. His palm crashed into the side of her face.

"Animal!" she screamed. She kicked at him and bit his hand.

A crazy rage boiled through him. In a wild frenzy he ripped off his belt and waved it over Phyllis as he rolled her on to her side. Crack! A sharp stinging pain cut into her buttocks. He raised the belt again, and again the exquisite pain streaked across her body. Crack! Crack!

As each lash of the belt seared her flesh, a strang new excitement began to race through Phyllis. Suddenly she stopped fighting. She lay back on the bed, pressing her head into the pillow. Her lips parted and a murky expression came into her eyes. Then her arms went up around his neck, and she pulled him down to her. Her mouth fastened against his.

"You sure know how to hurt a girl," she whispered, drawing him into her.

And that was the way they were when Bryan found them.

In the morning the shrill ring of the telephone woke Phyllis up. She sat up in bed with a start. Quickly she glanced at Rod asleep on her pillow, the rosy imprint of her teeth standing out on his shoulder. Then she picked up the phone and Bryan's voice, formal and businesslike, sent an icy chill into her heart.

"Phyllis, I've got to talk to you."

"What about, Bryan?"

"About you and Rod Talbot." He chuckled quietly. "I stopped in to see you last night but you were busy."

Phyllis felt the cold block of fear hardening inside her. She glanced again at Rod to make sure he was still asleep. "It . . . it wasn't my fault, Bryan," she stammered. "He forced me into it."

"It doesn't matter," he said quickly. "I don't care how it happened. I'm just glad that it did."

A stunned look came over Phyllis's face. "You're glad?" she asked incredulously.

"That's right." There was a pause. "You see, Phyllis, I want you to marry Talbot."

The color drained from her face and her mouth dropped open. "You what?"

He began to explain, a note of excitement creeping into his voice. "Look, Phyllis, Windfall opens in three months. It's a great picture, but Talbot's the only box office name in it. We've got to make the public want to see Phyllis Benson. How?" He took a deep breath. "By making her the new Mrs. Rod Talbot."

Phyllis was silent for a long moment. When she spoke, her voice was husky with hurt and disappointment. "But what about us? I thought you loved me."

He gave a short bitter laugh. "You should have known better than that, Phyllis. I don't have time for love."

She didn't answer.

"Well," he said finally, "will you do it?"

"What happens if I refuse?"

He snickered softly. "You want that five-year contract, don't you?"

There was a long silence. "All right, I'll play it your way," she said quietly. "But what about Rod? Doesn't he have any say in the matter?"

"He'll say yes. He can't afford not to," he answered. "Talbot's getting 10 per cent of the gross on Windfall. The wedding publicity will put a half million bucks in his pocket." Phyllis exploded angrily. "Is that all you men ever think about—your lousy, rotten money?" Bryan's voice was soft with mock reproach. "Now, now," he said. "Control yourself. You'll wake up your fiancé."

Phyllis heard the phone go dead in her hand and she hung up. She turned and looked at Rod, who was beginning to stir on the bed. She stared at him for a moment, her fingers lightly tracing the teeth marks on his shoulder.

Suddenly she smiled. Her long blond hair spilled across Rod's chest as she bent down and brushed her lips against his forehead. Then she leaned over the bed and slowly picked his belt up from the floor.

FOUR : June, 1944

They came down the steps of the church in a blizzard of rice, with flashbulbs exploding around them and police holding back the mob of screaming fans. The bride and groom walked to a big black limousine and stood at the door, smiling and waving at the crowd. The cheers swelled to a deafening crescendo. Then a uniformed chauffeur opened the door of the car, and with a final wave and a smile, the happy couple climbed inside.

Phyllis settled back and leaned her head against the seat. A surge of triumph swept over her. She'd made it. She had struggled, fought, and clawed her way out of nowhere to the very top of Mount Everest and now she stood at the peak: the Queen of Hollywood and the wife of Rod Talbot.

She turned toward her husband, and suddenly the triumph died inside her. He was sound asleep. Phyllis stared at his nodding head and a great realization came to her: it was going to be lonely at the top, frightfully lonely. There were too many people down below waiting for you to fall. And the ones at your side loved you only because there was something in it for them.

Silently the limousine turned onto the private road that led to Talbot's hilltop mansion. At the sight of the huge house Phyllis felt a faint glimmer of hope. Maybe she had a chance with Rod, after all. Maybe inside that big house they'd shake off the ugly cynicism of their Hollywood marriage and learn to love each other.

She reached for Rod's limp hand and held it. True, his wild brutality still terrified her at times, but he excited her as no other man had ever done before. And there was a tender side to him, she had noticed. She saw it in his devotion to his widowed mother, in the way he entrusted her with all his affairs, made her come live with him in the beautiful home. And in the touching way he always cried "Mother!" whenever he reached the climax.

He was a good son. And he would be a good father, too. She was sure of that. Gently she lifted his hand and placed it in her lap. She let it rest there, against the fullness that was already growing inside her stomach. The fullness that would one day be a child. Tonight, their wedding night, she would tell him about the baby. She could hardly wait to see the happiness in his face.

Phyllis sank into the big, luxurious bed and closed her eyes. She listened to the water running in the bathroom shower and the muffled sound of Rod's voice humming. Then it grew quiet, and she heard the door click open behind him. There was the soft thud of his bare feet on the rug as he padded over to the bed.

Then he was lying beside her and she came down into his

arms and sought his lips. "Darling," she breathed into his open mouth, "we're going to have a baby."

She froze as he scrambled out of the bed and turned to face her, his features twisted with rage. His lips stretched back across his teeth in a snarl, and his veins bulged in his forehead in thick, angry cords.

Phyllis shrank back against the pillows, trembling violently. "My God," she whispered in a horrified voice, "what is it?"

He seemed oblivious to her, blinded by some uncontrollable fury. With a demonic shout, he reached for a lamp and hurled it against the wall, smashing it to pieces. He ripped the sheets off the bed and threw them to the floor. He snatched a chair up and sent it crashing into a mirror.

Suddenly, his rage spent, he sank to his knees beside the bed and buried his head in his arms, sobbing pitifully. "I'm afraid . . . I don't want to be a father . . . I'm so scared."

Then he slid to the floor and screamed in terror.

Phyllis stared at him as waves of shock and revulsion swept over her. Instinctively she held out her hand to comfort him, when she heard the door open.

Rod's mother Lillian, an attractive grey-haired woman with a slim, youthful figure, stood in the doorway for a moment, then came into the room. Swiftly she crossed to her son's side and bent over him, caressing his head. "There, there. You'll be all right, darling," she said softly. She took his elbow. "You're just a little tired. Let Mother put you to bed."

Rod looked up at her, his eyes wide, his face white and strained. In a dreamlike stupor he slowly got to his feet. "I want to go with you, mama," he said in a small voice. Docilely he held out his hand and let his mother lead him from the room.

Phyllis sat up in the bed and held her hands to her throbbing temples. She felt sick inside. It was a nightmare. It hadn't happened. It couldn't have.

The door opened again, and Lillian came back into the room. She walked over to the bed and sat down next to

Phyllis. Gently, her eyes deep with sympathy, she took Phyllis's face in her hands.

"I'm sorry, Phyllis," *she said quietly.* "Rod's mentally ill, a psychomotor epileptic. *Most of the time he's perfectly normal, but under stress he becomes violent, he does things . . ." Her voice trailed off.*

Phyllis stared at her, a sudden chill piercing her heart. "Why didn't you tell me this before?"

"How could I?" *she asked bitterly.* "You wouldn't have married him if you'd known. And we'd have lost a half million dollars." *She dropped her hands and twisted them in her lap.* "You have no idea how much it costs—the psychiatric treatment, the drugs, the hush money. And who knows how many movies he has left, how long he can stand the pressure? The next time he goes into a rage, it could be the end."

"But what about me?" *Phyllis gasped hoarsely.* "I'm pregnant. I'm going to have his baby."

Lillian reached out to Phyllis and lightly stroked her forehead. Her voice was very low. "Get rid of it, Phyllis. What choice do you have? Rod's illness is hereditary—the chances are the baby would be born with it."

"Oh, no," *Phyllis sobbed.*

Lillian looked at her with compassion. "Don't make the same mistake I did, Phyllis. I wanted to have my baby at all costs, and I paid the price. When I married Rod's father I knew he was sick, but it didn't matter. I guess I was afraid of a real man. I felt sorry for him because he was like a little boy, so childlike." *She sighed deeply.* "Of course, he was a child emotionally. He killed himself when Rod was born. And now Rod is as sick as his father ever was."

Phyllis buried her face in her hands. The tears began to trickle through her fingers. She felt so hopelessly, bitterly alone. The way she'd felt ever since she was a little girl and her mother ran off and left her in that orphanage. Nothing had ever closed the awful void inside her, no man she had known had filled that terrible emptiness. If only she had a mother to turn to, to confide in, to love.

She felt Lillian's hand gently stroke her hair, moving over it like a soft whisper. Phyllis took her hands from her face. Slowly she raised her head and looked into Lillian's eyes. She saw her own pain and yearning reflected there.

Tenderly Lillian bent and kissed the tears from Phyllis's cheeks. "You're so beautiful," she said. "You mustn't cry." She put her arms around Phyllis and kissed her deeply on the mouth. Her hand slipped down and fondled Phyllis's breast. "Let me make you happy," she whispered. "I'll be good to you. I won't hurt you the way men do."

Lillian dropped her gown and pressed Phyllis's head to her naked bosom. Hungrily Phyllis sucked at the swollen nipples as a tingling excitement began to grow inside her. Her skin burned to the touch of Lillian's fingers tracing delicious patterns across it until her whole body caught fire and burst into flame.

With an agonized groan, Phyllis sank back onto the bed, her eyes tightly shut. She felt Lillian's head come down between her thighs. Then the final ecstasy exploded inside her, and over and over again she heard herself crying hoarsely, "Mother!"

Dimly she recalled hearing that same sad, angry cry before. Phyllis struggled to remember, and then it came to her— she'd sounded exactly like Rod.

F I V E : *October, 1946*

The plane rolled to a stop as the first tinge of twilight began to steal over Los Angeles. From her seat at the window Phyllis could see the reporters milling around the airfield like vultures

over a piece of carrion. A faint smile came to her lips. If they
were looking for a juicy divorce story, they had the wrong girl.

Not that she didn't have one to give them. Her two years
with Rod made Krafft-Ebing look like Mother Goose. For
openers, there'd been the abortion at Meadows Sanitarium,
alluded to in the press release as "minor surgery." Then there
were the wild, drunken parties, the lechery, the violent nights
with Rod, the passionate evenings with Lillian. And to complete her enslavement, there were always the pills, the blessed
pills—Phenobarbitals, Nembutols, Seconals, Doridens, Tui-
nals, Lotosates, Placidyls, Noludars, Libriums, Equanils—all
the angelic little transports that carried her from mindless
sleep to mindless sleep.

She'd been sledding downhill fast, and the crash was inevitable. It came one night when Rod suffered his first re-
lapse since the wedding night. The evening had started out
pleasantly enough, with both of them going to bed early after
a long day's shooting. Rod was whipping her with the beautiful leather riding crop she'd given him for an anniversary
present when he suddenly lost control. She was rushed to
Meadows Sanitarium with a broken nose, three missing teeth,
two cracked ribs, a collapsed lung, a fractured pelvis, and
a jagged gash in her back that required nine stitches to close—
all the result, the press release said, of a vague "accident in the
home."

She started the divorce proceedings quietly from her hospital
bed, with her lawyer filing in Reno. The grounds were incom-
patibility. She declined any alimony, and when it was over,
nothing was left of her marriage but the magnificient forty-
room house. And the scars.

Phyllis unfastened her seat belt. She reached inside her
handbag for a small bottle of Jack Daniels and a package of
pills. She put the pills on her tongue and swallowed them
down with a gulp from the bottle. Then she closed her handbag and stood up.

Quickly she walked down the aisle of the plane. She stood in the open doorway for a moment as a shout went up from the reporters. With a deep sigh, she squared her shoulders and lifted the famous jutting breasts. Then, with a toss of her golden hair, she turned toward the cameras and smiled.

Hack stopped reading and put down his papers. Airtight with expectancy, he looked up at Bonnie to see her reaction. He was shocked to find her quietly weeping. She was dabbing at her steamy eyes with her fingers and struggling to save her gelatinous features from collapse.

Hack's anguish at her tears was enormous. "Oh, please don't cry, Mrs. Ehrlich," he implored. "I know it's an atrocious piece of junk, but I was only following instructions. Maybe Mr. Shmeer's machines can fix it up." He flapped his hands in distress. "Anyway, if you want me to, I'll do the whole thing over."

Bonnie's face solidified on the spot. She stared at him in mascara streaked wonderment, her mouth working silently. Her words, when they came, were a leitmotif of incredulity. "Do it over? Are you out of your mind?" She shook her head. "It's absolutely perfect! Harold Robbins himself couldn't have done better."

Hack, vastly relieved, smiled shyly. "Do you really mean it?"

"Of course I do," she exclaimed. "I was only crying because it hit me so hard, and because I kept thinking as you read it, 'this is *mine*—all mine.' "

He looked at her, his eyes big with hope. "Then I have the job?"

"Are you kidding? I wouldn't have anyone else!"

"Oh, I'm delighted!" Hack said. He took an oceanic swallow of his drink and looked at Bonnie tentatively. "About the fee. Do you think you could pay me on a biweekly basis?"

"Twice a week?"

"No. Twice a month."

"Oh, that should be easy enough. Let's see now," she said, figuring aloud. "Shmeer said the book should take a year to write, twenty pages every two weeks. Suppose you bring me the twenty pages every two weeks and I'll give you a check for four hundred dollars each time." She tapped the pages in front of her. "You'll get your first check in the mail tomorrow for this. How's that?"

"Wonderful," Hack said. He inhaled deeply, seemingly tossing a pair of sandbags off his shoulders, and looked down at the papers he had brought her. "Are you sure you're satisfied with what I've done so far? Are there any changes you'd like me to make? Anything you want to add?"

Bonnie picked the papers up and scanned over them, her lips moving as she read random lines to herself. "There *is* something. Something missing," she said slowly. "I can't put my finger on it, but I have a feeling you left something out." She skimmed a few more paragraphs and suddenly cried, "Now I know what it is! There aren't enough dirty words!" She looked at him accusingly. "You didn't put one fuck in it."

Hack blushed furiously. "I-I know," he stammered. "My dirty word count is critically short." He appealed to her. "I tried to increase it, Mrs. Ehrlich. I really did. But I just couldn't bring myself to do it."

"That's all right," she said, nodding sympathetically. "You leave that department to me. I'll go over all your stuff and add the dirty words." She smiled at him. "At least there's something I can write by myself."

"It'll be a big help. I'm afraid obscenity's not one of my strong points."

"Maybe so," Bonnie said, "but you certainly did better with the sex scenes than I ever expected. Wow! I didn't think you were the type." She studied him closely. "But I guess you can't judge a book by its cover, can you?"

"I guess not." Hack felt flustered and he spoke hurriedly to cover his embarrassment. "But by the same token, you can't judge a person by his writings either. Some of the most torridly erotic passages in literature have probably been produced by homosexuals."

"Oh, Christ!" Bonnie gasped. "You're not queer, are you?"

"Good God, no! I only mentioned that to make a point."

"Well, you can't tell about anyone these days."

She reached out to put down her empty glass, and Hack's eyes were drawn like bees to the inviting mainland of her bosom. For a wild instant he pictured himself nose-diving into the canyon between her breasts, but he quickly swatted the notion out of his mind. How could he even think such a thing? A swinger like that was way out of his reach, in another league altogether. And besides, she was a married woman old enough to be, God forbid, his mother.

Bonnie caught him staring and she laughed. "I guess you're regular, after all," she said. "Do you have a girl friend?"

"Yes, a Wellesley girl," Hack said, his cheeks flaming again. "She's getting her Masters' degree in Social Work. She wants to work in the Poverty Program."

"Are you going to marry her?"

"I asked her," Hack said unhappily, "but she turned me down. She said she won't marry anyone who's not making a decent living."

"Why not?" Bonnie laughed. "You'd be a good credit when she goes to get a job."

"That's the trouble. She just wants to work in Poverty, she doesn't want to live in it. I suppose you can't blame her." His face brightened. "Anyway, I'm sure she'll be impressed when she hears I've got this job. Ten-thousand-a-year's not a bad wage."

"Yeah, but that's just *this* year. What about after that?"

Hack shrugged. "Who knows? Right now I'm living one year at a time."

"Maybe that's best," Bonnie agreed. She looked at Hack

and softly shook her head, smiling in private amusement. The poor slob was such a sad sack, but he was cute in his own way. And probably horny as hell once you got him into bed. She'd see. If he ever stopped treating her like Eleanor Roosevelt, maybe'd she'd have a little fun with him yet.

Hack finished his drink and glanced at his watch. "Oh, Lord, I've got to go! I'm driving up to Wellesley for the weekend and Brunhild—that's my girl friend—will be furious if I'm late."

He got up quickly and held out his hand to Bonnie. "I'm so glad you're pleased with my work, Mrs. Ehrlich. I'll have the next twenty pages ready in two weeks." He smiled bashfully. "And I'm sure our association's going to be a very pleasant one."

"So am I." She took his hand and pressed it affectionately. "Have a nice weekend, Percy," she said in a gracious tone. Then she added with a broad wink, "And give Wellesley one for me."

Chapter 5 The Middle

BONNIE SMILED lovingly at the half completed manuscript lying in her lap like a paper fetus. She was pleased at how remarkably it had grown in the last few months, taking on shape and substance as it gradually evolved into a fledgling novel. It thrilled her to think of its carbon-black words as thousands of tiny cells that would one day spring into life, informed with her own precious spark.

The doorbell rang, and she waited for the butler to bring Hack in. "My, don't you look handsome today, Percy," she remarked as he stood before her, resplendent in an obviously new suit. At least he's putting the money to good use, she thought dryly.

"Thank you," he said. "I've been on quite a shopping spree." He grinned sheepishly. "I never realized I had such a passion for clothes before."

Bonnie laughed. "That's the thing about having a little money. It brings out all your expensive tastes."

He sat down beside her, and she noticed he handled himself with a new assurance that was very becoming. He seemed more relaxed now, more poised and confident. He had dropped his old manner around her of a man cuddling up to a killer ape, and he was replacing it with a somewhat breezier style.

She nodded toward the papers in his hand. "Well, what goodies do you have for me today?"

"I've started the section on the second central character, and I think you'll like it," he said. "It's got a lot of punch."

"Good. The more punch the better. Let's hear it."

He waited for Bonnie to brace herself, and then he began to read:

O N E : *October*, 1946   Carol Gordon

The shrill wail of the ambulance siren mounted to its orgasmic climax. Inside, Carol Gordon lay strapped to a stretcher, a blanket wrapped around her body and her flaming red hair sprawled across the sheet. Her face was a chalky death mask drained of all color. Her lips were bloodless, and dark grey shadows etched the skin beneath her closed eyelids.

Careening wildly, the driver swung the ambulance onto the approach to Meadows Sanitarium and screeched to a halt at the emergency entrance. Quickly, the doctor seated inside scrambled to his feet and wrenched open the ambulance doors. He watched the night suddenly fill with white-clad figures running out to meet him.

"What's it this time, Doc?" an attendant asked.

"The same as usual," the doctor said, his voice flat with weariness. "An overdose of sleeping pills."

The attendant leaped into the ambulance with catlike grace and began to slide the stretcher toward the men waiting below.

"Easy now. Watch it." The doctor's staccato words darted at the men, directing their movements. He waited until the stretcher rolled onto the ground, then jumped down after it and trotted briskly alongside its speeding wheels.

Rapidly the stretcher glided across the gravel, a dark shadow surrounded by a ribbon of white coats. The men streaked to the hospital entrance where they paused for a second and flung open the doors. Then they swung into stride again, and the stretcher, bearing its silent burden, disappeared within.

"How are we feeling today?" the nurse asked cheerily as she came into Carol's room and stood beside her bed.

Carol forced a wan smile to her lips. "Fine. Just fine," she said in an empty voice.

"That's the spirit, dearie." The nurse popped a thermometer into Carol's mouth and reached for her wrist, placing her fingers on the pulse. "You don't know what a close call you had this time," she said, looking at her watch. "You're lucky you're alive."

Yeah, Carol thought dismally. Real lucky. A thirty-one-year-old has-been with nowhere to go but down. She waited for the thermometer to come out. "How long have I been stuck in this lousy dump?"

The nurse clucked in reproach. "Now what kind of a way is that to talk? You've only been here three days, and the doctor says you can go home tomorrow."

"Tomorrow?" Carol said hopefully, a faint tinge of brightness seeping into her pale face. "Brother! That's good news if I ever heard it." Only one more day to go. She'd go out of her mind if she had to wait much longer for a drink.

The nurse fluffed up her pillow. "Would you like me to get you something to read, a magazine maybe?"

Carol shook her head glumly.

"Well, try to get a little snooze then," the nurse said, retreating from the room. "The rest'll do you a world of good."

Carol waited until she reached the door, then stopped her. "Say, was I dreaming this morning, or is Rod Talbot here?

I thought I saw him walking down the hall a little while ago."

The nurse smiled. "You weren't dreaming, honey. Rod Talbot is here, in person in 714A. He came in yesterday for his routine twenty-four hour checkup." Her voice dropped to a confidential tone. "They say he's got some kind of brain disease that turns him into a dangerous maniac when he gets upset."

Carol stared at her informant, her mouth hanging open in surprise.

The nurse's face flushed and suddenly went blank as she realized she'd blurted too much. Abruptly, she turned toward the door. "I'd better get going. I've got the rest of the floor to see," she said quickly. "Take it easy now," she called to Carol over her shoulder, and she hurried out.

Carol sat up in bed, an eager excitement creeping over her. So Talbot was a real weirdo, dangerous when he got upset, was he? What a break! Now she had a chance to get even with his wife, the bitch, for stealing Windfall away from her. All she had to do was go down the hall and pay Roddy boy a little visit in . . . what was it the nurse said? . . . 714A . . . and tell him some of the stories she'd heard about Phyllis lately. By the time he got home to wifey, he'd be in one hell of a mood.

A cold smile tugged at Carol's lips. Quickly she swung her legs out of bed and thrust her feet into a pair of slippers. Then she threw on a robe and slipped out of the room.

She found Rod propped up in bed, smoking a cigarette when she came in. He glanced up at her. "Why, Carol, what a pleasant surprise," he said affably.

"I heard you were here, and I thought you'd like some company," she said, dropping into a chair beside the bed.

He watched as she crossed her legs, revealing a lush expanse of thigh. "It's always nice to have visitors. Especially such pretty ones."

Carol smiled and reached for a cigarette. She lit it and took a deep puff, letting the smoke scald into her lungs. "You know, Rod, I've always liked you," she said slowly. She paused, her large eyes veiled and mysterious. "That's why I have to tell you something you might not like to hear."

A dark look came over Talbot's face. His voice was tense. "What is it?"

Her eyes bored into his. "Your wife's been making a goddam fool out of you," she said grimly. "She's been screwing around with Lester Dale, the restaurant man."

She watched Talbot's face contort with rage as he gripped the sides of the bed, his knuckles turning pus white with effort. "Why, you lousy, rotten, no-good liar!" he shouted. "I'll kill you for spreading lies like that!"

Carol calmly ground out her cigarette, a faint smile playing around her lips. "If you don't believe me, ask his daughter Tina. A twelve-year-old kid wouldn't lie about a thing like that."

Talbot's face froze in its angry glare, and he raised his arms as if to strike her.

Quickly Carol sprang to her feet. She backed away from the bed and stood still for a moment, staring at him. Then, her eyes fixed on his, she reached for the sash of her robe and pulled on it. "I didn't come here to hurt you, Rod. I came to do you a favor," she whispered in a soft voice.

The robe fell open, revealing her naked body. She posed for him, cupping her hands under the protruding curve of her breasts and fingering the pink nipples with their hardening points. Her hands moved down the soft mound of her belly, caressing her hips and thighs. Her fingers grazed the silken russet thatch of her pubis. "Just what the doctor ordered. Right, Roddy?" she asked huskily.

She watched the anger in his eyes slowly give way to lust. She saw his lips part as her body began to undulate slowly, and she let her hips sway back and fourth in sensuous invitation. Then she started toward the bed.

"Move over, baby," she said, sinking down into his outstretched arms. "It's time to take your medicine."

The doctor discharged Carol after breakfast the next morning, and she was packing her bags when the floor nurse came in to say goodbye.

"My, we're looking cheerful today," the nurse remarked pleasantly. "Have a good night's sleep?"

"Not bad," Carol said. She glanced at her inquisitively. "Only what was that commotion I heard in the middle of the night? It sounded like the whole place was in an uproar."

"Don't you know?" The nurse's gossipy face lit up. "It was on account of Phyllis Benson. They brought her in at two A.M. in terrible shape."

Carol's eyes widened. "No fooling. What's the matter with her?"

"The story is she took a bad spill in the bathtub." The nurse shielded her mouth with her hand, a secretive expression on her face. "But from what I've heard, somebody must've given her a real working over."

Carol turned away to hide her smile. "Do they have any idea who did it?"

The nurse shrugged. "I don't know. But I wouldn't put it past that nutty husband of hers." She shook her head in disapproval. "You should have seen the mess he left his room in yesterday—the bed-clothes all tangled up, the buzzer cord pulled out of the wall—it was a real pigsty."

Carol laughed. "Well, you know how men are," she said lightly. She turned back to her packing, neatly folding a dress into her suitcase. She bent her head, and her long hair hid her ironic smile from the nurse's eyes. "When you get a chance, tell Phyllis I sent her my best."

T W O : *November,* 1947

It was a typical New York premiere—the crowds milling on the sidewalk, the bright lights beaming outside the theatre, the flock of elegantly dressed men and women streaming through the doors.

Inside, the special section roped off for studio guests was packed. Max Segal sat erect in his seat on the aisle, every inch the proud producer. A wave of elation swelled over him as he watched the picture unfold on the screen, and he glanced at Carol sitting regally beside him. In the darkness he could see the diamond tiara gleaming in her upswept red hair and the triumphant smile on her lips.

Segal shook his head. Go know from such a mixed up ME-SHUGGENEH. Last year they were saying KADDISH for her from the sleeping pills, and today here she was, big as life and UN-GESHTUPT with diamonds. The ghost was making the big come-back.

Segal's glance traveled from Carol to Bryan Young, seated next to her. Admiration glinted in his eye as he stared at the young executive. Such a smart GOY! He must have some YID-DISHEH blood in him. Where else would he get the SAYCHEL to drag a washed up Carol Gordon out of DRERD and star her in a BUBBAMEINSA like Tears for Tomorrow? The part was made for her. Drunken singers she could play with her eyes closed, the old SHIKKER; and she was so poor like a churchmouse she was willing to work for GARNISHT.

Segal smiled to himself as his eye stole back to Carol. The TSATSKEH never looked so good in her life—ten years younger at least. And she was a MECHAYA to work with for a change.

None of her old TSUROS with the staying out sick and the coming in late that you could GEHARGETVEHRN from the overtime. It was Young, the TUMMLER, who was keeping her so busy in bed she couldn't crawl out for a drink. The GOY must have a PUTZ like a wand to be such a miracle worker.

Segal turned his attention back to the screen. Tears for Tomorrow was nearing the end now, and it was time for Carol's big dramatic closing scene.

Alone in a shabby backstage dressing room, Evelyn Rush, the great torch singer, was putting on her makeup. On her dressing table stood an unopened bottle of champagne, a bottle she had sworn never to touch again.

She raised the bottle and looked at it, and the camera moved in for a close-up of her face. She was so near you could almost feel the texture of her skin, hear the sound of her breathing.

The moment froze, and all her torment was captured in it. You could see the deep struggle against temptation print itself on her face, the full lips twisted in pain and the high curving cheekbones drawn into lines of anguish. But it was her eyes that compelled you.

They were the eyes of a woman who had glimpsed hell. Eyes that had seen her own soul's degradation, and had looked on its private tortures with unspeakable sorrow and despair.

Slowly she put the bottle down, her face set with decision now. She drew back her shoulders and stood up. There was a look of serenity in her eyes as she walked out of the room.

In the wings the stage manager handed her a single long-stemmed red rose. She pressed it to her breast and stepped out of the shadows into the bright lights and the applause. She adjusted her eyes to the glare and began to walk toward the on-stage piano, her high heels striking sharply on the wooden floor, her beaded gold and green gown shimmering in the spotlight.

Gracefully she raised herself and settled down on the closed piano top, placing the rose beside her. She stared out at the audience, and the faces of the people peered back at her from behind the footlights. They were faces full of greed and defiance, begging her to entertain them, yet daring her to satisfy their demands.

Fear flickered in her eyes for a moment, and you could see her stiffen when she heard the soft piano behind her. Then she began to sing, and she lost herself in the blue notes. Her face and her body, even more than the famed husky tremulo, told all there was to know of love, heartache, and pain.

When it was over, the audience declared its approval with clapping hands and insatiable cries for more. All resistance had vanished, and in its place there was avid, total acceptance.

Evelyn Rush stared at the grinning, cheering faces, but she did not return their smiles. Her eyes were wide and solemn. An expression of sorrow came over her face. A bitter sorrow that the public's love was so fickle and demanding, that the cost of winning it was always too high.

She looked at the one empty seat in the front row, and the sadness in her eyes deepened. You could see how the emptiness of that seat tore into her heart, as if she knew that all the cheering in the world would never fill it again.

The roar of the crowd grew lustier, more persistent, but she seemed not to hear it. Her eyes blurred with tears, she picked up the long-stemmed rose lying beside her, raised it to her lips, and tossed it over the footlights. It fluttered in the air for a moment, then dropped onto that one empty seat, as the screen began to fade.

The sound of weeping filled the theatre when the lights came up. Segal blinked in embarrassment as he felt the tears in his own eyes. They were the tears of joy he always wept when he knew he had a winner. He turned to Carol and embraced her ecstatically. "BUBBALA, you were magnificent!" he cried. "Once in a PURIM you see a performance like that!"

Carol smiled. She glanced adoringly at Bryan who was beam-

ing at her with pride, then looked back at Segal. "Do you
mean it?"

"She thinks I'm kidding her," Segal laughed, winking at
Bryan. He patted Carol on the knee. "So you'll know I mean
TUCHES AUF DER TISCH, I'm starting you in Fallen Woman
three weeks from today. How's that, ZISSELEH?"

"It's fine with me, Mr. Segal," she answered. Again she
glanced at Bryan. "But you'll have to ask my husband first."

Segal stared at her, his eyes wide with surprise. "Husband?
What husband?"

Carol laughed. A faint note of triumph crept into her voice.
"Bryan and I were married tonight," she said. "We went to
a justice of the peace right before the premiere."

Segal jumped to his feet, a broad grin masking his shocked
expression. "MAZEL TOV! A better match you wouldn't find in
heaven," he cried. He held out his hands to them and pulled
them both to their feet. "Come, KINDERLACH. Such good news
it's a SHANDEH to keep a secret. Tonight we'll have a double
celebration."

As he led the way up the aisle toward the crowd of enthu-
siastic well-wishers, there was a strangely exultant expression
on Segal's face. How do you like that, he thought. So the GOY
went and married the SHIKKER. With her MESHUGASS, she'd
make mincemeat out of him in no time. It just goes to show,
a GOY was still a GOY, even a smart one like Young. When it
came to KNISH, they were all greenhorns.

"Oh, Bryan, it feels so good in here with you," Carol whispered. "I don't ever want to come out."

She clung to him in the shower stall as the soft, hot water
streamed down their glistening bodies. She could feel his
hardness rising against her, and she began to moan and writhe,
pushing herself upward frantically. "Oh, God! Give it to me,
Bryan!" she gasped. "Hurry! Give it to me!"

He backed her against the tile wall and slipped his hands under her buttocks. Gently he eased her down onto himself, and he felt her shudder, her whole body trembling as he impaled her. She squirmed wildly and dug her nails into his back. "Oh, Oh! Please. Oh, I can't stand it!" she cried. Then she suddenly stiffened in ecstacy and went limp in his arms.

Her eyes still closed, she rested her head on his shoulder. He kissed her wet forehead and held her for a moment, gently stroking her neck. Then he slowly reached up behind her and turned the water off. "Come on, baby," he said, his dark eyes smiling at her. "It looks like we're all washed up in here."

They dried themselves off and walked out of the bathroom arm in arm. Their room at the Plaza was like all hotel rooms— intimate and impersonal at the same time. The bureau was strewn with congratulatory telegrams, and on a table stood a big vase of flowers with a card that read "ZOL ZEIN MIT GLICK —Max Segal."

They lay down on the bed and Bryan reached for a cigarette. He put it between his lips and lit it, letting the smoke slowly drift through his nostrils. Then he flipped on the radio, and soft music poured into the room.

Carol leaned her head against the pillow. She took the cigarette from him and inhaled deeply on it. Then she placed it back between his lips. "Tell me something," she said softly. "Is Segal really signing me for Fallen Woman?"

Bryan smiled. "Of course he is," he answered. "You're the hottest property he's got now. Who else would he use?"

She turned on her side and stared at him. "What about Phyllis Benson?"

"What about her?" he retorted. Carol thought she heard a hint of bitterness in his voice. "Our friend Phyllis is on the way out. I'm afraid she's had it." He pointed at her with his cigarette emphatically. "You're Number One now, and you'll stay that way as long as I say so."

A soft look came into Carol's eyes. She leaned across him and pressed her lips to his. Her hand reached down, touching him gently. "You're too good to me, Bryan."

He laughed.

"No, I mean it," she insisted. "You're too kind, too gentle." Her eyes were suddenly serious. "You don't hurt me enough."

He stared at her. "You mean you'd like it better if I roughed you up a little?"

She nodded.

A faint trace of disgust came over his face. "But that's sick, Carol." He shook his head. "I couldn't do that."

"How do you know you couldn't if you never tried it?" she asked, her fingers tightening around him.

Quickly she bent down and seized his growing protuberance between her lips. She enclosed him in the moist warmth of her mouth and he felt her tongue moving over him. Then she lifted her head. She looked up at him, a taunting expression in her eyes. "Rod Talbot whipped me once, and he was great."

He exploded angrily. His hand shot down and pulled her head back by the hair. "You dirty bitch! he shouted hoarsely. "Don't ever mention that punk's name to me again!"

She stared at him, her eyes widening with sudden knowledge. "My God," she whispered. "You're still carrying a torch for Phyllis, aren't you?"

He didn't answer. He glowered at her for a moment, his face dark and menacing. Then a thin smile began to tug at his lips. "Okay, baby. If that's the way you want it," he said coldly. He let go of her hair, and his arm grabbed her around the waist, rolling her onto her stomach. She turned her head, and she caught a glimpse of his other hand coming toward her. There was a burning cigarette butt between his fingers.

She screamed as the fiery pain seared her flesh. Her screams grew louder, and Bryan turned up the radio to cover the noise. His hand touched the dial just as the announcement came

that Phyllis Benson and millionaire restaurateur Lester Dale
had eloped.

O N E : *January*, 1950   Phyllis

*The hot California sun crept under the umbrella on Phyllis's
chair beside the pool. She bent forward to adjust the metal
frame and glanced at her watch on the table beside her. One
o'clock. Another whole hour before Tina would be coming
home from school.*

*Languidly she picked her drink up from the table and lay
back, sipping it. Her eye scanned across the sparkling irides-
cence of the pool to the big white house beyond. There it is,
she thought grimly, the Dale mausoleum. And here she was,
buried alive inside it.*

*Marrying Lester had been a mistake, the way she'd known
it would be. He'd been a marvelous friend to her, but he was
a rotten husband. He was too old for her, too busy, too posses-
sive. Most of the time he wasn't even home. And when he was
home, what good did he do her? He was too tired to breathe,
let alone screw. She was going crazy with frustration. Hadn't
she seen the handwriting on the wall? She'd begged him not
to get serious after her divorce, to go on the way they'd been.
Why did she ever let him talk her into marriage?*

*Now she was like a prisoner. He wouldn't let her go any-
where without him, not even to the studio. He'd made her
quit acting because he said he didn't want his wife to work.
Who did he think he was fooling? Didn't she know how afraid
he was of losing her?*

*She'd have to be blind not to see it. He was getting so
desperate lately, he'd started using real Gestapo tactics. Imagine, hiring bodyguards to keep an eye on her. They were*

for protection, he said. What a laugh! There was probably one standing at a window in the house right now, "protecting" her through a pair of binoculars.

If it hadn't been for Tina she'd have left him long ago. The kid was the only thing that held her. She loved her face, with those big blue eyes and that red hair. She felt sorry for her, too. It must have been hard on her when the mother died. Maybe that's why she felt so close to Tina. The kid was a lot like her in a way—growing up so alone in the world.

Phyllis put her empty glass down on the table and stood up. It was time to go back to the house. She wanted to be there when Tina came home, and she was tired of sitting around in a wet suit, anyway.

She began walking toward the cabana, her suit clinging to her provocatively as she moved. She paused in the doorway for a moment until her eyes grew accustomed to the darkness. Then she stepped inside and saw him.

He was standing near the towel rack, a tall powerfully built man in his early thirties. He was wearing a pair of brief swim trunks, and he had a faintly Mediterranean look, with swarthy olive skin and a tousled head of thick black hair. His white teeth flashed at her in a smile.

Phyllis stared at him uncertainly. "Who are you?"

"I'm Vince DiStefano, your new bodyguard," he said smoothly. His eyes roamed boldly over her shapely figure, then returned to her face. "I can't remember when I've enjoyed my work so much."

Phyllis met his gaze steadily, then dropped her eyes. Her glance fell to the bulging front of his trunks. She felt a deep flush creep over her. Lester must have been out of his mind to hire a bull like this. What was he trying to do—torture her? She'd never seen such a stud in her life. Suddenly a knowing look crossed her face, and she glanced up sharply. That must be it. He was a stud. Lester had bought him for her to keep her happy. He wanted her to have someone safe to play with while he was away, someone he could control. From the looks of things, the old goat had picked a winner. She stared at him, her eyes on his. Slowly she moved toward him until she was very close. She stood there for a moment, then reached up and put her arms around his neck. A slow smile spread across her face. "I was just going to take my suit off," she whispered. Gently she drew his face down to hers. "How would you like to help?"

T W O : *March,* 1951

Vince rolled over on his side and looked at Phyllis questioningly. "What's the matter, honey?" he asked, propping himself on his elbow. "You're not yourself tonight."

Phyllis turned toward him, her blond hair spilling over the pillow. There was a note of deep concern in her voice. "I'm worried about Tina. She's been acting funny lately."

Vince laughed. "A kid that age can take care of herself," he said lightly. He looked at her. "Maybe she needs to get laid."

Phyllis sat up angrily, her naked breasts heaving. Her hand slashed across his face. "Don't you dare talk that way about Tina! She's my stepdaughter!"

He stared at her in surprise. "Take it easy," he said, his fingers rubbing his smarting cheek. "What the hell are you getting so upset about?"

She burst into tears and buried her face in her hands. "It's no good," she sobbed. "The kid read that item about you in Louella's column—that thing about your underworld past. Now she's afraid you're a dangerous gangster or something, and she's been after Lester to get rid of you."

Vince slipped his hand under her chin and turned her face up to his. "Tina's not afraid of me. She's jealous, that's all," he said softly. A faint smile came to his lips. "You let me have a little talk with her, and I'll straighten her out."

Phyllis stared at him, her eyes searching his. "You only want to talk to her? Nothing else?"

He laughed and pulled her into his arms. "I won't touch her," he said, brushing her forehead with his lips. "What do I need her for when I have you?"

She smiled and pressed her lips to his. A soft look came over her face as she reached down to him, her fingertips stroking the power back into his loins. Quickly he lowered her onto the bed and began to cover her with his body. Then he felt her hands pressing against his shoulders, stopping him. "Hurt me a little first," she whispered, her eyes half closed. "You know how I love it when you hurt me."

He straddled her with both knees and caught her hands, pulling her forward roughly. "Is this what you want?" he hissed as his strong brown hand seized her wrist and bent her arm behind her, forcing it upward.

She screamed with pain, writhing as he held her. He tightened his grip on her arm, and she screamed again. Then she felt the fire inside her racing downward. She grew wet with lust, and her hips began to churn uncontrollably. She thrust herself up from the bed, climbing wildly toward him. "Oh, please! Please!" she moaned. "Oh, God. Do it!"

He was just about to enter her when they heard the door open. Vince turned his head quickly and saw Tina standing in the narrow patch of light from the hallway. She glared at him, her face twisted with hate and rage. "You dirty Dago gigolo!" she screamed. "Get away from my stepmother or I'll kill you!"

He saw her start toward the bed, a knife flashing in her hand. Quickly he sprang away from Phyllis and snatched a pillow from the bed to protect himself.

Tina lunged at him, slashing savagely through the pillow. He flung it at her face and she tumbled backward onto the floor, the knife still in her hand.

"Tina! Tina!" Phyllis screamed in terror from the bed. "Get out of here before you get hurt!" She clawed at Vince's back trying to restrain him, but he shook her loose.

He leaped at Tina, his hand grabbing for the knife. She twisted away, and his fingers clung to her nightgown, ripping it down to her waist. He stared at her perfect young breasts and his breath caught in his throat. He could feel the flames begin to rise in him again when she suddenly thrust forward and plunged the knife into his chest. A stunned look came over his face as he clutched frantically at the knife. Then his hands slowly fell to his sides and he slumped to the floor.

Phyllis crept down from the bed and crouched beside Vince, pressing her ear to the dark rich stain on his chest. Then she lifted her head and stared at him for a moment. A look of surprise crossed her face. "My God," she whispered. "He died with a hard on."

Tina came out of shock and burst into tears, sobbing hysterically. "Oh, no. Oh, no," she moaned. "I killed him! I'm a murderer." She buried her face in her hands and her muffled voice came through her fingers. "Oh, Phyllis, I only did it for you. I wanted to save you from him. I couldn't stand the way he made you scream."

"I know, baby. It's all right," Phyllis said as she took Tina into her arms and gently stroked her long red hair. She seemed to drift away for a moment. Then her eyes cleared and her face took on a look of decision. She was the one to blame for Vince's death, not Tina. It was because of her that Tina had gotten into this. Now it was up to her to get Tina out. There was only one way.

She kissed Tina's bent head lightly, then released the girl from her arms and stood up. Slowly she walked toward the bathroom door and opened it, pausing with her hand on the knob. *She glanced back at Tina and looked away again as the tears formed in her eyes.*

Then she stepped inside the bathroom and locked the door behind her. Quickly she picked up a bar of soap from the sink and held it in her hand like a pencil, scrawling a note across the mirror of the medicine cabinet:

Lester—
Vince and I couldn't go on. Forgive us.
Phyllis

Then, with trembling fingers, she opened the medicine cabinet and reached for a bottle of pills.

"Jesus," Bonnie said when Hack had finished reading. She was obviously shaken. "You're not going to let Phyllis die, are you?"

"I don't know yet," Hack said. "I'd like to get rid of her for the sake of the story line, but it's not so easy. We've got a big problem."

"What's that?"

"She's still alive in real life," he said. "If she dies in the book, the public may get confused. They may not know who she is."

"She doesn't know herself," Bonnie said somewhat caustically. "She just divorced her sixth husband." She looked at Hack inquisitively. "Why do you want to get rid of her?"

"Because it'll give us a good deathbed scene, and the pamphlet says we should have one."

"Can't you work one in another way?"

"How?" he asked. "The other main characters are still alive, too. And they're not as expendable as she is."

"Then kill her off," Bonnie said. "We're supposed to blur the facts a little, aren't we?"

"Yes, but would you consider death a minor distortion?"

"I don't see why not," Bonnie argued. "You're not changing her life that much. You're just shortening it a little."

Hack nodded thoughtfully. "That's one way of looking at it, I suppose. But I'll stave off her demise until the end so we can make up our minds for sure."

"Okay. There's no rush," Bonnie said. "Let her suffer a little."

"Fine. Now what about the rest of the section? Did you like it?"

"I loved it." She grinned naughtily at him. "You're really starting to come on strong with those sex scenes, aren't you?"

"Do you think so?" He sounded surprised and flattered at the same time. "To me, my descriptions never seem clinical enough."

"Maybe I should have hired a gynecologist," Bonnie said laughingly. "But I'm satisfied. Your stuff sounds pretty good to me." She gave Hack a penetrating look. "Your girl friend . . . what's her name . . . Hildebrand?"

"Brunhild."

"Oh, yeah, Brunhild. She must be some hot ticket."

Hack colored profusely and looked away. "I wouldn't call her a 'hot ticket' exactly. 'Glacial' would be a better description. But she's been thawing nicely ever since I became what she calls 'husband material.' "

"Then tell her to keep on defrosting," Bonnie said. "It's good for your work. It sounds better if you know what you're talking about."

Hack looked at her, a thoughtful expression furrowing his brow. "You know, it's a funny thing, the difference between life and writing about it. Sex, for example, is much cleaner in dirty books than it is in life."

"What?"

"It's *neater*, I mean. You can do away with all the mess—

the zippers, hooks and eyes, bodily problems—you know, things like that. You don't have to worry about maneuverings; you just couple your people like boxcars. You make it simple and dramatic, like, 'her clothes ripped off in his hand,' 'her mouth pressed down on his,' 'she opened herself like a flower.' " His frown deepened. "But in real life it never happens that way. There are always so many little practical considerations that foul you up."

Bonnie studied him intently. "Maybe you need a more experienced woman to make you forget all that."

He stared back at her. "Yes, perhaps you're right," he said. Appalled at himself, he heard his voice speaking lines he never intended to say. "Lately I've begun to notice there's a kind of . . . heightened sensuality . . . about the mature woman. College girls are sexy in a bland, wholesome way, but they don't have the aura of excitement that a seasoned woman does."

Bonnie made a slight movement toward him. "You mean a woman like me?"

His eyes popped like flashbulbs. "Well, I . . . I . . ." He put his head down and blurted, "Actually, I suppose I did have you in mind, Mrs. Ehrlich."

She moved in closer. "You think there's something exciting about me?"

He nodded. "You're a very glamorous woman," he said faintly. His words seemed to come from an echo chamber. "You're quite lovely, really."

"Thank you." She came still closer, almost touching him now. "That was a nice thing to say, Percy."

Hack's alarm signals were beeping wildly, warning of imminent danger, but he stayed doggedly on course. "I-I really meant it."

She smiled radiantly at him and held out her arms. "Then do something about it."

He froze. "Do what?" he quavered.

"This," she said, nestling up to him and urging his arms around her.

He swallowed quickly, bleating in a panic-stricken voice, "Won't Mr. Ehrlich mind?"

She drew back for an instant, bristling. "No, of course not," she said testily. "He won't know about it." Then she folded herself against him again, all succulent tenderness, and lobbed her words into his ear. "Come on, Percy, relax. Pretend this is one of your bedroom scenes."

Her closeness assailed him, and he felt his inhibitions sliding away like melted wax on a candle. With infinite caution, he let his lips move down her cheek, scattering a packet of seedling kisses.

The moment hung suspended, poised and fragile, filled with heartbeats and fluttering eyelids. Then Manny's voice, booming from the vestibule like a cannon, shattered it to pieces. "Hey, Bonnie! I'm home early! Hurry up and get dressed. We're invited out for dinner."

"Oh, shit," Bonnie said.

Hack bounded up from the sofa, a mass of quivering nerve endings. He twitched about distractedly as Manny entered the room.

"Oh, hi, kid," Manny said, reaching for Hack's damp hand and shaking it. "I thought you'd be all through by now."

Hack stammered in confusion.

"As a matter of fact," Bonnie replied coolly from the sofa, "we were just about to start something." She gave Hack a meaningful glance. "But I guess it'll have to wait for later."

Hack stood still, red-faced and mute.

"Yeah, let it go 'til next time," Manny said. "Sit on it for a while. Things always go better when you start fresh." He gave Hack a playful jab on the arm. "Right, kid?"

Hack came to life with a start. "Oh, yes, certainly. There's a lot of truth in that, Mr. Ehrlich," he said, nodding vigorously. He began backing hastily out of the room. "Look, I know you people have an appointment, so don't let me keep you. I'll show myself out."

Bonnie waved to him as he left. "I'll see you, Percy." She smiled and called out gaily, "And don't forget. We'll take up right where we left off."

Chapter 6 The End

"I CAN'T believe it," Bonnie said, squeezing Hack's arm excitedly. "I just can't believe it's finished."

"Yes, it *is* hard to believe, isn't it?" he said quietly. "For a while I thought we'd never get here, but now here we are."

It was their last session together and Hack, a cathedral of solemnity, was preparing to read the final twenty pages of the manuscript. Sentiment weighed heavily on him, and in contrast to Bonnie's jubilation he felt curiously sad that they had come to the end. Relieved as he was to be finished, it seemed a shame to have to bow out now just when the real fun was beginning. For weeks she had been burbling to him about the excitement that lay ahead for her—the parties, the TV appearances, the magazine interviews—and he knew she was entering a world where he would have no admittance. He felt let down, shut out, like a wedding guest invited to the ceremony but not the dinner. It was foolish, he knew, but he couldn't help feeling that he was being carelessly discarded, resigned to the trash can like an old ball-point pen that had run dry. Bitterly, he thought of himself lying there, unattended, unremarked, the iron grey lid of anonymity closing over him while she, using his words for wings, went soaring like an eagle toward fame and glory.

Bonnie roused him from his mood with eager impatience. "Come on, Percy. Don't just sit there. Read to me," she said. "I'm dying to know how everything turned out."

"Yes, of course. I'm sorry." He coughed, dissolving the glob of self-pity lodged in his throat, and began to read the final portion:

March, 1951   Carol

The Beverly Towers, a shining cylinder of glass and steel, thrust skyward from the Sunset Strip like a giant phallus. The dome was Bryan Young's penthouse. Since his marriage to Carol four years ago they had lived there in virtual seclusion, shunning Hollywood's gaudy nightlife to spend quiet evenings at home in their soundproof bedroom.

Bryan smiled as he walked into the bedroom and saw Carol waiting for him. She was lying with her wrists manacled to the sides of the bed and her legs spread-eagled. He bent over her and inspected the rows of scars and purple bruises that lined her thighs. He ran his finger along the network of ridges and welts, and his smile broadened. "You look great, baby." He laughed softly. "Good enough to eat."

Quickly he lowered his head and seized the soft flesh of her inner thigh between his teeth. He held it until he heard her cry out in pain. Then he let go, and his lips moved slowly up her leg, his tongue skimming lightly across the surface of her skin. She moaned, stretching her legs wider for him as he began to nuzzle her. She felt his tongue probing her, darting forward and back with a maddening persistent rhythm, and she arched her back, her hips moving helplessly in and out in response. Then they suddenly stopped. The telephone was ringing.

"Oh, no! No!" Carol groaned, her teeth clenched. She twisted and turned on the bed. "Oh, God! Not now."

Angrily Bryan grabbed at the phone on the night table and picked it up. "Well?" he barked.

A young girl answered him. Her shaky voice sounded on the

verge of tears. "May I speak to Bryan Young, please? It's urgent."

"On the line. Who's calling?"

"This is Tina Dale. It's about my stepmother, Phyllis Benson. She . . . she's . . ." Her voice broke into harsh sobs.

Bryan felt an icy shock run through him, choking off his breath. "What is it, Tina?" he said hoarsely. "What do you want to tell me about Phyllis?"

The sobs grew louder. Then he heard Tina's voice blurt, "She's dying, Mr. Young. The doctors say she won't last the night."

"Oh, my God! No! Is it the pills?"

"Yes. She's at Meadows Sanitarium," she gasped. "And she begged me to call you. She wants to see you before she goes."

"I'll be right over!" he said grimly as he hung up the phone.

He glanced at Carol and he saw the mocking smirk on her face. An angry flush spread over him. "You knew about Phyllis, didn't you?" he hissed.

"Sure I did," she retorted. "And so did everybody else in this town." A bitter laugh rose in her throat. "You'd have known about her, too, if you weren't so busy screwing that little tart Lila Reed all day long. The Herald had the whole thing splashed across the front page this afternoon—a real sob story. One of those 'suicide pact' deals between Phyllis and her lover boy, DiStefano, a slimy Wop hood they found stabbed to death in her bedroom."

He stared at her. "Why the hell didn't you tell me?"

"What for?" she asked. "So you'd leave me high and dry to run over there and hold her hand?" Another harsh, bitter laugh escaped her. "You never could resist a piece of ass. Even a half dead one."

"Shut your filthy mouth!" He lunged at her as if to strike her, then lowered his arms in disgust. "Oh, what's the good of belting a broad like you?" he sneered. "You're so depraved, you'd only open your legs and beg for more."

Carol wrenched herself up, her bare breasts flouncing angrily. "You can go to hell," she snarled. "That's where you and your precious Phyllis belong."

He glared at her, his face twisted with rage. For a moment a look of pure hatred flashed in his eyes. Then it disappeared, and his voice was empty and flat. "It's all over between us, Carol. I've had it."

"Had what?" she asked scornfully.

"I'm through playing your sick, perverted games. You let your ambition destroy everything decent in you, but you won't destroy me, too."

She didn't answer him and he turned away from her, hurriedly pulling on his clothes. Then she broke her silence as she saw him start toward the door.

"All right, you bastard! See if I care! Go to her!" she shouted after him. She yanked savagely at the manacles. "But don't leave me here like this. Get me out first."

He stopped and turned toward her. A faint smile flickered across his face. "You made your bed," he said quietly. "Now lie in it."

The door slammed behind him and she stared fixedly at it for a moment. Then her lips began to tremble and she could feel the hot, acrid tears spring into her eyes. Damn it all! She could never win. Never. In the end all her victories turned to ashes.

March, 1951   Phyllis

The uniformed nurse behind the front desk greeted him with a polite smile. "Miss Benson's in room 509, Mr. Young," she said. An anxious note crept into her voice. "Take any elevator in the rear and go right on up."

"Thank you." He rushed past her down the corridor toward the elevators. Impatiently he jabbed at the button, a sudden feeling of panic lurching inside him. My God, what if he had come too late? Suppose she was already dead? No, she couldn't be! There was too much he wanted to tell her. He had to say goodbye.

Abruptly an elevator door opened and he went inside. He could feel the hard knot of fear tightening in his gut as he climbed upward. The blood began to pound wildly in his temples. Then the car stopped and the doors slid open again.

He got out, and the pungent antiseptic smell of the hospital corridor assailed his nose. An aura of illness, pain, and death pursued him as he hurried down the hall. His eye scanned frantically over the room numbers, searching for 509. Then he found it and stepped inside, the door closing softly behind him.

He stood still for a moment, staring into the room. An ominous chill gripped him as he saw the oxygen tent mounted over Phyllis's bed. His gaze fell on the grim, hopeless faces of the people standing beside her: Tina, a doctor and a nurse. They nodded faintly to him and watched in silence as he slowly approached the bed.

He looked down at Phyllis's ashen face, the closed, waxy eyelids, the haggard cheeks, the pale, lifeless lips. He turned to the doctor, his voice a hoarse croak. "She's not . . . ?"

"No, Mr. Young, she's in a coma," the doctor said quietly. "We've just given her some adrenalin to help her breathing, but she can't be roused for more than a few moments at a time."

Bryan looked at him imploringly. "Could I be alone with her now?"

"Yes, but only for a short time."

He waited for the three of them to leave, then dropped to his knees beside the bed. His hand crawled under the tent, desperately seeking hers. "Phyllis, Phyllis," he pleaded brokenly. "Say something! Answer me! It's Bryan."

There was no sign of recognition. Nothing.

Frenziedly he shoved the oxygen tent aside and bent over her. He pressed his lips down on hers. "Oh, please, Phyllis!" he breathed into her mouth. "Speak to me! I love you!"

He hung over her and waited, his cheeks wet with tears. Then he saw her eyelids slowly flutter open. She stared at him and a faint light came into her eyes. Her lips parted in a smile. "I love you, too, Bryan," she whispered.

He clasped her hand in both of his. "Then why did you do it, Phyl? Why didn't you come to me for help?"

"I couldn't," she whispered. "You belong to Carol now."

"Carol," he said bitterly. "You don't know what a monster she is."

"It's not her fault," she whispered. "The business did that to her."

"But I never loved Carol," he groaned. "I only married her on the rebound. It was you I always wanted." He twisted his hands in his hair. "I went crazy when I found you with Rod that time. I forced you to marry him out of spite. I tried to get even with you and I ruined everything!"

"Don't blame yourself," she whispered. "You only gave me what I asked for. Deep down I must have wanted you to punish me. I was trying to destroy myself even then."

"But why? You have so much to live for."

"No, I don't. My whole life's been a waste," she said hoarsely. She drew a tortured breath. "My death will be the only good thing I've ever done."

"What do you mean?"

"I'm doing it to save Tina," she whispered. "She's the one who killed Vince."

"Tina! But I thought the newspaper said it was a suicide pact!"

"I left a note to fool them," she whispered. "I'm telling you the truth because I want you to help me. You're the only one I can trust."

"I'll do anything you want, Phyl. What is it?"

"Take care of Tina for me," she whispered. "Be the father to her that Lester never was. Look how badly she needs him now, and he's in Europe somewhere."

"What do you want me to do for her?"

"She's got a beautiful voice," she whispered. "Help her to make it as a singer." Her frail fingers clutched at his sleeve. "But I beg of you, Bryan. Please. Don't let the business mess up her life."

He pressed her hand. "I'll watch over her, Phyl. You have my word."

She leaned toward him, her breath coming in harsh rales. "It's too late now for our happiness," she gasped. "But we can find what we never had in Tina."

She sank back and closed her eyes. Bryan looked down at her, then softly kissed her cheek. "I'd better go now," he said, "and let you get some rest."

"No," she whispered. She opened her eyes, but they were foggy and glazed. Her words were almost incoherent. "Don't go, Bryan. There's no time left. Take me out on the terrace and let me die in the sunlight."

He stared at her. "But Phyllis . . ." He caught himself and held the words back. How could he tell her that it was after midnight? That the sun had long since gone down and she would never see it rise again? No, he would spare her the truth. Let her hold on to her last illusion.

Gently he took her in his arms and carried her onto the terrace. She clung to him weakly. "It's like old times again, isn't it Bryan?" she whispered.

He nodded, unable to speak.

He watched as Phyllis slowly raised her head and looked out into the black night for a moment. Then he saw her feebly lift her hand and point, a faint smile spreading across her face. "Thank you, Bryan," she whispered. "I've always loved the sun."

Her hand dropped and she sagged lifelessly in his arms. He held her against his chest, his fingers softly stroking her golden hair. A tortured sob broke from his throat as he thought of the final, bitter irony. The orange glare she had seen in the sky was not the sun at all, but only the beam of a searchlight for another Hollywood premiere.

ONE : *February*, 1954   Tina

Tina stood at the window in her suite, staring out at the lights of New York. She looked westward toward Broadway and a surge of excitement coursed through her. She hugged herself ecstatically. Tomorrow night her name would be shining out there, too. Big as life on the marquee of the Booth Theatre. TINA DALE in Golden Girl.

She turned away from the window and poured herself a glass of champagne. She sipped it slowly, a thoughtful expression spreading over her face. Getting to the top had been easy. Too easy, really. There had been none of the groveling, the heartache, the sordidness she had thought she would find. Instead, the doors had all been opened for her, the path cleared. MCA had signed her right off the bat. Her first record, Cover Me With Kisses, had been a smash, and the offers had come pouring in: nightclub dates, TV appearances, concert tours, movie roles, and now the lead in her first Broadway show. It had all happened so fast it didn't seem real. She felt she was living in a fairy tale. And Bryan was her Prince Charming.

God, the things that man had done for her! The phone calls he'd made, the letters he'd written, the pressure he'd exerted. He'd handed her a whole career on a silver platter.

And with no strings attached. He'd never laid a finger on her, never even asked. At first she was glad he hadn't. She was so young and frightened then. But that was then. Now she was older and things were different. Much different.

She poured herself another glass of champagne, a warm flush creeping over her as she sipped it. She was in love with Bryan. Deeply in love. She had to be. How else would she have found the nerve to get him an adjoining room and wire him to come out? Even so, she'd had to lie to him. She'd told him she was scared stiff about opening and needed him there to hold her hand. She knew that would get him. And it had. He'd come running out on the double and he was there right now. In the next room. All she had to do was go to him.

Quickly, Tina put down her glass and walked into the bedroom. She stood in front of the mirror for a moment, pulling her negligee around her. Then she turned and moved toward the door to Bryan's room. She glanced under it, a slow smile spreading across her face. The light was out. He was already in bed. She reached for the latch and quietly unlocked it.

Bryan sat up with a start as he heard a noise at the door. His voice rang out sharply in the stillness. "Who's there?"

She stood in the doorway for a moment, then came into the room. "It's me, Bryan," she said. "I couldn't sleep."

His teeth flashed in the darkness as he smiled. "What's the matter? Opening night jitters got you down again?"

Her voice was very low. "No, it isn't that," she said, approaching the bed.

"Oh? What's wrong then?" he asked worriedly.

She stood beside the bed and looked down at him. "Nothing's wrong."

He reached out to turn on the lamp but she caught his arm. "We won't need that," she said quietly. "You don't have to hold my hand any more, Bryan. I'm a big girl now."

He stared at her, a puzzled expression in his eyes. "But, Tina, I thought . . ."

"It doesn't matter what you thought," she said quickly. She sat down on the edge of the bed and took his face in her hands. Her voice was husky. "Bryan, you've got to stop treating me like a child. I'm a woman. And I'm in love with you."

Gently he pulled her hands down and held them. "You know how I feel about you, Tina," he said. "But I'm not the right one for you. I'd only bring you unhappiness."

"That's not true," she insisted. "You've given me nothing but happiness." She felt the tears rush to her eyes. "I owe everything to you. And Phyllis."

A look of pain crossed his face. "But it wouldn't work out between us, Tina. I'm too old for you."

"No, you're not," she said angrily. "I don't want some young fool who doesn't know anything. I want a real man."

He stared at her for a moment, then slowly shook his head. "It's no use," he said bitterly. "Carol would never give me a divorce. She'd make our lives miserable."

Her eyes bored into his. "Only if we let her," she whispered. Tremblingly, she put her arms around his neck and drew her face up to his, covering his cheeks and mouth with tiny kisses. She took his hand and placed it inside her negligee, guiding his fingers over her budlike nipples. Then, with a sudden movement she slipped out of his arms and went down on her knees beside the bed. Her hands tore aside his pajamas and he could feel her lips grazing his belly as they moved toward his sex. Then her mouth enveloped him, her tongue and teeth plying his tumid flesh until he thought he would burst. He began to moan deep in his throat as a raging liquid fire poured out of his loins and boiled through his body.

Abruptly he reached down and pulled her up to him. "I think you're right," he gasped. "Why fight the inevitable?"

It was over an hour later when the door to the bedroom suddenly burst open and they saw Carol standing there in the room.

She switched on the lights and stared at them, her face flushed with liquor and rage. "My, what a pretty picture," she said, weaving drunkenly. "I'm sorry I didn't bring my camera."

Bryan rolled away from Tina and sat up, blinking at the light as he reached for a cigarette. He lit it and inhaled deeply, blasting the smoke into his lungs. "You shouldn't have come here, Carol," he said quietly. "It won't do any good."

"Won't it?" she flung back at him. "Maybe your little friend won't like you so much when she finds out what you're really like."

She came close to the bed, swaying in front of them for a moment. Quickly she ripped off her fur coat and threw it on the floor. Then she tore at her clothes, dropping them in a pile at her feet. While they watched in horror she began to circle about before them, a mocking smile on her face as she flaunted the ugly welts and bruises that covered her naked breasts and ran down her belly and buttocks. She paused in front of Tina, her fingers pushing her mottled thighs apart. "Get a load of this, honey," she sneered. "How do you like your boy friend's handiwork?"

Tina sobbed out loud and covered her face with her hands, the tears trickling through her fingers.

"Stop it, Carol," Bryan said harshly. "You're making a fool of yourself."

She glared at him. "Not as big a fool as you are, lover boy. You'll screw yourself to death some day trying to keep up with one of your little whores." She glanced at Tina and began to laugh. "Poor Tina baby. She thinks she's the only one. She should've seen those pictures of you and Lila Reed we got blackmailed with." She snickered loudly. "It's a shame we had them destroyed, Bryan. We should've kept them for training movies to break in your new girls."

"That's enough!" Bryan shouted. He leaped out of bed and grabbed Carol by the shoulders, shaking her violently. "For God's sake, shut up! Do you hear me?"

She broke away from him, gasping for breath. "No, I won't shut up. Not until I'm finished." Her eyes darted wildly toward Tina, then back to Bryan. Her voice was thick with contempt. "Does your little filly know how friendly you were with her mother? How the two of you were carrying on behind Lester's back all those years until she finally killed herself?"

Tina's hands dropped from her face. She stared at Carol, her eyes wide with shock. "Oh, my God!"

Carol lurched toward her. "That's right, baby. Your mama and lover boy here were a real hot item before you were even born." Her mouth curved into an evil leer. "In fact, there's a good chance Lester Dale's little girl is really Bryan Young's."

A look of horror crossed Tina's face. "No, it's not true! It can't be!" she gasped.

Carol laughed in her face. "What's the matter, honey? Didn't you like banging your own daddy?"

Tina screamed as Bryan lunged at Carol, slapping her savagely across the face. "You crazy vicious bitch, I'll kill you," he cried hoarsely.

He threw her onto the bed and fell on her, pummeling her furiously with his fists. She moaned and rolled onto her side, trying to escape the barrage of blows. Then she suddenly stopped resisting. Her arms reached out to him as her body began to writhe in the throes of a deep sexual excitement. She closed her eyes and pressed herself against him, her belly grinding against his. "Come on, baby. Make me happy," she whispered. "Hurt me, hit me, punch me, and beat the crap out of me. That's what I want."

Bryan turned to Tina. "Get me my belt!" he said harshly. "It's the only way to shut her up!"

Numbly Tina brought him the belt, her face flushed puce purple with shame and disgust. She watched as Bryan straddled Carol with both knees and raised the belt high above his head. Then she ran from the room, sobbing.

He found her in the bathroom, leaning weakly against the sink, her forehead damp and pale.

"Please, Tina," he said as he tried to take her into his arms. She pushed him away. Her voice was strained and husky. "No. Don't touch me."

"But I've got to explain," he insisted. "Those things Carol said about your mother and me . . ."

"I don't want to hear it," she cried, clamping her hands over her ears. "My mother's the only one who knows the truth, and she's dead. Why can't you let the dead rest in peace?"

She brushed past him into the bedroom and got dressed quickly. Then she threw her suitcase on the bed and began stuffing her clothes into it.

He watched her, a look of surprise on his face. "Tina, what are you doing?"

"What does it look like?" she retorted. "I'm packing."

"But you can't check out now! You've got to open in a show tomorrow."

She put down the brassiere in her hand and looked up at him. Her voice was so low he could hardly hear it. "I'm not opening in Golden Girl tomorrow."

He stared at her, a shocked expression on his face. "You can't mean that, Tina. If you walk out on Golden Girl tomorrow, you'll be signing your own death warrant. No producer will ever touch you again with a forty-foot pole."

Her eyes gazed steadily at his and her mouth settled into a firm line. "I don't care," she said quietly. "I don't want to be a star any more, Bryan. I used to think success was the only thing that mattered, but now I know better." Her lips began to tremble. "What does any of it mean if you can't live with yourself?"

She felt his hand on her arm. "Give yourself a chance, Tina," he said gently. "You've been through a lot tonight. You'll feel different tomorrow."

"No, it's too late," she said slowly. She looked into his face, and her eyes shone with a wisdom far beyond her years. "Tomorrow is already today, and today is yesterday's tomorrow."

He didn't answer.

She took his hand and pressed it to her cheek. "Don't think I'm not grateful, Bryan. You've been like a father . . ." Her face flushed and she looked away. "Please try to understand," she went on quickly. "I'm not doing this to hurt anyone. It's just that I've got to get out of this crazy business before it's too late. I've seen what can happen to you, and I don't want to wind up like . . . like that." She shuddered violently, as she pointed to the room where Carol lay sleeping.

Bryan nodded slowly. "I tried to shield you from all the ugliness, but I couldn't," he said finally. "You deserve a better life than this." A look of concern crossed his face. "But where will you go? What will you do?"

She stared at him, her blue eyes calm and clear. There was a radiance in them he had never seen before. "I'm going to join the Sisters of the Sacred Heart," she said softly. "There's a convent in Claremont."

His mouth hung open in shock. "Are you sure that's what you want, Tina?"

"Yes," she answered, her voice firm and strong. "God has been calling me for a long time, Bryan, but I was always afraid to heed His call. Now I have the courage I need." She looked at him, and he saw the deep springs of serenity and faith flowing within her eyes. "Where else but in the shelter of His house can I find true peace and contentment? What greater glory could my voice bring me, Bryan, than in the singing of His Word and His praises?"

Slowly, almost shyly, she held out her hand to him. "Do I have your blessing?"

He grasped her hand and pressed it to his lips. Her palm felt cool and soft as he spoke the words into it. "Go in peace, child. May God be with you."

She buried her face against his chest, her tears dampening the soft wool of his robe. "Thank you, Bryan," she whispered. Then she raised her head and looked at him, and her eyes were clear and serene once more. A note of humility came into her voice. "Before I go to take the vows I want to do penance for my sins. I need to be chastised for the weakness of my flesh. Will you help me?"

He stared at her. "How, Tina?"

She looked into his eyes. "You know how," she said quietly as her fingers slowly reached for the thick leather sash on his robe.

TWO : March, 1954

Max Segal stood at the French window of his beach house and watched the moonlight gleaming on the waves. Then he turned back to his visitor, Lila Reed, perched prettily on the low sofa beside the fireplace. "So, NU, ZISSELEH, the FARSHTUNKENEH beach I can look at anytime. You got maybe something else for me to see?"

A faint smile lifted the corners of her mouth. "You bet I do, Mr. Segal," she said as she held out a large white envelope to him.

He came over and sat down beside her on the sofa. Silently he took the envelope from her and tore it open. A dozen photographs poured into his lap, showing Bryan, Tina, and Carol in a series of obscene naked poses.

Segal stared at the photographs, his eyes popping. He held them up to the light one by one. "OY, GEVALT! GUTTENYU! Like VILDE CHAYEHS they look! It's a regular three-ring circus."

He put the photographs aside and turned toward Lila, a questioning look on his face. "So how does a HAYMISHA little MAIDELEH like you come to such SHMUTSEKEH pictures?"

Lila helped herself to a cigarette from the silver box on the table and leaned back, blowing the smoke out in a thin stream. "You see, Mr. Segal, it's like this. I've got this friend of mine who specializes in hidden camera work. He took some pictures of Bryan . . . I mean Mr. Young . . . and me a couple of years ago when I was trying to get Carol to divorce him. She wouldn't go for the divorce, but they sure paid through the nose for the negatives. I guess he was scared to death of a scandal because the word was out that they were kicking you upstairs and he was going to get your job."

"Over my dead body!" *Segal exploded.* "A MOCKA and a KRENCK he'll get!"

Lila took a deep drag on her cigarette and went on, ignoring the outburst. "So he destroyed the negatives and then he dropped me like a hot potato. He got busy all of a sudden promoting Tina Dale, but she was such an innocent little thing everybody figured it was strictly business. God, she always came on so pure and holy you'd have thought she was the Virgin Mary in drag."

"Some virgin," *Segal said. He spat into the ashtray.* "Phuie!"

Lila laughed. "I knew Bryan would get to her sooner or later. So when I heard she was staying at the Waldorf before Golden Girl opened, I hired my photographer friend to plant some equipment in her suite. But I never thought I'd get a haul like that," *she added as she glanced at the photographs lying on the table before them. A note of righteousness crept into her voice.* "I thought that as president of the company you should know about this, Mr. Segal. And that's when I called you."

Segal grinned as he reached across and pinched her cheek. "You made a smart move, BUBBALA. Who needs to PATSHKA with second fiddles when you got the big MAHOFF himself?" *His grin broadened.* "And believe me, CHUNNALA, Maxie Segal is staying the big MAHOFF for a long time. With these pictures you brought me I'll have that PASKUDNYACK Young thrown out on his TUCHES at the next board meeting." Abruptly Segal jumped to his feet and held out his arms to Lila. "CUM, ZISSELEH. When a person does Maxie Segal a MITZVAH, they don't go empty-handed. A SCHNORRER I'm not." Lila ground out her cigarette and let Segal help her up. She stared into his eyes. "I thought the lead in First in Line would be a nice reward." Again Segal pinched her cheek and smiled. "It's yours, SHAINELEH. Don't I know talent when I see it?" He patted her arm. "But that's, EPISS, business. I got something personal I want you should have, too."

"Oh, thank you, Mr. Segal," she said, embracing him. "You're an angel."

Segal, beaming, led the way to a huge closet in the corridor off the bedroom. He threw open the closet doors and turned to her. "There, GIB A KUCK."

Lila gasped as she saw the magnificent array of dresses and fur coats hanging inside. "Good Lord, Mr. Segal," she exclaimed. "I've never seen clothes like this in my life."

Segal snatched a lustrous dark mink coat off a hanger and held it out to her. "So try one of my SCHMATTES on already. See if you like it."

She slipped into the coat and admired herself before the full length mirror in the bedroom. "Oh, it's beautiful!" she cried. "And it's a perfect fit."

"Sold!" Segal said. "You'll take it home with you."

Carefully Lila removed the coat and draped it over her arm. Then she walked back to the open closet and stood there for a moment gawking. Suddenly she turned toward Segal, an ironic smile on her face. "If you'll pardon my saying so, Mr. Segal, you must be quite a ladies' man to keep such a collection on hand."

Segal stared at her, his eyebrows lifted in indignation. "Vus

MEINS DU a ladies' man?" he demanded. "Thirty-five years I'm in this COORVEHSHA business and I never once laid a finger on any NAFKA. Never! As God is my witness, Maxie Segal's skirts are clean."

Lila looked at him, a puzzled expression on her face. "Then I don't understand," she said. "Why do you have all these clothes."

"For myself, BUBBALA." He laughed at her shocked expression. "For VUS NISHT? What's the matter, I'm not allowed to like nice things?"

She backed away from him, her face twisted in revulsion. "My God, Mr. Segal! You don't mean you actually wear them, do you?"

Segal reached out and fondled one of the dresses, a peculiar expression coming over his face. His voice sounded strained and far away. "VU DENN?" he answered. "What do I need them to hang in the closet?"

Suddenly he tore the dress off the hanger and began pulling it over his head, his chubby fingers clawing at the buttons.

"Mother of God!" Lila whispered as she ran from the room, dragging her mink coat after her. Quickly she let herself out of the house and stumbled toward her car, a wave of nausea churning inside her.

She threw the car into gear and roared off, but not before she caught a final harrowing glimpse of Segal as she passed the bedroom window. He had forgotten to close the drapes and she could see him standing there, his stocky body encased in a blue silk dress, his trouser legs rolled up, and his fat bare feet stuffed into a pair of high-heeled shoes. He was just starting to pirouette before the mirror when she wrenched her head away.

For a moment she thought she was going to be sick. Then the feeling passed and she began to laugh, softly at first and then harder and harder. By the time she reached the freeway

she was doubled over the wheel, wiping helplessly at her eyes
with the back of her hand.

April, 1960   Carol

Carol grimaced as she withdraw the hypodermic needle from
her arm. She stared at the tiny red puncture mark for a moment, then sank back on the bed and waited for the heroin
to take effect.

Good old horse, she thought, as she felt the sudden rush of
euphoria overpower her. It was so fast and delicious, not like
those slowpoke pills she used to take. Bah! Those crummy red
dolls and yellow jackets were never like this.

Dreamily, her eyes dilated and hazy, she gazed out the
window at the dingy grey buildings of the Boulevard Raspail.
She could see the sign of La Coupole, the popular hangout of
the Left Bank café set. What did Bryan see in that big dump,
she wondered. A bunch of freaky looking slobs sitting around
drinking beer and coffee and talking in circles all goddam
night. Paris. It was a far cry from the Hollywood rat race.

She reached for a cigarette and lit it, letting the smoke
come out slowly. Hollywood was a thing of the past now.
They had Lila Reed to thank for that, the blackmailing little
bitch. It was funny though. She really didn't give a damn about
losing her career. As long as she still had Bryan, that was all
that mattered. And she knew he'd never get rid of her. He
was even worse off than she was.

Poor Bryan. What a comedown for him, from Segal's right-
hand man to making underground movies in an old ware-
house. No wonder he was on drugs, too. She didn't think he'd

give in to it, but those crackpot cronies of his wore him down. And the sex stunts they were teaching him! Where the hell did they think those things up? It was getting so she never knew what to expect from him any more.

She heard the front door slam and the sound of footsteps coming up the long flight of stairs to the apartment. Another door slammed and the footsteps were inside now. Then Bryan and a young man with a camera slung over his shoulder walked into the room.

Bryan put down the large box he was carrying and came over to the bed. He bent to kiss Carol and she saw how glazed and distant his eyes looked. "Hello, baby."

"Hi," she answered as she ground out her cigarette. She nodded toward the young man, standing politely in the background. "Who's your friend?"

Bryan smiled. "Lucien Porter, the cameraman on my new picture. He said he wanted to meet you, so I invited him up." He motioned to the young man. "Don't be shy, Lucien. Come over and meet my wife. I'll hold your camera while you say hello."

The young man stumbled forward, his eyes cloudy with drugs and alcohol, and silently handed the camera to Bryan. He bent over Carol as if to kiss her hand, then suddenly pressed his lips to her breasts, finding the nipples through the thin gown.

Carol looked up, startled, as Bryan burst out laughing. "Atta boy, Lucien!" he shouted jovially. "Give her a real French hello."

Abruptly the young man slipped his hand under Carol's gown, his fingers moving busily for a while. Then he threw the gown up over her belly and sank his head between her thighs.

She could hear Bryan howling with laughter as she began to wriggle and squirm, her hands fluttering blindly about the boy's head. At first she tried to push him away, then she was reaching for him greedily, her legs spread wide. "Come on! Oh, come on, come on!" she moaned as he rose and covered her with his body.

Later, she opened her eyes and saw Lucien sprawled exhaustedly beside her, snoring softly with one arm thrown across his face. She turned her head, dreamily aware of Bryan standing alongside the bed.

He was looking down at her, the camera still in his hands. "That was a great performance, Carol," he said, an odd half smile on his lips. He tapped the camera. "I got some terrific footage out of it. I hope we can use it in the film."

She sat up, staring at him angrily. Then the anger faded and she began to laugh in a low voice. "You bastard."

Abruptly he put the camera down and reached out to her, pulling her to her feet. "Get up. There's something I want to show you."

Wide-eyed, she reeled after him as he went to retrieve the large box he had brought home. She watched him carefully set it down on a chair and open it. A bewildered look came to her face as he lifted out the contents and showed them to her: a leather saddle, a riding crop, a flesh-colored dildo, a pair of cowboy boots with spurs, and an eerily lifelike mask in the form of a horse's head.

She stared at him blankly. "What's all this for?"

"You'll see." Quickly he tore off his trousers and fastened the dildo around his hips with a series of straps. He thrust his feet into the boots and slipped the horse mask over her head, the thick black mane obscuring her red hair. Then he picked up the riding crop and began to dance excitedly around her. "Get down on all fours, Carol!" he shouted. "Hurry up! Get down!"

She jumped as he cracked the whip on the floor at her feet. A vague anger rose inside her, but she was too sluggish and dizzy to care. Nothing seemed real to her any more. It was all happening to someone else.

Meekly she dropped to her knees, bracing herself with her hands on the floor. She felt the weight of the saddle on her back as he strapped it around her waist. Then another, more crushing weight pressed down on her and she knew he had lowered himself onto the saddle.

A sudden pain tore through her side as he kicked her with the spur on his boot. "Giddy up!" he cried. "Come on, you old nag. Giddy up!"

She staggered for a moment and almost fell. Then she felt the dildo nudging her from behind as the spur ripped into her again. A warm stickiness began to trickle down her side. The pain blazed across her body, a strange, unbearable agony that trembled on the brink of delight. Suddenly she threw back her head, shaking the long black mane, and whinnied. Then, setting one hand slowly before the other, she began to move across the floor.

Hack sighed, filling his lungs in the manner of a long distance runner breaking the tape, and laid his papers down. He sank back onto the sofa awaiting some loud outburst from Bonnie, full of praise and pyrotechnics.

But none came. Not a word. Alarmed at her ominous silence, he opened his eyes and glanced sideways at her. She was sitting hunched forward, trancelike, with her chin resting on her closed fists. "Well," he prompted softly, "what did you think?"

The sound of his voice made her start, and she turned toward him slowly, looking, he thought, rather stunned. "My God," she said finally. Her voice had a breathless quality, as if someone had slapped her too hard on the back. "What a boffo ending! Phyllis commits suicide, Tina joins a convent, and Carol becomes a dope addict, galloping around like a horse." She sucked in her breath and let out a whoop of joy. "Oh, wait'll Shmeer sees this! He'll go out of his frigging mind!"

Hack smiled. He could see the expected display of emotion on its way now and he leaned back to enjoy it.

She had begun to hug her elbows and rock back and forth on the sofa in a vaulting transport of happiness. "Christ! I don't know how you swung it, but you didn't miss a trick. You name it, buster, we got it. We've got them making it on the beach, in the shower, with whips, in costume, taking pictures, going down on each other, homos, incest, murder—and you even made Segal a . . . whatjamacallit . . . a transvestite." She cackled gleefully. "Oh, that was beautiful." Then she went on, rocking harder as she gathered steam. "Do you realize what we've done here? Do you have any idea what we've accomplished? We got in every queer sex thing there is and we still managed to tell a story. And what a story! I never saw anything so powerful in my life. It says what the public wants to hear and it says it in their language." She stopped rocking and her voice hit a quivering note of pure elation. "I tell you, Percy, this book is a goddam masterpiece!"

Hack chuckled quietly, his sense of well-being restored. He tried not to sound too smug. "Considering the genre, I think we've turned in a rather creditable job."

Bonnie looked at him and laughed. "Oh, Percy, you're too much." She bounced up from the sofa and began moving off to the bar. "Let me get some drinks. This calls for a celebration."

As he watched her retreating back, not unmindful of the sensuous way she moved, the poignancy of the occasion returned to haunt him. He would probably never see her again after this. And even if he should see her, it would be only the slick public image. Never again the woman, vulnerable and real.

She returned with the drinks and handed him one. "Thanks," he said as she sat down opposite him. "I think I could use this now."

They raised their glasses and touched.

"To *The Broadbelters*," he said.

"And to Bonnie Ehrlich, the famous author." She smiled as she said it, but her eyes burned like a tiger's.

She continued to gaze off in space with that strangely incandescent look as they sipped their drinks. "It's finally going to happen," she said. "When the book comes out six months from now they'll be talking about it all over the country. And they'll be talking about *me*, baby. That's the main thing. After all these years I'll be a name." She gave a soft, triumphant snort. "You know, it's funny. The autograph hounds always stop me whenever I come out of Sardi's and ask me who I am. They want to know if I'm *somebody*. It's a real bitch. Well, pretty soon they won't have to ask any more. They'll know."

"I'm sure it'll be a wonderful feeling," Hack said quietly.

Something in his tone caught her ear and she looked up sharply. Then she smiled reassuringly at him. "Don't worry, Percy. You're going to make it one of these days, too. I've told Shmeer all about you."

"You did?" He seemed genuinely surprised and pleased. "Why?"

"Because he asked me," she said, laughing. "I told him someone was helping me, and he wanted to know who you were. I think he's got a real hot proposition for you."

"He does?"

She nodded. "He said he'll discuss it with you at the kick-off party for the book." Then she added, "You're invited, you know."

"I am?" Again he sounded happily surprised. "That's very kind of you, Mrs. Ehrlich."

"Don't be silly," she laughed. "You didn't think I'd leave you out, did you?"

When he didn't answer she said, "If it hadn't been for you, there wouldn't be any reason for a party. An invitation was the least I could give you." Her eyes twinkled at him. "I'd have given you a lot more, but it didn't work out that way, did it?"

"No, I guess not." He blushed and studied his drink. The memory of the day Manny had walked in on them rose up like a specter. He had never gotten over it and had ruthlessly suppressed his desire for Bonnie in all their subsequent meetings, giving vent to it only in tormenting sexual fantasy. Now, suddenly, all these fantasies sprang startlingly to life, crowding in on his psyche like ambushers hidden behind some dark foliage. Curiously, he had no desire to escape.

He looked up at her and spoke in the low, guilt-edged voice of a sinner making his confession to a priest. "Last night I spent hours sitting in my room, playing your tape over and over again."

"What the hell for?" she asked in surprise. "You've heard it all by now and you don't need it any more, anyway."

"I know," he said, "but I just wanted to listen to your voice. I . . ." He looked away. "I'm going to miss you, Mrs. Ehrlich."

He felt her fingers on his cheek and he turned back to her. She was smiling at him affectionately but with a trace of exasperation. "Damn it, Percy. You always acted like such a Boy Scout. I thought you weren't interested."

"I *was* interested—until that day when Mr. Ehrlich came home."

"Oh, Christ. I should've known that was it." She looked at him and began to laugh. "Well, you're in luck. Manny's out of town for a couple of days, so you have nothing to worry about."

He swallowed thunderously. "But that's just it. I do worry. I feel guilty."

"What about? Manny?"

He nodded.

"But that's ridiculous," she said in annoyance. "Manny wouldn't mind even if he knew about it. All he wants is to keep me happy—in a way, you'd be doing him a favor."

Hack sipped his drink and stared ahead thoughtfully. "There's a lot of sense in your point of view," he said at last. "Guilt's such a drag. It's really the only thing that separates the squares from the swingers." He turned to her in abject perplexity. "The trouble is, I can't decide which one I want to be."

"Oh, Percy. You're such a clown." She smiled at him indulgently, slowly shaking her head from side to side. He was so pathetic in his uncertainty, and at the same time, oddly appealing.

She put down her glass and took his face in her hands. "I can see you have a hell of a time making decisions. You'd better let me help you." Then she bent forward and kissed him on the mouth.

"Come on," she said, getting up. "Before you change your mind."

He put his drink on the table and stood up, feeling that sudden delightful airiness that rushes in when the initiative is taken away. He watched her legs moving like blades as she drifted off toward the bedroom, and inexorably, as a satellite orbits the sun, he began to follow her.

She turned to him when they reached the bedroom and kissed him lightly on the cheek. "Wait here," she said. "I'll be right back." Then she disappeared into another room, leaving him piteously on his own.

Like a trespasser he approached the great canopied bed and sat down on the edge, removing his shoes as though he were about to enter a shrine. He looked around furtively and then took off his jacket, shirt, and trousers, his movements so stiff and awkward he might have been a mechanical doll undressing itself. Stripped to his underwear he sat down on the bed again, feeling unbearably out of place, the absurdity of his situation rushing at him from every direction. What was he doing here in this preposterously elegant bedroom, waiting, half naked, to make love to a stranger nearly twice his age? What did he hope to prove by it? Why was it so important? He sat there, confused and uncertain, and listened to the Whys buzzing inside his head like a swarm of gnats.

"Percy," Bonnie was calling him. She had come back into the room, wearing a graceful smile and very little else.

He caught his breath. "Oh! Oh, how beautiful you are, Mrs. Ehrlich."

She came over to him and sat beside him on the bed, and they held each other for a long time, kissing, gazing, touching. Neither spoke but their senses shouted, and all about them they heard the crash and roar of barriers falling away to rubble. His questions in that time of trembling and wonder were not answered. But they vanished anyway, dissolving, finally, into the larger unknowable mystery.

They lay down together on the bed and yielded themselves up to the eddying onrush of desire. As the waters closed over them at the moment of union, which contained for each of them both a surrender and a conquest, he called out her name. "Oh, Mrs. Ehrlich," he gasped.

And she answered him, her voice floating up to him as if from a great distance. "Please, Percy. Don't you think it's time you called me Bonnie?"

Chapter 7 The Party

THEY WERE all there: the rich and the famous, the powerful and the semiliterate. The big room at the St. Regis teemed with "interesting people"—the scenemakers making the scene —laughing, drinking, eating, and being relentlessly sophisticated. Beneath the enormous chandelier that threw down its light on them their voices swelled like a symphony, cigarette smoke haloed their heads, and everywhere could be seen the sparkle of raised glasses and the flash of pinky rings.

Shmeer was giving *The Broadbelters* its coming-out party, and no debutante could have asked for a finer bash: free flowing liquor, filet mignon, and music by the Militant Prune Juice. There were over four hundred guests, the women dressed in feathers, fur, and shimmering minis, and the men in anything from velvet cutaways to 1890 French field marshals' uniforms. Shmeer had overlooked no one—critics, columnists, show people, producers, artists, writers, agents, jetsetters. And most important of all, there were the booksellers, Shmeer's "chosen people." While the others preened and traded conversational gambits and absorbed each others gloss, it was the booksellers, drab and colorless as they were, to whom Shmeer had given the ringside tables and on whom he kept his most watchful eye. For he knew, in his homely wisdom, that the stars only glitter, but the booksellers order books. And so he kept his vigil and waited, looking for the right moment to unleash the big guns and fire the opening shots of *The Broadbelters'* campaign.

As he threaded his way through the crowd, pausing now and again, particles of the swirling conversation clung to Shmeer like lint.

"What on earth is he doing with that riding crop in his hand?" he heard a young man ask a female companion as he brushed past their table. "He looks like a jockey in search of a horse."

The girl, whom Shmeer recognized out of the corner of his eye as an assistant buyer at Brentano's, giggled coquettishly. "That's Shmeer's 'wailing whip.' You mean you haven't heard about it?" She sounded mildly reproachful. "It's a teaser he sent out to promote the book. It's like a talking toy. When you crack it, a woman's voice starts to moan and sob."

"Good Lord. You're not serious, are you?"

"Oh, yes. He's got a fabulous promotion department. They do such clever things!" Her voice bubbled with admiration. "They sent press releases out on paper smeared with mud and they said, 'If you think this paper is dirty—wait until you read the book!' Then they put out a paperback version of the first chapter and enclosed a free package of birth control pills with the announcement: 'AFTER READING THIS ONE CHAPTER OF *THE BROADBELTERS* YOU'LL WANT TO MAKE LOVE TO SOMEBODY—BE OUR GUEST.' Then they . . ."

"Please, please. No more. Not while I'm eating."

Shmeer, smiling inwardly, moved on. Standing near the bar he spied Durston Flatus, the essayist, engaged in a heated discussion with a friend.

"Yes, but the *Partisan Review*," Flatus was saying, "blasted Larry's book to pieces. They said it was full of 'phony obscurantism,' 'metaphysical pretensions,' and 'bogus existential profundities.' "

"Well, the review in *Commentary* put it down, too," his friend answered, "but they praised the writing as 'occasionally brilliant.' "

"Really? The *New York Review of Books* said it was written in 'moth-eaten pseudo-Joycean rhetoric,' and the *Times Book Review* called the prose style 'absurdly anemic.' "

"Have you read the book at all?"

Flatus grunted disdainfully. "With those reviews—are you kidding?"

Shmeer turned away, and long-haired, fourteen-year-old Priscilla Roundheel, the British girl-novelist, caught his eye. Piquant in a transparent vinyl dress, she was chattering antimatedly to a TV talk show producer.

"Yes, it's true I had a book of poetry published when I was eleven," she was telling him, "but *A Worm in the Ivy* is my first novel and I'm terribly excited about it."

"I can imagine," the producer said. "What's it about?"

"Oh, it's a rather gay, frothy story about two wayward girls in a convent school and the things they take up—you know, masturbation, Lesbianism, buggery, and all that."

"Sounds interesting. Would you like to come on our show and discuss it?"

"*Sooper!*" she cried. "I love your American telly. It's so mad and crazy, and I just *adore* mad, crazy things."

"Do you like New York?"

"Oh, it's smashing! Your discotheques are *wild*." She giggled. "I haven't seen much else, but the rest can wait. I've simply *got* to do the mad, crazy things now, while I'm still young."

"Do you have any plans for the future?"

"Yes. I'm *terribly* ambitious. I'm going to work at being a teen-aged wonder for the next few years. Then I guess I'll have to retire when I'm nineteen or twenty and be a lady novelist or something."

"I see. Does anyone else in your family write?"

"Oh, we all do. My sister Regina—she's twelve—does these *marvelously* bleak short stories for the better magazines. And Cecil, my seventeen-year-old brother, is a screen writer in

Hollywood and lives in a tree house in Big Sur. And Archibald, that's my . . ."

A loud noise diverted Shmeer's attention and he turned around to find Daddio Brashbattle, the famous middle-aged author of fashionably avant-garde novels, crouching in a fighter's stance and growling ferociously at a bearded literary critic.

"Grr . . . grr . . ." said Brashbattle, feinting sharply with his left hand while his right held firmly to a triple shot of Scotch.

The critic, looking badly frightened, tried to back away, but Brashbattle closed in doggedly as the onlookers formed a startled ring around them.

"I'll get you, you mother, for that biased bad-ass review," Brashbattle snarled, dodging and jabbing wildly at the critic's midsection. His words poured out in a bibulous stream of semiconsciousness that held the crowd mesmerized. "What you don't know is I'm a Spook writing like a Kook, which is to say, a red hot cock. For the Spook is the spark of the white man's cock, and when we die the big death we send our semen, see men sprouting in the genes, seamen bulging in blue jeans, sailing aboard the big stick Nigger prick into the wide open cunt of white immortality. That's right," Brashbattle said, ignoring the shocked gasps of the people staring at him, "what if I'm not the white Abraham, Isaac, Jacob middle-class son of Brooklyn, New York, and Hear O Israel shit but am instead black as a tarry stool in a pool of blood, yes Lord, black as the entrance to the Harlem tunnel, ever see a colored boy glued, arms out, to the side of a building while some chill-grey-iron cop feels him up and down? Dig this!" Brashbattle cried, wagging his finger at the cowering critic. "Reason is the technique of the alienated to discover truth under sterile conditions, just as emotion is the technique of the involved to discover truth under instantaneous but mythic, penetrating, pervasive conditions of fertility." Brashbattle smiled grandly. "That's where it's at, professor, for if implosion comes can the message be far behind?—and now Daddio is off to piss in the john, son, piss on Johnson's peace, for Daddio is, mean to say, *has* got to go. Keep the fart, baby."

And with that, Brashbattle poured his glass of whisky down his throat and lurched off to find the Men's Room. The stunned silence he left behind him gradually dissipated as the people resumed their conversations. Shmeer, convinced more than ever that serious authors were all hopeless psychotics, began inching toward the bar for a drink. As he maneuvered through the mob he though he heard a familiar voice at his elbow. Glancing around, he found Manny, a look of not-quite-pain on his face, being mercilessly harangued by Augustus Bleak, president of the prestigious Bleak House and a pompous old windbag who attended every publishing party whether he was invited or not.

". . . because, unlike other publishers," Bleak was saying, his lips puckered into a malicious little smile, "we have steadfastly refused to traffic in pornographic trash. We have bravely resisted the temptation to give the public what it wants." He thrust out an armored vest of honor society keys, dangling them under Manny's nose. "Instead, we have courageously taken the high road of shaping and elevating public taste with such outstanding works as Akim Zygote's *Reflections on a Yapok.*"

"That was a big one," Manny said.

"It's not out yet," Bleak snapped. "We're releasing it next month." He chuckled. "Akim's a bit disappointed the book hasn't had any advance sale, but I keep telling him that's not important. Staughton Slunj, editor of the *Nahuatian Quarterly*, hailed it as a 'nonwork of surprising unintelligibility.' "

"No foolin'."

"Oh, yes," Bleak replied. "Believe me, my good fellow, I've been a guiding force in the career of many a prominent writer. Take Jeffry Jordan, for instance."

Manny's eyebrows shot up. Jordon, the first recognizable name Bleak had spoken, was a world famous novelist.

"Jeffry came to me," Bleak explained, "when he was still a complete unknown, a budding young author with a manuscript he was desperate to get published. It was a piece of rubbish—a lurid, action-paced sex story that thoroughly offended my editors. You have no idea how shocked they were by that manuscript! It seems incredible, but they couldn't put it down even for a moment, and one of them went so far as to carry it out with him on his lunch hour.

"But I ignored their reaction," Bleak went on, "because I was determined to help the struggling young writer. I promised him we would consider the manuscript if he would only eliminate all the explicitly detailed bedroom scenes and replace the glamorous characters and setting with something more commonplace." Bleak laughed ruefully. "Anyone else would have leaped at such an opportunity, but Jeffry was a pig-headed young rascal. He stubbornly refused to cooperate, leaving me no other alternative than to reject him. And it was my rejection that forced Jeffry to bring his material to another, less discriminating publisher, who hastily snapped it up. The book, *Time in the Sack*, established Jeffry Jordon as the most popular big-name author in the country and broke all records as a money winner. It sold over two million copies in hardcover, twelve million in paperback, was reprinted in forty-three languages including minor dialects, and was bought by MGM for nine hundred thousand dollars."

Manny was overwhelmed. "There's no question about it," he said. "You sure done Jordon a big favor."

"Yes," Bleak agreed. "But the truth is, if Jeffry had taken my original advice, he'd be infinitely better off today. Don't laugh, my good man. It's true. Just think how empty and meaningless his life is—a vulgar marriage to an international sex symbol and a life of spoiled luxury on Capri, which he leases yearly from the Italian government as a summer place.

What satisfaction can he have blindly churning out his trashy billion dollar novels year after year when he knows that none of them will ever win the Esoterica J. Younes Award or the Ulfelder R. Crock Prize? I ask you, deep down inside himself, in his innermost soul, do you think he's really happy?"

"I don't see how he could miss," Manny said. Then he blurted impatiently, "All this highfalutin crap aside, do your books make any money?"

Bleak recoiled as if struck by a rattlesnake. "Making money is something we leave to the crass commercialists," he said icily. "We're more interested in quality. If a book is good we'll publish it even if we know it won't sell three copies."

"But how can you afford to?"

"A matter of simple economics," Bleak said. "We make the author guarantee us against loss."

"What if he can't?"

Bleak looked uncomfortable. "Well, then we have to reject him. But of course," he went on quickly, "most of our authors are very cooperative. They usually buy out the first edition as gifts anyway."

"That lets *you* off the hook," Manny said, "but what about your authors? How do they live?"

"Oh, if their work is obscure and experimental enough, they might be awarded a literary prize. Or they could pick up a grant or a fellowship, maybe even a foundation year abroad or a writer-in-residenceship at a university, if they're lucky."

"And the unlucky ones?"

"They starve."

Just then they were accosted by a pale, shaggily bearded young man in a threadbare suit who knelt before Bleak and dutifully kissed the keys on his vest chain. "Excuse me, Mr. Bleak," he said reverently, "but I've just returned from a fellowship in Rome and I've brought you some portions of my new novel-in-progress."

"My dear boy . . ." Bleak began expansively.

Manny seized his opportunity for a getaway and swam off through the crowd with salmonoid frenzy. At the bar he met up with Shmeer, falling over him happily. "Dave! Oh, Christ, am I glad to see you!" he cried. "Some old cocker got ahold of me and damn near bent my ear off."

Shmeer laughed. "I know—I saw you back there with him. I didn't think he'd ever let up."

"Neither did I." Manny took his drink from the bartender and swallowed half of it down in a big gulp. "Whew! That's better. I'm startin' to feel like myself again."

"Good," Shmeer said. He took Manny by the elbow and began propelling him away from the bar. "Come on. It's no good standing still too long at these things. You're an open target for all the bullshitters."

"I know what you mean," Manny said, falling into Shmeer's brisk stride. "Where are we going?"

"Let's get back to the table. I want to talk to Bonnie for a minute."

On the way back they passed Nicky Acrylik, the well-known pop artist, making a spectacle of himself as he sat at a table, trying to cross his legs in a transparent miniskirt.

"Jesus," Manny said, staring at Acrylik. "How can that jerk wear that thing without a jock strap?"

Shmeer, on the other hand, was more intrigued by the conversation of a theatrical producer discussing his latest Broadway venture with a prospective backer.

"We're following the proven formula," the producer was saying, "of taking a time-tested classic property and updating it with a message of social protest."

"I see," the prospect said. "And what property are you using?"

"We're doing a modern version of *Snow White* with Sammy Davis as the lead."

"You mean he's going to play the Prince?"

"No, no. Sammy's cast for Snow White." The producer

hurried on enthusiastically, "You see, we had to change the love interest a bit to give the story intellectual significance, to make it relate to the moral issues of today. So we replaced the old-fashioned girl-boy romance with a hip black-white, he-he-she triangle. In the play, Snow White is a militant Black Power advocate with a homosexual problem and the seven Dwarfs are moderate Negro leaders. As I told you, we've signed Sammy Davis for the lead. Then we have Rex Harrison as the Queen, and we . . ."

By this time Manny and Shmeer had reached their table. They found Bonnie seated beside the press agent Shmeer had assigned her, Milton Flugelhorn, an intense ferret-faced man who perspired a lot and whose sincerity of manner bordered on chronic anxiety. He was frantically fielding the questions of a clutch of newspapermen while Bonnie smiled affably and nodded in agreement with everything he said. She glanced up as Manny and Shmeer approached and she rose to greet them, looking radiant as the sunrise in a white sequined dress boldly slashed to the navel. "I was wondering when you'd get back," she said. "You've been missing all the fun."

Shmeer chucked her under the chin. "As long as you're enjoying it, sweetheart, that's what counts."

"Oh, I am!" She smiled ebulliently. "Believe me, Mr. Shmeer, I've been waiting for this party a long time. I hope it never ends."

"I'll remember that six months from now," Shmeer laughed. "You'll be so tired of parties like this in so many cities, you'll hate the thought of one."

"That'll be the day." Bonnie felt a light tap on her shoulder and whirled around to find Hack smiling at her, taller than she remembered him and boyishly handsome in a well-tailored dinner jacket. "Percy!" she cried, throwing her arms around him. "I'm so glad you're here."

He accepted her embrace and then stood back from her, looking mildly embarrassed. His face glowed with his old chagrined blush as he turned to the girl beside him. "Bonnie, this is Brunhild, my fiancée."

"Oh, how nice to meet you," Bonnie said. "Percy's told me so much about you." She programmed a big smile at Brunhild while her eyes scrutinized the girl carefully. She was big-boned, big-featured, and nearly as tall as Hack—the type of unpretty girl who would later be called handsome. A cold-hearted horse, Bonnie decided. She'd drive him up the wall in no time. What the hell did he ever see in her?

"I'm delighted to meet *you*, Mrs. Ehrlich, and I want to congratulate you on the book." Brunhild smiled pleasantly enough but her voice had a bitchy, overeducated quality that made everything, even a compliment, sound like a dig. "I've heard quite a bit about you, too," she added.

"You have?" A tiny frown peeked through Bonnie's smile. "Well, I hope it was flattering."

Shmeer broke in, quelling the bad vibrations. "Allow me to introduce myself," he said as he grasped Hack's hand. "I'm Dave Shmeer, Mrs. Ehrlich's publisher. Aren't you the young man who helped her with the book?"

Hack nodded so vigorously that his neck seemed to have acquired springs. "Yes, sir. I'm Percy Hack. This is a real honor, Mr. Shmeer."

"My pleasure, Hack. I want you to know what a fine job you did on *The Broadbelters*. You're a writer of real promise." Shmeer beamed at him. "You know how to follow instructions."

"Oh, thank you, Mr. Shmeer. You're most kind."

"Not at all. I'm always on the lookout for fresh new talent." Shmeer threw an arm around Hack and drew him aside. "I've been wanting to talk to you about a project I have in mind that might interest you, Hack. Now listen carefully. How would you like to do a book for me all by yourself, with your name on the cover? Same format as Mrs. Ehrlich's but a different theme, naturally." He smiled. "Matter of fact, something in *The Broadbelters* suggested the theme to me. I'd like to do a book about prominent men in business and government who are secretly all transvestites. We could call it *TV Is a Person*, and we could build the plot around four main characters—patterned after real ones, of course—you know, Monica, the labor leader; Giselle, the Senator; Delores, the steel executive; Olivia, the Pentagon official. Well, what do you say?"

Hack fumbled and sputtered in a spasm of confusion. "Gosh, Mr. Shmeer, I don't know what to say. You've hit me with this so unexpectedly. I . . . . naturally I'm terribly grateful, but . . . well, perhaps I ought to straighten something out before we go any further." He licked his lips nervously. "You see, I only took on Mrs. Ehrlich's assignment because I needed the money. I never intended to make this kind of writing my career. I'm a poet actually. I'd hate to be judged on the wrong basis." He looked around desperately, hoping to be rescued, and then went on, "What I mean is, Mr. Shmeer, I don't know that I'd want to be personally responsible for a book like this, to lay my literary reputation on the line for it. I mean, it's one thing to write a book for somebody else, but to put your own name on it, well . . ."

"I understand how you feel," Shmeer interrupted, nodding sympathetically. "That's a perfectly normal reaction for somebody with your high esthetic standards. But I assure you"—he gave Hack a heartening smile—"you won't have to be ashamed of this book. We can handle it in such a way as to overcome all your misgivings."

Hack stared at him, hope flooding into his eyes. Shmeer was a man of sensitivity, after all. "You can, sir? How?"

"We'll have you write it under a pseudonym."

"Oh." Hack's face collapsed.

"What's the matter?" Shmeer asked. "Don't you know what a great little gimmick that is for selling books?" He began to cackle. "All you have to do is leak it out to the public that the author is using an assumed name. That starts a whole big guessing game as to the author's real identity, and the first thing you know, everyone is buying the book to see if they can figure out who wrote it. Pretty clever, eh?"

"Yes, it's quite clever, I suppose. But what happens when they find out who the author really is?"

"What can happen?" Shmeer retorted. He patted Hack's shoulder encouragingly. "Take my word for it, no one'll think any worse of you when they know you wrote it. They can only admire you for trying to hide your identity."

Hack chewed his lip. "But how will I ever achieve critical acclaim . . ."

"Oh, come on," Shmeer pooh-poohed. He glanced pointedly at Brunhild making uneasy smalltalk with Bonnie and Manny. "We all know that critical acclaim doesn't pay the bills. Why should you starve for the sake of artistic integrity while the public sits in front of a color TV set watching *Peyton Place* twice a week? You have plenty of time to turn out highly praised books that no one reads *after* you've made your first million."

"Million?" Hack stared at Shmeer's unsmiling face and he began to laugh giddily.

"What's so funny?" Shmeer asked. "I'm speaking literally. You can't make less than a million if the book is a smash—$300,000 if it flops."

Hack's knees sagged and he would have fallen if Shmeer hadn't held him up. "You mean to say, at the very worst this book will earn me"—he took a big breath—"three hundred thousand dollars?"

"That's if it's a bomb. But it won't be," Shmeer added quickly. "You've got a real way with the blockbuster formula. You're a 'natural' at it."

Hack grimaced. "Yes, I suppose I am," he sighed. Lost in thought, he looked away for a moment and caught sight of Brunhild signalling wildly to him over the top of Bonnie's head, her lips moving in silent exhortation. "Say yes," she was pleading, "say yes." He stared at her, amazed at her perception. Here she was, almost beyond earshot, thoroughly absorbed in a conversation of her own and she hadn't missed a word of his.

The insistence in Brunhild's eyes, painful in its intensity, found its mark in Hack as an arrow cleaves a bull's eye. He turned back to Shmeer with a small ironic smile on his face. "Well, when do you want the first twenty pages?"

"Good boy!" Shmeer cried. "I knew you'd see things my way. Drop by the office Monday and we'll work out all the details." He flashed a high wattage grin at Hack and gave him a helpful shove toward Brunhild. "Now go tell your girl friend the good news."

Hack stumbled off just as Milton Flugelhorn, looking more harassed than ever and in an obvious state of anguish, bustled up to Shmeer. "Those newspaper guys are murder," he said, shaking his head. "I'm trying to sell Mrs. Ehrlich to them, but all they want to do is discuss the reviews." He waved a bunch of papers at Shmeer. "And look at them! They're all ruinous. There's not a good one in the bunch."

"Let me have those," Shmeer said. He dropped the riding crop he was still holding, which fell to the floor with a faint, girlish whimper, and took the papers from Flugelhorn. Then he reached inside his breastpocket for another set of clippings and handed them to the press agent. "Here, you take these. They're the pre-pub notices. We knew we'd get lousy reviews so we piled up a whole slew of rave quotes in advance. Take a look at that one from the Swinging Nun. It's a beaut."

Flugelhorn's face brightened as he read, "*The Broadbelters* raises physical suffering to the level of the tragic sublime, its erotic elements stimulating the reader to a breathtaking, rapturous, transcendental experience." He looked up at Shmeer. "Now that's more like it. This is the kind of stuff I can work with." He hoisted the clippings like a flag as he hurried away. "Just let anyone mention reviews and I'll show 'em these." "That's the spirit," Shmeer said, waving him off. He frowned at the reviews in his hand and started to tear them up. Then he changed his mind. He remembered a saying he'd heard somewhere—probably one he'd made up himself, it was such good advice—"If someone hands you a lemon, make lemonade." Smiling cagily, he tucked the reviews into his breastpocket and glanced at his watch. Ten o'clock already. Time to get the show on the road.

He picked his riding crop up from the floor and strode resolutely past the tables and up onto the stage. He nodded at the leader of the Militant Prune Juice and the music suddenly stopped. The bandleader, wearing a ponytail, hot pink bell-bottom trousers, and strands of multicolored love beads on his bare wire-haired chest, stepped to the microphone. "Will everyone please be seated," he cried. "Please take your seats, folks. Your host, Mr. Shmeer, would like to say a few words."

Shmeer waited patiently while the noise and motion gradually subsided and the guests settled into an expectant silence. When he finally spoke, his voice was firm and strong, and it throbbed with the nightclub m.c.'s overtones of intimate excitement.

"Good evening, ladies and gentlemen. It gives me great pleasure to welcome you here tonight on the occasion of this important publishing event: the release of the sensational new novel certain to become the nation's number one bestseller—*The Broadbelters* by Bonnie Ehrlich. I know you're all anxious to meet Mrs. Ehrlich, our lovely, talented, and charming author, and I'll present her to you in a little while.

"But first, I have a wonderful surprise in store for you that I'm sure you'll find most entertaining." He paused significantly, waiting just the right length of time. Then he suddenly raised his riding crop high in the air and brought it down on the ground with a resounding crack. There were murmurs of surprise in the audience followed by startled, embarrassed giggles as the sound of feminine moaning filled the air. When it was quiet again, Shmeer continued. "What you have just seen me demonstrate, as many of you know, is the symbol of *The Broadbelters'* underlying theme. To bring this theme vividly to life for you tonight, on an advanced artistic level of total involvement, we are fortunate in having with us a thrilling and boldly original new 'psychodramatic dance troupe'—The Marat-Sades."

Like an eclipse, the lights slowly dimmed until the room was completely black. A long moment of silence followed, and the audience waited it out, their curiosity stiffening into tension. The silence persisted, coiled and mysterious, deep and still as a well. Then the beat of a drum began to throb in the darkness, pounding out a pulsing, tribal rhythm. A spotlight struck the center of the stage, revealing six male dancers, stripped to their shorts, whips at the ready. Lying at the feet of each was a seminude woman with a flaming candle rising out of her navel. Behind the couples loomed a distorted movie screen across which shadowy filmed images shifted and wriggled as they depicted erotic scenes from *The Broadbelters.*

While the crowd watched in fascination, the whole room suddenly erupted into a wild, tumultuous uproar of sight and sound. Strobe lights splashed flickering colors across the stage, spotlights strafed the audience, the Militant Prune Juice shrieked and screamed electronically like a flock of hi-fi loons. And through it all, the dancers ran, leaped, whirled, writhed, and flung themselves at each other in an explicit, savagely uninhibited portrayal of sexual sado-masochism. The men sailed into the air and cut spectacular curlicues as they flogged the women's buttocks, while the women evoked libidinous passion by gyrating shamelessly on the floor or blending their bodies with the men's in sensuous arabesques.

At the climax of the production the whirlwind of noise and

light abruptly ceased. Once again the room plunged into darkness, and no sound could be heard save the tireless beat of the drum. In the stark glare of the solitary spotlight the stage seemed strangely bare. The movie screen was empty now, and the lighted candles in the women's navels had burned down. In a mood of gathering menace the male dancers, still brandishing their whips, slowly began to circle the cowering women. Suddenly the six coiled whips lashed out as one, catching the women's flesh-colored bikini panties and ripping them to shreds. Naked, the women writhed convulsively in time to the quickening drumbeat while the men danced around them, flailing them with the whips and lashing themselves into a frenzy. Finally, in an ecstatic swoon the dancers sank to the floor, the bodies piling up in a babel of orgiastic abandonment that represented every conceivable variety, natural and perverse, of sexual congress. Uttering violent cries and moans, arching in passion, bouncing in the act of love, the troupe capped their performance with a rousing finale that ended, not a moment too soon, in an opportune blackout.

When the lights came on again, the room was strangely quiet. It was a sober, drained silence unbroken by any clapping, as though the audience had just witnessed some powerful religious rite—a ritual of purification, perhaps—and to applaud it would be a desecration.

Even Manny was profoundly moved. He turned to Bonnie and whispered, "That Shmeer is something, ain't he? When he puts on a smoker, it has class." He looked around the room at the rapt audience. "You see that? All these big artlovers are sitting here like they just seen Shakespeare."

Bonnie hushed him up nervously. "Shhh. Be quiet. Shmeer's getting ready to announce me."

Back in the center of the stage, Shmeer rocked smugly on his heels as he surveyed the audience, savoring their awed reaction. He glanced at the booksellers rooted to their ringside seats, and his pleasure deepened. He could tell by the slavering expression on their faces that he had them in the palm of his hand.

He cleared his throat. "And now, ladies and gentlemen, the moment we've all been waiting for. It is with the deepest pleasure that I present this evening's guest of honor, and the next leading lady novelist in the country, Bonnie Ehrlich."

While the band played "Cover Me With Kisses," a song from *The Broadbelters* that a top male vocalist had already recorded in a deal set up by Shmeer's indefatigable p.r. department, Manny slowly escorted Bonnie to the stage. Flashing a winsome smile and impressive cleavage, she stood at Shmeer's side and graciously accepted the applause.

"Isn't she lovely?" Shmeer asked, beaming at Bonnie proudly. "And she's a great little writer, too. I'd like to read you, if I may, what some of the critics have to say about her."

Bonnie shuddered imperceptibly. She watched Shmeer reach inside his breastpocket, and her smile turned to wax as she saw him take out the packet of reviews. Oh, no, she thought, no, no, no. How could he do this to her? Didn't he know what was in those goddam things? She looked toward Flugelhorn, hoping for a reassuring sign from him, but he had sunk down so low in his chair he seemed to be sitting in quicksand. He, too, had obviously been taken by surprise.

The hell with it, Bonnie decided. Everyone knew reviews were something to wipe your ass with. Let him read them if he wanted. She was tough. She could take it. She'd had plenty of experience. Gamely, she tilted her chin skyward and riveted her smile into place as she listened to Shmeer read from The Critics.

"According to Amos Vitriol of the *San Francisco Examiner, The Broadbelters* is, and I quote, 'a smorgasbord of pornographic filth with a juicy tidbit for everyone. The fare ranges from exotic delicacies like incest to the meaty old staple of fornication.' Unquote." Shmeer grinned. "How about that, folks. Isn't that something?

"And here's another one from Lisa Hatchet of the *Miami Herald*: 'The sick sensationalism and sewer-level obscenity of this tawdry novel will appeal to voyeuristic perverts everywhere.'

"And here's something from the *Cleveland Plain Dealer*," Shmeer went on, blithely ignoring the snickers spreading through the audience like a measles rash—'A trashy tale of three show-biz stereotypes hooked on drugs, alcohol, and masochism, that makes *Valley of the Dolls* look like a Girl Scout manual.' "

The snickers grew louder, and Bonnie felt herself losing control, her granitic aplomb threatening to crack with each succeeding insult.

But as Shmeer read on, she was distracted from her pain by an undercurrent of puzzled murmuring in the audience. Scanning the room, she suddenly discovered the cause: a number of uniformed men, frighteningly armed with guns, had begun to file in and station themselves against the walls. My God, she thought, it's a raid! Her heart thumped and boomed, knocking crazily against her ribs for a moment. Then she realized, as she stared at the uniform of the man nearest her, that he was not an ordinary policeman at all but a security guard.

Shmeer, seemingly oblivious of everything except the endless diatribes of the critics, was still reading away with obvious relish. ". . . funky, melodramatic soap opera badly in need of a detergent.'

"And finally, this last statement from *Publishers' Weekly* that pretty well sums it up: 'The Broadbelters, a below-the-belt peek at the cruelly travestied but still identifiable lives of a trio of Hollywood stars, remains, from first page to last, a tawdry, scabrous "sexploitation" novel.' "

Smiling broadly, Shmeer stuffed the reviews back into his jacket. He stood silently before his restless audience and coolly assessed them. Over sixty armed guards had infiltrated by now, and the tension was sizzling like a fuse. He waited, forcing the anticipation still higher. Then he leaned into the mike and began to speak in a sober, low-key tone. "You've heard the reviews now, ladies and gentlemen—every last one of them—and let me tell you this. When the critics uniformly label a book tawdry, trashy, scabrous, pornographic, and obscene; when they accuse it of 'sexploitation,' sick sensationalism, and melodramatic soap opera; when they deplore its cruel travesties of the lives of famous real people; when that happens, you can be sure of one thing." He pointed his finger at them and escalated his voice to a roar. "YOU CAN BE SURE THAT BOOK WILL BE THE MAJOR HIT OF THE YEAR!"

As he delivered this last line, a bandwagon emblazoned with the words "The Broadbelters" rolled out of the wings onto the center of the stage. There were guards riding in the bandwagon, and when they jumped off and stood at attention, the people gasped in amazement at what they saw. The entire inside of the wagon was heaped with great, towering chimney stacks of dollar bills.

Shmeer's voice rumbled through the mike again. "Everyone knows what a major hit means. It means money. *Lots* and *lots* of money." He detached the mike and walked over to the bandwagon, dipping his hand into the mountainous agglomeration of bills. "Ladies and gentlemen, do you know what this is? This is *fifty million dollars*." He listened to the fresh wave of gasps that came up to him. Then he fixed his eye on the booksellers, punching his words out at them like blows. "We expect *The Broadbelters* to gross every cent of this—fifty million dollars—and some of it could be *yours*."

Suddenly Shmeer leaped onto the bandwagon. Still clutching the microphone, he flung his arm out to the audience and cried, "Now I ask all of you here tonight to climb on *The Broadbelters'* bandwagon and ride with me to success!"

The crowd went wild. Caught up by Shmeer's theatrics and by some deep inner pull, they jumped up from their tables, pent-up emotions spilling over, chairs clattering to the floor, in the delirium. While the band blasted them onward with "Happy Days Are Here Again" in a thumping Boogaloo beat, they began a laughing, shouting, pushing, scrambling stampede toward the stage, the booksellers out in front, leading the herd.

Before the mob could reach her, Bonnie ran to the bandwagon and climbed up next to Shmeer. She threw her arms around him, shouting at him over the din. "You did it, Mr. Shmeer! You really grabbed them!"

He grinned in sheer delight and pointed happily toward the barrage of flashbulbs popping off in front of the stage. "Look at that publicity, will you? We'll make every wire service, newspaper, radio and TV station in the country. You couldn't buy that for a million!"

One of the reporters called out to him. "Any plans for a second printing, Mr. Shmeer?"

"Not yet," he answered. "But there will be after tonight."

"Where did you get all the money for your bandwagon?" another shouted.

"Rented it from the banks," Shmeer answered.

The rest of the questions were lost in the noise and commotion as the people began swarming across the stage, dancing excitedly around the bandwagon. A cordon of guards held them off at arm's length, but that didn't curb their exhilaration. The very nearness of all that money was enough for them; they were intoxicated with the scent of success.

And so was Bonnie. "Oh, Mr. Shmeer!" she cried. "This is so exciting!" Her hands swept over the walls of cash that surrounded them. "So much money! I can't believe it's real."

A strange smirk stole over Shmeer's face. Her remark seemed to have triggered off a private joke.

Bonnie stared at him—at the odd little pussycat smile—and suddenly she surmised the truth. She began to giggle. "You mean . . ."

He nodded.

"Oh, that's too funny! Oh, Shmeer, you're unbelievable!" She threw back her head and howled with laughter at the thought of Shmeer's chicanery. The old bastard hadn't rented the money from any banks. No, that would have been too expensive. Instead, he must have found an old ex-con somewhere who printed the stuff up in his basement. The whole fifty million was counterfeit. Phony as a three dollar bill. And sixty guards with rifles were standing there to protect it.

The bandwagon began to roll across the stage, the exuberant crowd laughing and cavorting as they trailed after it. Bonnie leaned back against her cushion of bogus bills and smiled with happiness. She looked at Shmeer, and a glorious feeling of confidence sang inside her. She was in good hands. The man was like P. T. Barnum, Mike Todd, and Billy Rose rolled into one. He could play the public like a piano. He could sell them anything—even nothing.

With such a captain at the helm, how could she fail to reach the beckoning shores of fame?

Chapter 8 The Campaign

A CAR WAS already waiting for them when *Satyr* magazine publisher Sydney Crotchnick's mini-jet, a speedy little five-seater called the *Satyrn,* swooped down onto the airstrip like a graceful exotic bird.

"Welcome to Lake Loot," the chauffeur said as Bonnie, Manny, and Flugelhorn climbed out of the plane and approached the black Maserati. "How was your flight up from Chicago?"

"Wonderful," Manny said. "How could a six-minute flight be bad?"

"It was more like an elevator ride," said Bonnie, bile-faced. "Where do we go from here?"

"Down to the dock," the chauffeur said, helping them into the car. "There's a speedboat waiting for you . . ."

"Speedboat! Oh, my God," Bonnie groaned.

". . . that'll take you out to Mr. Crotchnick's yacht."

"To his yacht?" Flugelhorn looked at him in surprise. "But this isn't a social visit. Mrs. Ehrlich is here to pose for *Satyr's* centerfold. She's a 'Nymph-of-the-Month.' "

The chauffeur glanced appreciatively at Bonnie's legs drawn up to her chest on the back seat of the low-slung car. "Yes, I understand that. But Mr. Crotchnick lives in seclusion on his yacht now. He still maintains the estate for visitors, but he moved the magazine offices and the Nymphet dormitories onto his yacht along with his private quarters so he could work without distraction."

Manny smiled. "I don't blame him. If I was in his line of work, I wouldn't want to be distracted either."

The chauffeur nodded toward Bonnie's overnight case. "Is there any more luggage on the plane, ma'am?"

"No, I'm traveling light this trip," Bonnie said. "I figured I'd be taking my clothes off, not putting them on."

"Very well, then." The chauffeur closed the door and they were soon tearing down the stony road in the Maserati like riders clinging to the back of an uncaged animal, banging and lurching against the sides at every turn, until they came to Crotchnick's estate.

At the entrance the chauffeur slowed down and carefully steered the car past the luxuriant formal gardens toward the enormous Tudor mansion surrounded by a quadrangle of new guest chalets, each with its own bathroom, all modern conveniences, and two nymphet-maids in permanent attendance. Then he veered off to the left, skirting the stables large enough to house a dozen horses and the miles of riding paths visible through the thicket, and came, finally, to a jetty where a speedboat with the *Satyr* emblem on it—a leering faun— was tied up.

A nautical-looking man waved to them from the cockpit. "Hi, there, folks," he called. "Have a good trip? You're ready for the last lap."

"Beautiful," Bonnie said. "Where can I get some Dramamine?"

"Come on. You can make it," Manny said, taking her by the elbow. He and Flugelhorn helped her into the boat and jumped in after her. Then, with a roar of the motor and a nasty lunge that almost brought Bonnie to her knees, they were off.

Churning at madcap speed, the boat skimmed through the green-glinting water and entered a canal. "There she is!" cried the man at the wheel as they approached the yacht.

And there she was—tall and majestic, her white hull gleam-

ing in the bright sunlight—the 2,000 ton *Pride of the Pru-
rient*. Nestled against the lush vulva-shaped island that
Crotchnick had bought to ensure his privacy, the ship rose up
before them like a fortress of polished elegance.

The speedboat pulled up alongside to let them off, and
Bonnie, looking sodden and quite curdled in the face,
climbed up the accommodation ladder with Manny and Flugelhorn following on her heels.

They were welcomed aboard by a lovely young Nymphet,
her nudity covered by the traditional Nile green gauze of the
Satyr Club hostess, who offered to take them on a tour of the
ship. "Perhaps you'd like to see the Sinerama Room, our
famous salon and private theatre with reclining pubic-hair
seats; or the swimming pool with its secret "Peeping Tom
Grotto" and underwater vinyl mermaids with wind-up tails;
or the bar with our unique collection of miniature nudes
under glass; or the . . ."

"Listen, don't give me that jazz," Bonnie broke in.
"Where can I find the ship's hospital?" She staggered a bit
and put out a hand to steady herself. "I'm not feeling so hot."

"Sometimes it takes a little while to get your sea legs," the
Nymphet said, smiling at Bonnie sympathetically. "Suppose
your skip the tour, and I'll have someone take you down to
the Nymphet cabins so you can rest awhile before posing.
There's a sauna and a beauty shop down there, and if you
want anything to eat . . ."

"No!" Bonnie barked. She grimaced nauseously. "Don't
even talk about food. All I want is a little rest."

The Nymphet signaled to another green-gauzed girl who
came forward promptly. "Yes?"

"Libida, will you take Mrs. Ehrlich below now?"

"Certainly." The girl held out her arm to Bonnie who
clutched it gratefully and reeled along beside her as they
headed toward a staircase.

"If you don't mind," Flugelhorn said, turning to Manny, "I

think I'll skip the tour myself. I want to meet with the editors and discuss the copy that'll go with Mrs. Ehrlich's layout. It's important to give her an intellectual image."

Manny stared at him. "How the hell are you gonna do that?"

"Oh, we'll work in something about how the course of her life changed when she read Nietzsche's *Thus Spake Zarathustra* or about her avid interest in figurines and paintings relating to commedia dell'arte." He turned to the Nymphet. "Where can I find the editorial offices?"

"I'll take you there if you like." She smiled at Manny. "What about you, Mr. Ehrlich? Is that where you'd like to go?"

"Not really," Manny said, peering wistfully at the stairway leading to the Nymphet dormitories.

"They're off limits," the Nymphet said.

"That figures." Manny sighed. "Well, I guess I ought to pay my respects to old Sydney while I'm here. Come on, let's go."

The Nymphet led Manny and Flugelhorn down an elegant circular staircase to the bridge deck and Crotchnick's private quarters: a suite of offices, a TV taping studio, and a three-room apartment. Flugelhorn stayed in the offices, blending at once into the frantic confusion, while Manny continued on into Crotchnick's study.

"Please make yourself comfortable," the Nymphet said, "and I'll tell Mr. Crotchnick you're here."

Manny paced around the huge room, stopping to admire the immense oil portrait of Alfred Kinsey and the gallery of nudes and abstract paintings, also nudes, that hung on the walls. He glanced at the shelves lined with books by Crotchnick's favorite authors—Havelock Ellis, Krafft-Ebing, the Marquis de Sade, Henry Miller, Vatsyayana, folio editions of Kinsey. He gazed at the most precious of Crotchnick's objets d'art, a delicately sculptured Sienna marble bust with inlaid nipples of lapis lazuli, and at the enormous seventeenth-century Spanish hutch filled with voluptuous Egyptian, Greek, and Roman antiquities, graphic pre-Columbian statuary, and engraved trophies from the Scatological Society, the League of Moral Permissiveness, and the Fraternal Order of Paroled Disk Jockeys.

Manny could only marvel, as he sank into a plush automated love seat that immediately threw its arms around him, how far Sydney Crotchnick had come. He thought of Sydney in that time so long ago when they were a couple of kids in tattered knickers growing up in the old neighborhood in Brooklyn. He remembered him as a frail, bespectacled boy of uncertain complexion whose nose was always buried in a book, a serious-minded student with no time for games. While the other boys were having fun hustling pool, gang-banging a local girl, or amicably stoning each other in the streets, Sydney could be found holed up in the library poring over thick textbooks on Italian Renaissance art and slobbering over all the pictures of the nudes. He was clearly destined for greatness.

But it was Manny, strangely enough, who had achieved greatness first. On his early triumphal return from the Coast as head of United Misalliance, he had bumped into Sydney at a party and had been shocked, though not without a certain amount of smug satisfaction, to learn that Sydney was a shabby sixty-dollar-a-week clerk for some girlie magazine and was married to a skinny disaster named Minerva Spleen whom he had met while working his way through N.Y.U. as a male housemother in a sorority.

At the party, Crotchnick had been overjoyed to see Manny. Forsaking his customary shyness, he drew Manny off into a corner and began babbling excitedly to him about an idea he had for starting his own magazine. "You see, Manny, this wouldn't be just another ordinary girlie slick. Oh, no. This one will have style, taste, and sophistication. It'll raise the nude photograph to an art form. And what's more important, it will stand for something editorially. It'll be a girlie magazine with *relevance*. It'll be"—he broke into a proud smile as he said the words—"the house organ of the sexual freedom movement."

Manny looked at him. "Do you think it needs one, Syd?"

"My God, yes!" Crotchnick cried. Perspiration had begun to break out on his brow. "There are millions of suppressed people in this country being held in moral restraint—frustrated, unhappy second-class sexual citizens—who need an authentic spokesman for their cause. We'll be their voice, crying out against our unenlightened Victorian moral code and upholding the basic right to carnality of every man, woman, and child of consenting age." He mopped his forehead with his handkerchief. "But that's just the editorial page. The rest of the magazine will have plenty of bawdy cartoons, dirty jokes, spicy fiction, racy reportage, and the complete inside track on how the fashionable Lecher-About-Town dresses, drives, drinks, dines, and makes out."

"And lots of good-looking nudes with big knockers, right?" Manny asked.

"Oh, certainly. They'll be the backbone of the magazine— the hard core, you might say—pages and pages of nudes in glorious color. And not just unknowns either, but big-name actresses."

"Go on, Syd. Where are you gonna get big names from?"

Crotchnick smiled. "You've heard of doctored photographs, haven't you? Well, in our first issue we're going to tinker around with the shots a little, that's all."

"What d'ya mean?"

"We're going to take off the model's head and put on Marilyn Monroe's."

Manny stared at him. "But you can't get away with a deal like that! Monroe will sue."

Crotchnick clasped his hands together prayerfully. "From your mouth to God's ears. A lawsuit like that would put us on the map." He smiled slyly. "Of course, if I had enough money

I wouldn't have to resort to such trickery. I could do everything open and above board."

"How's that?" Manny asked.

"I could buy the rights to her nude calendar pictures and run them without her consent."

Manny studied Crotchnick shrewdly. He was beginning to sound less like a sex nut and more and more like a businessman all the time. "How much money do you need, Syd?"

"I've already raised five thousand," Crotchnick said quickly, "and I figure another five thousand would put us in business."

Manny took out his checkbook and stared at it for a moment, his pen poised precariously over the lined paper. Then he hastily wrote out a check and handed it to Crotchnick. "Here you are, Syd. Buy the calendar pictures and whatever else you need. I got a feeling you're onto something big."

Crotchnick stared at the check and his stifled face burst like a firecracker into an open, reckless smile. "The whole five thousand!" he exclaimed. His eyes blinked rapidly behind his glasses as he reached for Manny's hand. "I promise you, Manny, you'll get your money back a hundred times over. This magazine is going to make publishing history. It'll hit America where she lives—right between the thighs."

Crotchnick gave Manny's hand a final, fervent squeeze. "Give me a few years and we'll have the biggest circulation in the country. Then they'll all come crawling to us on their knees, stars and would-be stars alike, begging to pose for our centerfold. Mark my words," he said. "Those two pages will have more exposure inch for inch than anyone ever dreamed."

As it happened, Crotchnick couldn't have been more prophetic. Much to Manny's amazement and probably to Crotchnick's as well, the first issue of the magazine, dubbed *Satyr* by a mythology-minded editor with odd, pointed ears, sold over a hundred thousand copies. Circulation quickly spiraled into the millions, and Crotchnick plowed the profits into a fertile string of Satyr Clubs with comely Nymphet hostesses. The skinny little kid from Brooklyn became, in less than a decade, a swashbuckling millionaire with an empire built on a centerfold. In time, the centerfold itself took on the grandeur of an institution—careers rose or fell on its rolling planes. Bonnie's, Manny hoped, would be one that rose.

A Nymphet appeared in the doorway. "Mr. Crotchnick is ready to receive you now, Mr. Ehrlich. Come this way, please."

Manny leaped up from the loveseat's embrace and followed the Nymphet out of the study into Crotchnick's bedroom. He stood in the threshold for a moment, accustoming his eyes to the heavy shade-drawn gloom. An acrid mustiness sprang out at him, the stale odor of a hermitage or a sickroom. Crotchnick, wearing pajamas and a faded blue silk robe, sat cross-legged on a huge circular bed, a pile of papers spread before him. His face was bent in scowling profile as he studied the papers.

"Hello, Syd," Manny said loudly. "How've you been?"

There was a long silence while Crotchnick continued to peruse his papers. Finally he said, "Not bad, Manny. Not bad." Absent-mindedly, he reached behind his back to the panoply of buttons on his headboard. He pushed one, and the bed slowly revolved toward Manny. When it stopped, Crotchnick looked up at him, his piercing contact-lensed eyes staring out of his gaunt, saturnine face like chunks of coal set in a death's head.

"You look great, pal," Manny said unconvincingly. He drew near the bed and waited for the Nymphet to leave. "But you oughta come up for air once in a while. Leave the broads alone for a change and get a little sunshine."

"Who has time for sunshine, Manny? I've got work to do." Crotchnick turned grimly back to his papers. "Next month we're opening a luxurious year-round Satyr resort in Haifa. If the Arabs don't louse us up with a war or something, we'll turn Haifa into the Miami-of-the-Middle East."

Manny sat down on the edge of the bed and appraised Crotchnick's cadaverous face with its hollowed-out cheeks and deeply shadowed eyes. Who's he kidding, he thought. No one looks that bad from a successful business. The broads were killing him. "How's Minerva?" he asked casually.

"Minerva? Didn't you hear about us?" He glanced up at Manny's questioning face. "She divorced me six months ago."

"Oh, I'm sorry to hear that, Syd."

"Yes, it was one of those messy, name-calling things the newspapers have a field day with."

"What were the grounds—adultery?"

"No," Crotchnick said sadly. "Impotence."

"*No!*" Manny was astounded. "*You*, Syd? Of all people. I mean, I always thought you were such a big lover . . ."

Crotchnick cut him short with a wave of the hand. "Yes, well, I *was* until I got bogged down with all this work. Do you think it's been easy leading the crusade against puritanism in this country? I can assure you, spreading the gospel of hedonism has taken a lot out of me."

"Maybe all you need is a little vacation."

"How can I take one?" Crotchnick asked. "I'll never rest as long as there are still people left in our Society ruining their lives with that old antisex, antiplay, antipleasure ethic of the pre-*Satyr* days." He put aside his papers for a minute and sighed nostalgically. "It's a funny thing, Manny. I can't say that I miss Minerva—I'm too busy for that—but we did have a beautiful relationship. Especially in the beginning, when we were college sweethearts. I'll never forget the night I came into her room at the sorority house and we spent hours together reading aloud from Kinsey. Then we made savage, wildly abandoned love, and it was like the whole world opened up to me. Afterwards, I took her in my arms and I said to her, 'Now I know what I'm going to do with my life, Minerva. I'm going to become a Freedom Fighter in the Sexual Revolution. I'm going to wage war against cruel, irrational repression so that one day in this land of ours there'll be sexual freedom and libertinism for all.' "

"What did Minerva say?"

"All she said was, 'I hope I'm not pregnant.' Minerva was a bit of a worrier, you know." He sighed wistfully. "Ah, well, that's all water over the dam now."

A face suddenly appeared on one of the ten closed circuit television monitors in the room and announced: "The editorial page is ready for your approval, Mr. Crotchnick. Shall I bring it in?"

Crotchnick glanced at the monitor and pressed a button on the headboard. "All right, Angst, let's see it."

Minutes later, the head on the television set, scaled down to human size and supported on a long, stalklike body, hurried into the room. Crotchnick introduced the materialized Angst as an executive vice-president of the company and promptly went into conference with him over the papers he had brought in.

"Yes, yes, the lead article's fine," Crotchnick said. "I like it —'Masturbation: A Do-It-Yourself Answer to Your Sex Problems'—it's got just the right note of forthright sincerity. Quite convincing, I'd say." He riffled a few pages. "Now let's see. What else have you got here? 'Fetishes Can Be Fun.' Hmmm. Yes, it's engagingly written and I like the persuasive approach." He turned a few pages more and stopped dead. " 'Let's Liberate the Homosexual,' " he read, scowling. "What's all this slop about? You know how we feel about fags."

"Yes, I do," Angst said quickly, "but how can we champion sexual freedom for one group of people and not speak out against the sexual enslavement of another?"

"Because the perverts are in the minority," Manny explained. "We're selling sexual freedom to the masses, and we can't afford to turn them off by sticking our neck out for a handful of queers."

"But that's just the point . . ."

"The point is," Crotchnick snapped, "that you'll tear this damned thing up and replace it with something from our files —something on censorship, maybe. That's always timely and it won't get us in any trouble. You've got to remember, Angst, the people we write for are straight."

Angst shriveled with contrition. "All right, all right. You're the boss. I'll dust off the censorship article and run it instead." He scooped up the papers and was on his way out when Crotchnick's voice stopped him at the door.

"You don't have to throw that faggot piece out, Angst. Just shelve it temporarily." There was a placating smile on his face. "If public sympathy for fairies gets strong enough, we may have to champion their cause."

Angst, mollified by this concession, nodded brightly. "That's a wise decision, Crotch," he said and left.

His departure was followed by the arrival of a bearded and mustached art director who sidled in bearing hundreds of transparencies of nudes. He spread them out on the bed and discussed them with Crotchnick while Manny stood by, ogling. The comments of the two men seemed singularly cold and businesslike to Manny, especially when he realized they would be discussing nude shots of his wife in much the same terms only a month from now. For all the emotion they exhibited, they might have been rummaging through a pile of old door hinges.

"This shot of her face is good, but I don't like the breasts. The nipples are too aggressive."

"The angle of that shot makes her hips look too whorish. We want to titillate the reader, not offend him."

"There's something wrong with the navel on this shot. It's not making a clear statement."

"Don't you think the thighs lack conviction here?"

They continued in this fashion for almost a half hour, meticulously examining breasts, thighs, hips, and navels until the right Nymphet-of-the-Month shots had been selected. Then the art director took his leave and Crotchnick, exhausted, slumped back against the pillows. He passed a hand wearily over his brow. "Lord, I'm glad *that's* over."

Manny smiled in amusement. "You sound like you just had a tooth pulled or somethin'. That's a real hardship, to lay in bed and look at naked broads all day."

Crotchnick sat up, an injured look on his face. His voice was filled with reproach. "I'm surprised at you, Manny. You ought to know better. The selection of nudes is an art—like diamond cutting—that requires the utmost skill and concentration. We've got to take these naked broads as you call them and work them over until they're so clean and wholesome looking that no one thinks they're real."

Manny scratched his head. "But they *are* real. Why don't you want 'em to look that way?"

Crotchnick's lips formed a tiny smile. "Because real sex frightens people. It's the real stuff that's obscene. Give people the *illusion* of sexuality and they're happy." He cocked his head to one side. "Haven't you noticed something about our Nymphets, Manny? They all look the same—young, perfect, and completely dehumanized. They're great for gawking at, but they'd be no different in bed than a Barbie doll."

"But Bonnie's not like that," Manny objected.

"No, she isn't," Crocketnick agreed, "But we never would have used Bonnie if we weren't promoting her book as a favor to you. First of all, she's too old. Women over twenty-one tend to develop brains or other complications that make them potentially dangerous. And then, too, even when she was younger Bonnie was always a bit too, uh, overripe, you might say. Not that she wasn't always enormously attractive," he added quickly, "but there was something a little too earthy about her, frighteningly physical."

Manny felt a sharp pang of annoyance. Where did Crotchnick, an impotent crackpot who couldn't even hold onto a dog like Minerva, get off passing remarks about Bonnie? He glanced abruptly at his watch. "Speaking of Bonnie, what the hell's keeping her? She's been down there for hours. How many pictures do they hafta take?"

"Nonprofessional models are sometimes a problem," Crotchnick said. "Let me check in and see how she's doing." He pushed one of the headboard's numberless buttons, and another disembodied head appeared on a TV monitor, this one high-domed and esthetic-looking with a trim goatee.

"Are you finished with Mrs. Ehrlich yet?" Crotchnick asked. "Her husband's waiting for her."

"Yes, we're just about through," the face said. "We'd have gotten done much sooner, but we had some trouble with her left breast."

Crotchnick's eyebrows went up. "You did? What was the matter with it?"

"It had this funny birthmark on it. Damnedest thing I ever saw." The face tittered softly for a moment. "Looked just like a dollar sign."

Crotchnick glanced at Manny, whose expression was stonily impassive, and then turned back to the monitor. "Did you get rid of it?"

"I think so," the face said. "We covered it with cosmetics, and the airbrushes should do the rest."

"Okay. Send Mrs. Ehrlich in to me . . ."

"No, no. Tell her to meet me in the bar," Manny interjected quickly. "I'm gettin' a little restless in here."

"Oh. Tell her Mr. Ehrlich will see her in the bar when she's finished." Crotchnick clicked off and turned to Manny. "Say, I hope you and Bonnie will stay and have dinner on the ship. The cuisine is marvelous—everything from bouillabaise to brandy. And tonight in the Sinerama Room we're showing two great film classics—the foreign versions."

Manny's eyes lit up. "Oh, I know all about them European export jobs. What've you got?"

"*The Sound of Music* and *Mary Poppins*."

"Oh." Manny shook his head slowly from side to side. "If you don't mind, I think we'll pass, Syd. Bonnie's probably got other plans for tonight, but thanks, anyway."

He stuck out his hand to Crotchnick who shook it limply. "Well, it was nice seeing you, Manny, and good luck with the book. I'm glad *Satyr* could be of help." Immersing himself in his papers again, he added absently, "And remember me to Bonnie."

"Thanks, Syd," Manny said. "I know she's very grateful." On his way out he caught a glimpse of Crotchnick reflected in the eighteenth-century Venetian mirror that rose over the dresser. Startled, he paused and stared. It was a compelling image. In that strange play of light and shadow the cross-legged Crotchnick hunched over his tear sheets, ascetically gaunt and saturnine in his faded blue robe, looked for all the world like a mendicant friar poring over the precious pages of his Bible.

Girlie Curlie sat in her dressing room at the TV studio, one slender booted leg crossed over the other, and waited for the glue on her false eyelashes to dry. When she was sure they were set, she blinked rapidly in succession a few times to test them. "Perfect," she said aloud, evidently pleased with her flutterability.

Rising, she crossed the room to her full length mirror and planted herself in front of it. She smiled slightly as she hailed the woman in the mirror—a tiny woman, sleek and seductive in a viperish way, who managed to look both cool and smoldering at the same time as though she had been chiseled out of dry ice. It amused Girlie, slowly revolving before the mirror like a chicken on a spit, that her diminutiveness was such a constant source of surprise to people. "But she's so *little*," they would whisper to each other, seeing her for the first time.

Somehow they expected the country's most famous sex evangelist to be a woman of ampler proportions. They soon discovered, though, that what Girlie lacked in size she more than made up for in intensity. It was the intensity of a revivalist, and when it came to winning converts to the new morality, Girlie had no equal. Single-handedly, she had brought more women into the fold of promiscuity than any other spiritual leader in the world. As the self-appointed savior of the meek and flat-chested of the earth, she had been given her own weekday talk show, *Open Up!*, on which she never failed to seduce her celebrity guests, no matter how tight-lipped, into babbling the most intimate minutiae of their sex lives. These taped confessions, aired each afternoon in millions of homes like a year's wash strung out on a line, worked wonders in propagating her faith. Even the most hardened nonswingers, watching her program, were persuaded to cast off their sins of drabness and virginity.

Girlie turned from the mirror as the show's assistant producer, Aphrodisia Rodenbusch, came into the room. Aphrodisia, who pre-interviewed all the guests, had on an outfit that looked like a cheer-leader's uniform, the big red "O" on the back of her sweater theoretically the emblem for *Open Up!* but symbolic of other things as well.

"We'll be taping in a few minutes, Girlie," Aphrodisia said. "I'd better go over the fact sheet with you."

"Okay, Aph. What do we have?" Girlie slipped into a chair, careful not to muss her size 6 hot pink ("Passion in fashion" was a Girlie byword) wool dress.

"It's going to be a bit tricky," Aphrodisia said, handing Girlie a typewritten sheet and keeping a copy for herself. "First we have those two orgasm experts, Drs. Voyeur and Fettish—Voyeur is the lady. They're pretty dull, so for a touch of glamour we threw in one of Shmeer's authors, a Bonnie Ehrlich."

"Oh, that one. I had to endorse her book. Let's see now
. . . " Girlie had an amazingly retentive memory. "*The
Broadbelters,* isn't it?"

"Yes, that's it. Now the problem is, this Ehrlich dame is a
real glamorpuss but she hasn't got a thought in her head."
Aphrodisia permitted herself a wry smile. "I read somewhere
that she's a real Nietzsche lover but if you ask me, she probably thinks Nietzsche is the name of a Chinese laundry." She
went on, "And of course Shmeer's got her so brainwashed with
that TRAP course of his that she won't discuss anything but
her book. So you've got to find a way to draw her into the
orgasm discussion on a *personal* level. Get it?"

Girlie sat forward, tapping her front teeth with a fingernail.
She was worried about Shmeer. He was getting to be a
problem, always throwing her tough customers like this. But
of course, how could she turn him down? If it hadn't been for
Shmeer, she herself would still be sitting behind a desk in the
same Fricke, Fryor, Cisyk, and Drookas Advertising Agency
where she'd started out as a mousy thirty-five-dollar-a-week
clerk and had endured fifteen years of answering to "girlie"
simply because nobody could remember her real name (Ger-
trude). Where would she be now if Shmeer hadn't spotted
that true confession piece she'd sent in to *Office Party,* de-
scribing how her whole life had changed the day Bullock laid
her in the supply closet, an event recorded for posterity on a
stack of carbon paper? Along with her virginity the supply
closet caper had freed her from the torment of acne and
menstrual cramps; and transformed by new vitality she had
meteorically risen from clerk to copywriter to vice-president
of the company. She'd hoped the revelation of her experience
to that vast army of other faceless, flat-chested ciphers wast-
ing away in unsung office jobs would inspire them to do
something about their plight. When Shmeer had pointed out
to her that she could reach millions more by expanding her
story into a book called *How to Get Ahead in a Closet,* she

had embraced the opportunity eagerly. She had gone along with all of Shmeer's demands, zealously promoting the book to the top of the best-seller list, and had emerged victorious from the campaign as the sexual shepherd of the career-girl flock. With her sequel, *Beyond the Closet*, she had achieved the status of a guru. But it was Shmeer, she knew, who had been the real power behind her rise to eminence. And knowing this, how could she refuse him her help in powering the rise of others?

Girlie continued tapping her tooth as she studied the fact sheet. "I've got an idea," she said at last, looking up at Aphrodisia. "You leave it to me. I'll get Ehrlich involved in this program like she's never been involved in anything before."

Aphrodisia clapped her hands together and for a moment seemed about to let out a mighty "Yea team!" but she merely said, "I know you'll come through, Girlie."

The two women left the dressing room and went into the studio where Bonnie and Flugelhorn were waiting. Inside a wooden enclosure, which looked like a small cabin but was actually a vastly enlarged orgone box, sat the other two guests warming up for the start of the show.

At the sight of Girlie, Flugelhorn sprang forward and introduced Bonnie like a curator unveiling a treasure.

Keyed up and determinedly gracious, Bonnie said, "I'm a great fan of yours, Girlie. I watch your show all the time."

"Thank you. We're glad to have you with us." Girlie smiled cordially as she fought down an involuntary prickle of dislike. It was impossible for Girlie, even at this stage in her life, not to resent a woman as effortlessly erotic as Bonnie. Bonnie was sexy without even thinking about it, while she, Girlie, had to think about it all the time. Women of Bonnie's ilk always seemed to remind her that no matter how impenetrable the façade she had developed, underneath the proud dunes of her falsies beat the heart of a shy, plain mouse.

Flugelhorn handed Girlie a copy of *The Broadbelters*. "We had the jacket design pre-tested for TV," he told her proudly. "When you hold the book up, the letters and coloring will jump right out of the tube."

Girlie smiled as she tucked the book under her arm. "Shmeer doesn't miss a trick, does he?"

Aphrodisia said, "You can stay out here and watch the show on the monitor, if you like, Mr. Flugelhorn." Then she nodded anxiously toward the wooden structure. "Girlie, I think you'd better take Mrs. Ehrlich in now. It's time to begin."

Bonnie looked apprehensive. "Why do you tape in there? Is it some special kind of sound stage?"

"You might call it that," Aphrodisia said. It's really a giant orgone box."

"A who?"

"An orgone box."

"What the hell's that?"

Aphrodisia started to explain, but Girlie stopped her. "Never mind—let's just get in there," she laughed, hooking her arm through Bonnie's. She gave Aphrodisia a faintly reproving look as if to say, "Why waste your breath on a yo-yo like this?"

Inside the orgone-studio the cameramen were waiting. They manned their machines like gunners preparing to open fire, the red tips of their cigarettes glowing in the darkness. Their target was a shabby-genteel living room stage set consisting of a small Chippendale settee, two armchairs of indeterminate period, and an end table on which reposed an ivory-colored phone. The settee was already occupied by Drs. Voyeur and Fettish, both dressed in white lab coats and looking frostily composed. They gave scarcely any sign of recognition as Girlie and Bonnie entered and took their places in the armchairs, Girlie stationing herself next to the phone.

"All right, everybody, let's put on a great big smile," Girlie said. She tilted her head at an angle favorable to her plastic nose and parted her lips over a sea of perfectly capped teeth. Dutifully, the others followed suit. As soon as all four on-screen grins were firmly affixed, Girlie signaled to the camera pointing at her. Its red eye winked on, and the tape began to roll.

Girlie's voice, sultry yet athrob with the promise of joy and redemption, filled the room. "Hello, America. This is Open Up! asking you: Have you had your Big O today?" She paused for a moment as though listening to the answer from her unseen audience. Then she continued, her voice filled with compassion. "You poor little lambs. You don't even know what the 'Big O' is, do you? Well, thank goodness you have me to tell you. It's the 'insiders' ' term for the female orgasm, your God-given birthright as a woman."

Girlie's camera blinked off and another came up on her guests as she went on, "Here with me today are three people whose intimate knowledge of the orgasm, through one means or another, qualifies them as experts. On my right is Dr. Julius Fettish, senior consultant in gynecology at . . ."

Flugelhorn, pacing nervously in the outer studio, his eye peeled to the monitor, waited for Bonnie to be introduced. He was terrified that she might freeze up and forget the scores of pointers they had drilled into her all these weeks.

"And on her right," Girlie was saying, "is Bonnie Ehrlich, former actress turned novelist whose book . . ."

And there she was: Bonnie at her most relaxed and self-assured. She was leaning back in her chair, her legs crossed at a discreet but alluring angle, an engaging smile on her face. Flugelhorn thought she looked especially lovely in contrast to the matronly and rather frumpish Dr. Voyeur. And he was certain, as Girlie led off the questioning with her, that Bonnie would not let him down. She seemed to be holding onto her cool with both hands, tossing off her prepared one-liners and delivering her ready-made answers as though they were completely spontaneous while doggedly refusing, all the while, to be drawn off the track.

"Mrs. Ehrlich," Girlie was saying in the coquettish voice she used to soften up all her guests, "over and over in your marvelously sexy book you describe your characters in orgasm. Are these passages based on personal experience?"

"They certainly aren't based on *impersonal* experience," Bonnie said banteringly. Shifting quickly to a more serious tone, she continued, "Actually, it's not how much *I've* experienced that counts; it's how much I can make the *reader* experience. And believe me, anyone who reads *The Broadbelters* in bed alone at night is in real trouble."

"Anyone in bed alone at night is in real trouble to begin with," Girlie said. She persisted, boring like a drill. "But tell me, to get that ring of truth in your work, don't you have to write about something you know?"

"Does a person have to sleep on a bed of nails before they can write about pain?" Bonnie countered. "Speaking of pain," she went on in the same breath, "the sadism scenes in *The Broadbelters* are probably the 'realest thing' I've written, and I don't go in for that kind of thing at all."

"What *do* you go in for, Mrs. Ehrlich?"

"The same things as any other healthy, red-blooded American woman," Bonnie smirked. "But the women in *The Broadbelters*," she raced on, "are different, exciting, with all kinds of crazy hang-ups. Phyllis Benson, for example—and I don't know who started that wild rumor that Phyllis is patterned after . . ."

Flugelhorn almost laughed out loud. He wanted to kiss the monitor, he was so happy. Bonnie was performing like a pro. She was making an impact, coming across with charming insouciance as she deftly pushed her book. He thought of all the copies that were being sold—and of the bonus Shmeer might give him—and he began to relax. Slipping into a seat, he lit a cigarette and settled down to watch the remainder of the show.

Having temporarily given up on Bonnie, Girlie was now pummeling daintily away at Drs. Voyeur and Fettish, hoping to pry loose some of the more titillating details of their sex research project.

"Isn't it true," Girlie was saying, "that to obtain your data your spent months filming live volunteers in the act of intercourse?"

"That's correct," Dr. Fettish answered crisply. "The primary purpose of our experiment was to film the orgasm in its native habitat."

"And tell us the truth, Doctor," Girlie wheedled, "didn't you ever get the teeniest wee bit 'excited' watching all that take place right under your nose?"

The Doctor's craggy white eyebrows shot up and he sputtered for a moment, unable to answer. But Dr. Voyeur, stung into maternal protectiveness, saved the day for him. "Certainly not," she snapped. "We never get personally involved with our subjects. We're much too busy operating the camera equipment."

"Yes, our equipment is extremely sensitive and costly," Dr. Fettish chimed in, making a quick recovery. "We use a Mitchell camera with a 16 mm projector and a special 'instant rushes' video system in case we have to do retakes. And as a teaching aid, we've developed the remarkable 'Polaroid Plunger,' a camera-equipped mechanical phallus."

Girlie decided to take a different tack. "I understand there are some very famous celebrities among your subjects, isn't that so?"

"Yes, and they come to us because we never violate their privacy," Dr. Voyeur said icily, "by revealing their names. We don't even allow their faces to be photographed—all of our shots are taken from the pubis down."

"And what is it exactly that you shoot?" Girlie asked coyly. If she couldn't wring anything confidential out of them, she wanted to get on to the provocative part as quickly as possible.

Dr. Fettish reacted to her question like a track star at the sound of the gun. He immediately launched into a detailed description of the female orgasm, but in a manner that was flat as a wallboard. To Girlie's misery, his language was so dry and clinical as to remove any trace of humanness, let alone pleasure, from the act. By the time they were ready to break for the commercial, he was still droning away in textbook tones of unbearable monotony . . .

". . . the outer one third of the vagina—which is known as the orgasmic platform—swells and thus markedly decreases in diameter. This is in contrast to the upper two thirds of the vagina which expands in diameter. The clitoris enlarges and retracts to a higher position on the mons, away from the vaginal opening and away from the penile thrusting."

"And we'll have to move away from the penile thrusting ourselves for a moment," Girlie said lightly, "as we pause for this message from our sponsor."

Out of camera range, Girlie pressed a hand nervously to her forehead and snatched the phone up from the table beside her. In low, urgent tones she spoke to Aphrodisia, seated outside in the control booth. "Yes, yes, I *know* it's dull as dishwater . . . I tried to, but they won't . . . all right, I'll put more pressure on . . . no, I can't bring her back in yet . . . I'm saving her for the end . . . that's right, a big finish."

She hung up in time for the end of the commercial, a surreal fantasy in which a scrawny, unendowed spinster, dining out with a date, swallows a name-brand estrogen pill and forthwith sprouts an omnivorous bosom that reaches across the table, engulfs her escort, and carries him off to a grinning justice-of-the-peace.

Back on camera again, Girlie pounced on Dr. Fettish with renewed zeal. "What an exciting eyewitness report on the

orgasm, Doctor! Now could you tell us—in *laymen's terms*
—how your subjects reached that point?"

"Generally, they engaged in foreplay and then had intercourse. Sometimes the foreplay alone was sufficient to effect
orgasm."

"Really!" Girlie moistened her lips expectantly. "And what
kind of things did they do during foreplay?"

"Of the married women in our female sample more than
90 per cent experienced simple kissing, manual stimulation of
the breasts and the genitalia, oral stimulation of the breasts
and manual stimulation of the male genitalia by the female.
Eighty-seven per cent experienced deep kissing, 54 per cent
reported oral stimulation of the . . ."

And on he went, a sex manual come to life, mechanically
jabbering an endless litany of data and statistics.

Bonnie, schooled against being upstaged, tried to cut in on
him several times. "I'd like to add something to that . . . May
I say a word or two . . . Listen, if I could butt in for just a
moment . . ."

But it was no use. Dr. Fettish rolled on, inexorable as the
tide.

It was Girlie, finally, who stopped him. Desperate that time
was running out, and goaded by Aphrodisia's frantic signals
from the control booth, she gave the Doctor what amounted
to a command. "I think we have all the facts and figures we
need, Dr. Fettish. Now could you give us a demonstration?"

". . . whereas in 85 per cent of the cases, tactile stimulation
of the erogenous zones . . . uh, eh . . ." Dr. Fettish faltered in
mid-stride and ran down to a halt. "What's that? What was
the question?"

"The erogeneous zones, Doctor. Could you show us where
they are?"

Dr. Fettish looked startled for a moment, and then he
meekly placed a forefinger on his lips. "Well, the mouth, for
one. The lips, the tongue . . ."

"No, no. Don't show us on yourself, Doctor—not when you have such a pretty model like Mrs. Ehrlich sitting there."

The camera followed Dr. Fettish's gaze and swung around to Bonnie. She smiled prettily, glad to be back on view.

"Go ahead, Doctor," Girlie urged. "As you can see, Mrs. Ehrlich has all her zones in the right places."

Dr. Fettish cleared his throat. "Yes, well, in the absence of a mannequin, I suppose she'll have to do." Briskly he leaned across the stone ledge of Dr. Voyeur and reached out toward Bonnie's head. He touched her ear, and the camera moved in for a close shot. "In addition to the mouth," he said, "another cranial area of erotic sensitivity is the ear." He took hold of her lobe and rolled it gently between his thumb and forefinger. Then he released it, and his hand slipped down behind her neck. "Next we have the nape of the neck." He stroked it softly. "Then the throat." His fingers caressed her windpipe. "And the armpits . . ."

"Ooch," Bonnie giggled, "that tickles."

". . . and the breasts . . ."

"Hey! Cut that out!"

"No, don't stop now, Doctor!" Girlie cried. "You're doing fine."

The Doctor was on his feet now, bending over Bonnie, the camera following the movements of his hands as they played over her body. ". . . and the navel area," he was saying, ". . . and the abdomen . . . and the whole pubic area . . ."

"Say! Get out of there!" Bonnie squealed. "What do you think this is?"

"That's it, Doctor!" Girlie shouted, her eye on the clock. "Come on, you two. Open up! Open up!"

". . . and the lower end of the back . . . and the buttocks . . . and the inner surface of the thighs . . ."

"Stop that! Take your hand away!"

"Keep going, Doctor! You're beautiful! Open up!"

"Open up! Open up! Open up!" Aphrodisia had come out

of the control booth and was jumping up and down in the studio, rooting the team on.

Even Dr. Voyeur had lost control. "Turn her on, Doctor! Turn her on!" she hissed, as she slipped out of her seat and crouched beside him, a Minox camera in her hand.

Dr. Fettish was on his knees now, running his hands down Bonnie's legs. ". . . and the feet," he was muttering, "the feet are . . . the feet are . . . Oh, my God! They're beautiful." Suddenly he tore off Bonnie's shoes and began kissing her feet. "Oh, those toes," he gasped, his arms clamped around her legs like a vise. "I've never seen such toes."

Aphrodisia raced back into the control booth, screaming, "Get him off her feet, Girlie! You've only got a minute left."

"Please, Doctor. Don't get hung up now," Cirlie pleaded. "She's got to have a big O."

"Remember, Doctor. It's for Science," Dr. Voyeur whispered, clicking her Minox.

"Thirty seconds to go!" Aphrodisia yelled.

As the camera angled in for the last close-up, Dr. Fettish's hand shot up from Bonnie's legs. Half rising, his face aflame with the febrile, wild-eyed expression of the Ancient Mariner stumbling on a bucket of rain water, he uttered a ululating moan and fell on Bonnie deliriously.

"Goodbye, all you wonderful people out there," Girlie cried, drawing the camera back on her for the final seconds. With a beatific smile, she raised her arms and delivered her parting line like a benediction: "*Open Up!* has just presented a television first."

Outside in the anteroom, Flugelhorn stubbed out his cigarette—he had packed the ashtray with butts in the last five minutes—and stared numbly at the monitor. He watched it go blank, unable to turn away. What a show—a real shocker if he ever saw one. A knockout! He knew Bonnie would be furious, but he couldn't worry about that. She wanted publicity, and she was sure as hell going to get it.

Was she ever, he thought, as he turned and looked at the switchboard on the wall of the control booth. He let out a cackle of glee. It was all lit up with telephone calls like a jackpot.

Her telephone was ringing. It was Shmeer. "Bonnie, darling! Have you seen the Best-Seller List? You jumped from ninth to fourth place overnight! One hundred thousand copies sold in twenty-four hours—triple what we did after the *Satyr* spread. It's fantastic!"

"My God! Really? Oh, Mr. Shmeer, this is wonderful! I'm thrilled."

"You should be. I've already arranged with the network for a rerun of your *Open Up!* performance. And they're going to do an hour-long special on it in *prime time*." He chuckled. "That is, if Manny won't mind."

"I don't know," she said worriedly. "He still isn't speaking to me."

"Oh, he'll get over it," Shmeer said. "He's a good sport." He went on excitedly. "The Georgie Hayseed people have been ringing my phone off all day. They want you to do a series of three guests shots on the *Bedtime Show* in the next five weeks."

"I won't have to get laid again, will I?"

"Don't be silly," he laughed. "All you'll have to do is go on and talk. I'll have Flugelhorn write you up some nice late-night special material—a lot of risqué conversational stuff. We'll make it blue enough for you to get bleeped a few times so we can raise a big stink about censorship. The controversy will put you over the top." He chortled. "I guarantee you, after the *Bedtime Show* you won't be number four any more. You'll be Number One."

"Do you really think so?"

"I *know* so. And I'll tell you another thing," he went on. "I'm really pouring the heat on now. I'm throwing Europe in on the autograph circuit and I'm doubling the advertising budget. You'll be getting two-page ads—fold-outs yet—in the *New York Times Book Review, Life,* and *Time.*"

"Oh, Mr. Shmeer. You've been so good to me. How can I ever thank you?"

"Don't thank me, Bonnie," he said. There was a note of pure admiration in his voice. "Believe me, dear. You earned it."

They said their goodbyes and hung up. But Bonnie stayed at the phone, staring at the receiver and replaying Shmeer's conversation in her mind. The Georgie Hayseed Show wanted her! Go figure it. When she'd gone there for her audition, four producers in turtlenecks—three men and a dike—had grilled her in a little room for hours and finally told her she couldn't be on the show because her book was too dirty. Now, after she'd gotten banged on *Open Up!,* they were begging her to come on and be as dirty as she wanted. And what about the Pal Buddyboy Show, she wondered. Shmeer hadn't said anything about it, but they'd probably come groveling now, too. It would serve them right. The nerve of those smart-asses —making her think up four sado-masochism jokes and learn six karate chops, and then canceling her for some goddam politician at the last minute. Well, they could take that canceling bit and shove it. They wouldn't dare push her around any more. She was too hot for that now. And she was going to get a lot hotter.

Boston . . . New York . . . Philadelphia . . . Baltimore . . . Washington . . . New York . . . Houston . . . Dallas . . . St. Louis . . . Cleveland . . . New York . . . San Francisco . . . Los Angeles . . . Houston . . . Miami . . . Washington . . . New York . . .

She had hit the campaign trail, zigzagging across the country on an endless round of appearances, interviews, and autograph parties that blurred indistinguishably into each other as she doubled back on her tracks like a stymied hamster in a maze. Time was a tunnel that led into a grey-walled studio that led into a bookshop that led into an auditorium that led into a restaurant that led into a hotel room that led back again into another faceless grey-walled studio. Half of her life she spent riding in planes, on trains, and in taxis, with Manny beside her and the back of Flugelhorn's head, which looked like a sheared-off coconut, in front. She was tired much of the time, and often rushed, and occasionally bored. But she was never unhappy. The spotlight and applause had been like blood plasma to her ailing self-esteem. They had nourished her and she had thrived, her shrunken ego stretching little by little, like an empty inner tube pumped with air, until it spread and filled the image that had been molded for her. Now she was ready to take her place in the world of other inflated images, and she knew they could not deny her a certain measure of respect.

Her acceptance into this world was ritualized by her appearances on the *Bedtime Show*. The host, Georgie Hayseed, a bland Midwesterner with the impishness of a slightly horny Elk, gushed and fawned over her and gave her a free reign. She delighted the audiences with her sophisticated patter, carefully tailored for her by Flugelhorn in raunchy shades of blue. And her last time on the show, she brought the house down by engaging in a verbal exchange with Velda Paprikash, the loquacious Hungarian charmer, in which she called Velda, her sense of gender blurred by rage, a "hunkie mother-fucker." Her words were bleeped, of course, but the studio audience went wild. They loved her. She was a glorious smash.

And as Shmeer had predicted, the impact of the show jolted *The Broadbelters* straight into first place on the Best-Seller List. Bonnie got the news when she was in Hawaii with Manny—and Flugelhorn in an adjoining room—resting between laps around the autograph circuit. Lonesome for news of home, she had gone down to the hotel coffee shop for a *New York Times*. Back in their room, she had opened the paper to the book section, cried out, and handed it to Manny. He looked at it, and they were soon kissing and hugging each other and dancing around the room.

Then, as if for the first time, they tumbled into bed and made love. And it was good. Very good. Better than she had ever remembered. This was the way it felt, she thought, when you were Number One.

Chapter 9 The Celebrity

"You'll have to rent a dog," Flugelhorn said.

Bonnie stared at him. "What the hell for? I *hate* dogs." She shuddered involuntarily. "I'm scared to death of them."

"I'm sorry," he said, "but you'll need one when the *Life* team comes out tomorrow to do their close-up on you. A dog'll give the place a more homey effect."

"Why?" she countered. "Am I supposed to live in a kennel?" She glanced around the apartment and shrugged. "I don't know, it looks homey enough to me."

Flugelhorn shook his head. "No, you need a pet," he insisted. He extracted a pamphlet from his briefcase. "Now I've already spoken to the Rent-a-Dog place, and they say a Yorkshire terrier is very popular with the big feminine stars today. Elizabeth Taylor, Audrey Hepburn, Sandra Dee, and Sonny of Sonny and Cher all have Yorkshires." He consulted the list and his mouth dropped open in awe. "Even Frank Sinatra has one. Well, what do you say?"

Bonnie waved her hand in a vague gesture of indifference. "Why don't you rent me a couple of kids while you're at it," she grumbled. "Oh, all right. Get a Yorkshire."

"Good." Flugelhorn put the pamphlet away and took out some mimeographed sheets which he handed Bonnie. "Now here's something else I want you to do for tomorrow. You'll have to be prepared in case their reporter gets tricky and starts throwing you questions about the current book scene or the theatre. So to help you out, I got you a copy of Waldo

Psudosmith's *Standard List of Knowledgeable Opinions.*"

"Who's Waldo Psudosmith?" she asked, scowling at the list.

"He's a culture expert," Flugelhorn said. "He tells people what to think about books they haven't read or plays they haven't seen so they can discuss them intelligently at cocktail parties. He's what you might call a one-man crash course in instant hipness."

Bonnie groaned as she glanced over the list. "My God, look at the names on this thing, will you? 'Rosencrantz and Guildenstern'—they sound like a Jewish comedy team in the Catskills."

"Well, don't let it throw you," he told her. "Just try to remember the key words I've underlined for each author or playwright, and you'll be all right. For instance, if James Baldwin's name comes up, say something about the 'polemicism in his novels'; or if they mention John Updike, talk about the 'Dutch Calvinist influence' on his work; or if they get on the subject of black comedy in the theatre, toss them a line about the 'crackling menace' in Pinter's plays vs. the 'bursts of passionate poetry' in Ionesco's."

"Lots of luck," Bonnie said. "I'll be lucky if I can remember my own name after all this."

"Oh, you'll do all right. I'm not even worried." Flugelhorn riffled through the batch of press releases he always carried with him like a second skin and added, "And one other thing. If they ask you what you intend to do after this book, tell them you're working on a sequel: *Return of the Broadbelters* or something."

"Will there really be one?"

"Are you kidding? It's in your contract," Flugelhorn laughed. "And the way this book is going over, Shmeer'll milk it for an eight-volume series, six movies, and a five-year TV serial. In case you don't know it, owning *The Broadbelters* is like owning the Brooklyn Bridge."

Bonnie smiled. "With a little Shmeer in every toll booth."
Flugelhorn snapped his briefcase shut and looked around
the room as if checking it over. His eye roamed proudly over
the neat rows of brand new leatherbound classics and bright-
jacketed unopened Book-of-the-Month Club selections he had
crammed into Bonnie's once half-empty bookcases, and the
superb collection of oils and lithographs, mostly on loan, with
which he had covered her living-room walls. There were paintings by Klee, Rouault, Picasso, Miro, Matisse, Braque, Chagall,
and even one by Van Gogh, the bold, whirling "Road with
Cypresses," a fake requisitioned by Manny from the United
Misalliance property department. "I must admit," he said
finally, with a touch of pride, "the place does have class. That
reporter ought to be pretty impressed tomorrow."

"I hope so. I feel like I'm living in a goddam museum."

Flugelhorn tucked his briefcase under his arm. "Well, we'd
better get moving—it looks like another busy day today.
You've got an autograph party at Porno's Book Store at 11:00;
you're commentating a maternity fashion show at the Fanny
Hill Home for Unwed Mothers at 1:00; you're being inter-
viewed by Kitty Crone on the *Tooth and Nail Radio Show* at
3:00; and you're co-hosting the *Pal Buddyboy Show* tonight."
He waved to her as he went out. "And tomorrow be ready for
Life."

Bonnie screamed when she saw the dog gallop in with
Flugelhorn. It was big—big as a bison—and it had a panting,
cavernous mouth stuffed with yards of unlovely tongue and
teeth. Powerfully built, with a thick coat of black-and-white
fur, it stood stiffly at the end of the leash gripped in Flugelhorn's two white-knuckled hands, looking for all the world as
if it should have been out pulling a sled across the tundra.

Bonnie cowered against Manny on the sofa in raw terror
and gasped, "Jesus . . . Oh, my God . . . what's *that?*"

"It's a malamute," Flugelhorn said. He smiled sheepishly.

"They didn't have any Yorkshires left so I got you this. His name is Tootles."

"*Tootles!*" Bonnie glared at Flugelhorn and her terror swiftly turned to rage. "Get that thing the hell out of here!" she bellowed. "Now! Do you hear me?"

Flugelhorn tried to placate her. "Now take it easy," he said. "It's a very fine dog. Jill St. John has one."

"To hell with Jill St. John!" Bonnie screamed. "Get that mother out of here before I call the S.P.C.A.!"

They heard the doorbell ring.

Bonnie paled as she sat up quickly and smoothed out her dress. "Oh, God, that's the reporter," she wailed plaintively. "Now what am I supposed to do?"

"Just forget Tootles is here," Flugelhorn said, dragging the dog over to an armchair and unleashing him. He stuffed the leash under the seat cushion and sat down on top of it.

"How can you forget a hyena like that?" Manny asked as the dog pranced gracelessly around Flugelhorn's chair. "Get him to be still, for Crissake."

"Heel, boy," Flugelhorn said tentatively. "Heel, fella." When the dog gave no sign of understanding, Flugelhorn reached out and belted him across the hocks, and the dog promptly flopped down on the rug as though he had truly found a home.

The butler brought in the reporter, a svelte, coolly super-confident English major ten years out of Sarah Lawrence, accompanied by a rumpled photographer. The reporter, who introduced herself as Nancy Skewer, displayed in her mien and speech that finely honed edge of malice of the dedicated female journalist. She took the seat that was offered her as soon as the introductions were finished, Flugelhorn having been presented as an intimate friend of the family, and whipped out a yellow stenographer's pad. Across the top she scrawled, "*A Candid Close-up of the Ehrlichs at Home with Their Press Agent.*"

The butler glided in with a tray of drinks and tea sandwiches and disappeared again like an apparition.

"Help yourself," Manny offered, at which the photographer sprang over to the tray and attacked it with gusto. Miss Skewer, on the other hand, declined with a prim "No thank you," too preoccupied with her computerlike reading of the room's decor to brook any distraction. Her penetrating eye alighted on each object in the room and recorded it with an instantaneous, indelible impression: the Scalamandré silk drapes and upholstered sofa, the cushions of antique Greek embroideries, the Bavarian mirror above the Louis XVth commode, the 18th-century Swedish benches, the 17th-century Chinese altar table, the Louis XVIth bergère chair, the antique bouillotte lamp, the Russian icons, the Chinese-lacquer screen, the throw rug made from the skins of Greek jackals.

Finally she pronounced judgment. "You have a lovely home here," she said grudgingly.

"Oh, thank you," Bonnie said. "I had some help in furnishing it, but I picked a lot of the things out myself."

"Really? You have good taste," Miss Skewer commented, scribbling on her notepad, "*The living room faithfully reflects its mistress—patently evident throughout are the discreet imagination, elegant taste, and sophisticated self-expression of the highest-priced decorator in the business.*"

"I don't know how good her taste is," Manny laughed, "but it sure is expensive." He pointed to the open terrazzo fireplace with its white Louis XVIth marble mantel. "That thing alone cost me four bucks a square inch."

"*The style,*" Miss Skewer noted accordingly, "*is* Haute Nouveau Riche." Her gaze returned to the painting above the mantel. "I notice you have quite an impressive art collection," she said. "That's a Van Gogh, isn't it?"

"Yes, and it was a real bargain," Bonnie answered, turning to Manny with an impish smile. "My husband picked it up in California for next to nothing."

"How fortunate," Miss Skewer remarked. *"Owners of an impressive art collection (Van Gogh, Picasso, and others), the Ehrlichs are the kind of avid collectors who tend to remember paintings by how much they paid for them."* Her eye traveled to the bookcase and leapfrogged over the titles. "I see you manage to keep up with your reading, Mrs. Ehrlich," she observed in a smirky voice. "How did you like James Baldwin's new novel?"

Bonnie glanced at Flugelhorn who shook his head faintly from side to side. "I didn't like it," she answered quickly. "I thought it was . . . ummm . . . banal in construction and content and lacking in . . . uh . . . credible characters with real problems." She saw Flugelhorn's lips form a P, and she added offhandedly, "Of course I've always found his fiction marred by too much polemicism."

Miss Skewer looked staggered. "I'm afraid I have to agree with you," she said. *"Mrs. Ehrlich is surprisingly familiar with the works of our serious contemporary artists,"* she wrote, appending after a moment, *"although her opinions seem to have a vaguely secondhand ring."*

At this point the dog, who had been lying peaceably until now gnawing on the cabriole leg of Flugelhorn's chair, suddenly leaped up and began clambering over the photographer's legs in an effort to wrest a tea sandwich from him. Miss Skewer looked down with wry amusement as Flugelhorn, enticing the dog with a deviled ham and watercress sandwich, managed to bribe him into submission again. "That's a malamute, isn't it?" she asked. "I seem to remember Jill St. John having one when we did a close-up on her. What's his name?"

Bonnie and Flugelhorn answered together.

"Doodles," Bonnie said.

"Tootles," Flugelhorn said.

Miss Skewer looked from one to the other in mild confusion.

Bonnie laughed good-naturedly at her own mistake. "I

don't know what's the matter with me—his name is Tootles,"
she said. Then she added, "Doodles is our Yorkshire terrier.
She's at the vet's."

*As the title of her book suggests, Mrs. Ehrlich is none too
good with names. Understandably, she has trouble remembering the names of her two pet dogs: Tootles (a malamute) and
Doodles (a Yorkshire terrier).*" Miss Skewer read over her
notes hurriedly. "Goodness," she exclaimed, glancing at her
watch, "We've spent all this time on preliminaries and we
haven't said one word about *The Broadbelters*. My editor will
kill me."

Bonnie smiled, unabashedly pleased both at the prospect of
Miss Skewer getting "killed" and at the mention of *The
Broadbelters*. What a relief it was to be approaching safe
territory after so much perilous treading in the minefield of
strange topics. "Fire away," she said agreeably.

Miss Skewer turned to a fresh page of her notepad. "Suppose you begin by telling me how you came to write *The
Broadbelters* in the first place."

Bonnie sighed, almost as if clicking on some internal tape
recorder, and went into her routine, spinning out her spool of
lines with an electronic ease and precision achieved in count-
less such interviews. She began by relating her experiences as a
struggling young actress in Hollywood who had supported
herself by waiting on tables in the studio commissary. Any
reference to her stint at "Auto-Erotica" was, of course, stu-
diously avoided; but she larded her story with as many cute—
and promotable—anecdotes as possible. ("My screen test was
one of the most expensive in the studio's history. I did it
without a brassiere, and one of the grips got so excited he fell
off a scaffold and broke his collarbone and twenty-five
hundred dollars worth of equipment.") As Bonnie retold it,
her acting career became not the dismal failure it had been
but rather a pearly strand of minor but nonetheless brilliant
performances. She embellished her achievements by claiming

she had won the "most curvaceous bit player, male or female" award five years in a row. That this title had been conferred on her solely by Flugelhorn, no other performer ever having won it before or since, was a fact that invariably escaped the attention of all the reporters who dutifully parroted it to the public.

Even when Miss Skewer raised some of the touchier questions concerning *The Broadbelters'* success, Bonnie was glibly prepared. "Isn't it true," Miss Skewer wanted to know, "that you were helped rather *considerably* with the writing of your novel?"

"No more so than any of Mr. Shmeer's other authors," Bonnie countered. "I was simply very fortunate in finding a publisher with such a marvelous editorial staff."

"Aside from editorial assistance," Miss Skewer demanded, "didn't someone help you write the book?" A venomous smile puckered her upper lip. "To put it bluntly, Mrs. Ehrlich, there's a nasty rumor going around that you hired a ghost-writer."

"Absolute nonsense!" Bonnie snapped. "That's just what I call 'literary envy.' Every time an unknown lady author comes along and writes a smash hit, everyone accuses her of 'having help' with it because they never heard of her before. Well, what they don't know is that I've been writing for years: one-act plays, short stories, even poetry—haiku's my favorite —all exciting, terribly original things I just never bothered getting published."

"How interesting," Miss Skewer said as she observed on her notepad, "*Although previously unpublished, Mrs. Ehrlich bravely shoulders full responsibility for* The Broadbelters *by claiming to have written it herself.*" Then she asked, "What about the unfavorable critical reaction to the book. Did it bother you?"

"Certainly not," Bonnie said. "Why should I care what the critics say? As Disraeli put it, 'You know who the critics are?

They're the men who have failed in literature and art.'" She grinned wickedly at Miss Skewer. "In my own phrase"—Flugelhorn's really—"they're like capons at a chicken orgy."

Miss Skewer permitted herself an amused sniff and continued, "And how do you feel about the charge that your book is nothing more than 'a vulgar triumph of promotion?'"

"As far as I'm concerned," Bonnie said tersely, "I'd much rather have a vulgar success than a dignified failure." (Another Flugelhorn original.)

And so it went, Bonnie neatly parrying each of Miss Skewer's vicious lunges and coming back at her opponent with a telling riposte. Did the hostility of the people she'd scandalized in the book upset her, Miss Skewer wanted to know? No, Bonnie told her, because the people she'd written about were all characters she'd made up, and if the shoe fit anyone living it was because of their own clay feet. How, Miss Skewer asked, making a last-ditch effort, could Bonnie reconcile her notoriously permissive views on sex with a happy marriage? Here Bonnie grasped Manny's hand in hers and smiled fondly at him. "To paraphrase Bertrand Russell," she said—Flugelhorn leaned heavily on Russell for lively quotations— "'marriage achieves dignity only by the freedom of the partners to cherish other relationships.' It's precisely because of my permissive views on sex that my husband and I have such a successful and enduring marriage." She leaned toward Manny and kissed him tenderly on the lips. "Right, darling?"

This was too much for the photographer. He jumped up and recorded the kiss with a flash of his camera. "Beautiful!" he exclaimed as he reloaded the camera and took several more shots of Bonnie and Manny in fond connubial poses. The dog, meanwhile, had begun to growl ominously, following the photographer's movements with wary, narrowed eyes. He seemed to bear the photographer a grudge for not sharing his tea sandwiches, and considered any of his actions suspect.

Distracted by the dog's growling, Bonnie missed the next

question. "I'm awfully sorry," she said. "Would you repeat that?"

"I said," Miss Skewer iterated, "after this book, what do you plan to do next?"

A glimpse of the dog's teeth, now bared in menace as the photographer crouched before the bookcase for a shot, threw Bonnie off the track for a moment. "Why, I . . . uh . . . I'm looking forward to appearing in the movie." As soon as she said the words she realized her mistake. Something buckled inside her and she felt uncomfortably exposed. Now why the hell did I say *that*, she asked herself.

Miss Skewer sniffed the scent of a scoop hanging in the air. "Has United Misalliance signed you?" she asked.

Bonnie shot an anxious glance at Flugelhorn. He shook his head ever so slightly up and down and with his thumb and forefinger made a gesture to indicate something very tiny. "Yes, they have," she answered. "It's only a small role"—she looked at Flugelhorn's fingers again—"a bit part, actually, but it should be lots of fun."

"Yes, I'm sure it will be," Miss Skewer said. "*Mrs. Ehrlich assured us that acting in the movie version of her book would be 'lots of fun,'* " she wrote, "*but she failed to specify whether she meant for herself or the audience.*" She looked up at Bonnie. "Could you tell me how much you're getting paid for the part?"

Bonnie, misinterpreting the four fingers Flugelhorn held up to indicate $4,000, blurted grandly, "Four hundred thousand dollars."

Flugelhorn stifled an apoplectic gasp while Miss Skewer jotted down, "*In what must surely be one of the most magnanimous gestures in film-making history, United Misalliance will pay Mrs. Ehrlich a record $400,000 for her cameo appearance.*"

After a few more questions, some of which were directed at Manny and elicited answers that delighted her with their tortured syntax, Miss Skewer looked up from her notepad. "Well, I think that ought to do it," she said. She smiled at Bonnie and Manny in a polite, formal way. "I certainly want to thank you for being so cooperative."

"Oh, don't mention it," Bonnie answered.

"It wasn't nothing," Manny said.

Miss Skewer looked for the photographer and found him snapping the Van Gogh. The dog stood poised at his side, waiting to retrieve the ejected flashbulb, his animus for the photographer having been forgotten in the excitement of this new game. "I'm ready to go now, Herbie," she called. "Do you have all the pictures you need?"

The photographer turned and gazed thoughtfully around the room, his lips pursed. "I think so," he said slowly. Then his eye came to rest on the dog grinding a flashbulb to powder between his teeth, and an inspired smile lit his face. "How about a shot of Mrs. Ehrlich with the dog? The readers would love that."

Bonnie felt a constriction in her chest not unlike the beginnings of a coronary. "Oh, no, don't bother with that," she quavered. "It's too corny."

But with that obsessive conviction of all artists, the photographer insisted. "No, no, it's the perfect shot. It'll make the whole spread."

Bonnie rolled her eyes toward Flugelhorn in a silent appeal, but he merely shrugged back at her, a helpless what-can-I-do look on his face.

"Go ahead," the photographer urged. "Get the dog over there and I'll take the picture."

"Here, Tootles," Bonnie called. She sounded as if she were summoning her own executioner. "Come here, boy."

The dog looked up from the mound of masticated flashbulbs he had deposited on the rug and stared at Bonnie. But he didn't move.

She patted the sofa beside her and called him again. "Here, Tootles."

This time he obeyed. He suddenly bounded over to the sofa and jumped into Bonnie's lap with such exuberance that he knocked the wind out of her. She tumbled to the floor and rolled onto her back, her dress riding inelegantly up her thighs, while the dog romped over her in a binge of playfulness, pummeling her with his paws and lapping at her face with his paddlelike tongue.

"Beautiful!" cried the photographer, darting forward. His camera flashed. Then he came still closer, crouched, and shot several more pictures in quick succession. "Great! That's it. Perfect!"

Finally Miss Skewer tugged at his sleeve. "Okay, Herbie, that's enough. Give the poor woman a break." She turned to leave, and her lips slithered into her snaky smile once more. "After all," she said, "Mrs. Ehrlich spends enough time on her back as it is."

"You and your goddam dog," Bonnie moaned. She was propped up on the sofa against a mound of cushions, holding an ice pack to the small, plum-colored bruise on her forehead that she had sustained in her fall. A decanter of brandy and a bottle of spirits of ammonia stood on the cocktail table.

Flugelhorn, back from returning Tootles to the Rent-a-Dog place, where he had received a discount for misbehavior, sat scrunched up in an armchair, a look of feral concentration on his face. "Well, I still think he added a lot to the interview," he said.

"Yeah, a bump on my head and three cracked ribs." Bonnie sighed heavily. "And it was all his fault I screwed up when she asked me what I plan to do next. 'I'm looking forward to appearing in the movie,' " she said, mimicking her own sultry interview voice. She grunted in disgust and scowled at Flugelhorn. "Now how are you going to get me out of that one, wise-ass?"

Flugelhorn pursed his lips. "That's just what I've been thinking about," he said. "And to tell you the truth, I've decided not to get you out of it at all."

"*What?* Oh, no, you can't mean that!" Bonnie put down her ice pack and stared at him incredulously. "You don't really think you're going to get me back in Hollywood again, do you?"

"Why not?" Flugelhorn jumped up and began pacing the floor excitedly. "Look, I know how you feel about Hollywood, but this time it'll be different. They'll welcome you with open arms. You're not some little run-of-the-mill unknown any more. You're a celebrity—a famous author starring in the movie of her own best-seller." He slapped his thigh jubilantly. "What a double-edged sword! Think of it—we'll use the movie publicity to push your book and the book publicity to promote your movie role."

Manny, too, seemed excited as he sat up on the sofa. "And four hundred thousand smackers in our pocket is nothin' to sneeze at neither." He turned to Bonnie persuasively. "Why should the studio waste that money for talent when they can give it to you and get box office for it? We can save dough by usin' a bunch of cheapies for the leads."

Bonnie looked carefully from one to the other, signs of nascent interest flickering in her eyes like candlelight. "Well, maybe . . ." she wavered. Then she shook her head firmly. "No, I can't. If I go back to that jungle out there they'll only tear me apart all over again. Who needs it? I've got it made now."

"But it's only a minor role," Flugelhorn coaxed. "You told the reporter, in your own words, it was a 'bit part.' How could a mere cameo possibly hurt you?"

She stroked her chin, ruminating. "Mmmmmm . . . a walk-on. I don't know . . . it depends."

Flugelhorn pressed his advantage. "The director will show you what to do. It'll be as easy as breathing."

"I know, but . . ."

"It's somethin' you always wanted, Bon. You'll have that Hollywood crowd at your feet," Manny urged.

The glimmer in her eyes turned to a hard, bright flame, and she began to nod slowly. She wondered whether her slip to the *Life* reporter had been all that unintentional. "I guess with a little help I *could* manage a walk-on," she said finally. She looked at Flugelhorn. "Especially if it's a nude one."

He flashed an eager grin. "Oh, it will be—don't you worry about that. It'll be a juicy part in every way except dialogue."

"Not too many lines?"

"No, no. We'll keep them down to a minimum, mostly a few cries and moans and some heavy breathing."

"That's right up her alley," Manny interjected excitedly.

Bonnie's excitement, slow-starting, was now galloping apace with theirs. "Hey, you know the more I think about this, the more I like it. I'll be the first lady author who ever pulled a stunt like this." She reached for the ice pack and tossed it into the air. "Christ, I can't wait!"

"It's a deal," Manny said. "I'll have 'em sign you up in the morning."

Flugelhorn turned to him. "Do you think we ought to tell Shmeer about it first, just as a kind of courtesy?"

"What for?" Manny laughed. "If we let him in on it now he'll want a piece of the action. You know Shmeer—he's got a handshake like a one-armed bandit."

"Manny's right," Bonnie said. "What Shmeer doesn't know won't hurt him. Let him find out about it when the time comes."

It was only a month later that the time came. It arrived on the heels of the *Life* interview, a subtly less-than-loving spread highlighted by a full page photo of Bonnie romping on the floor of her apartment with her dog Tootles. The day after it appeared, seventy thousand animal lovers went out and bought a copy of *The Broadbelters*. And the day after that, in a summons cunningly veiled as a spider web, Shmeer called Bonnie to his office.

"Go right in, Mrs. Ehrlich," the receptionist purred, motioning with her blond Prince Valiant head and a ringed forefinger. "Mr. Shmeer's expecting you."

Ensconced behind his enormous rosewood desk, Shmeer greeted Bonnie with a broad, unctuous smile that had all the warm invitation of a swamp. "Hello, darling. It's good to see you," he said, rising as Bonnie came toward him and stamped a kiss on his cheek.

"Yes, and you, too," she burbled, responding to his benevolently jovial manner. As she settled into the armchair opposite his desk, she spotted among his papers a copy of *Life* magazine, open to the page of the close-up.

Seated behind his desk again, Shmeer folded his arms across his paunch and continued to smile at Bonnie with wily, heavy-hooded eyes, a genial Buddha in a Bernard Weatherill suit. "I've been reading about my favorite author," he beamed, pushing the copy of *Life* toward her, "and I want you to know how delighted I am that you're starting such a brilliant new career."

Bonnie looked at him quizzically. "A new career?" She noticed the thick brackets around the portion of the interview referring to her movie role, and she began to laugh. "Oh, that," she said, dismissing it modestly. "I'm afraid you're exaggerating a little. It's only a bit part, a cameo."

"For $400,000," Shmeer observed dryly, "it's an expensive cameo." He added quickly, "Not that you don't deserve every penny, darling. No one worked harder for their success than you did." He smiled at her with oily affability. "Believe me, it couldn't be happening to a worthier person."

"Oh, that's very sweet of you," Bonnie said, warmed by the wine of his compliments. She felt moved to reciprocate. "You know I couldn't have done it without you, Mr. Shmeer. Whatever success I have is all your doing." Her voice throbbed with gratitude. "I owe everything to you."

Shmeer looked at her, his face still wreathed in smiles. "I'm glad to know you feel that way," he said. He paused for a moment, his eyes narrowing cagily to slits. "To be perfectly honest with you, I feel the same way myself."

Bonnie stiffened at this unexpected boomerang, suddenly wary and on the defensive. "Wh-what do you mean?"

"I mean that after all I've done for you," Shmeer said, a martyred note cropping up in his voice like a black kernel in an ear of corn, "I thought you might want to pay me a small token of appreciation."

Bonnie stared at him. He had that avid look he always wore when he was about to put the bite on someone. "What kind of token did you have in mind?"

"A cut of the $400,000 you're getting from the studio," he said simply.

Her mouth dropped open. "Why, you've got some hell of a nerve . . ."

"No, I don't," he cut in quickly. "I'm not asking for anything unreasonable. By rights, you should have offered it to me yourself." He held his hands out to her in an exhortatory gesture. "Listen, you've got to remember where you'd be today without me. I'll tell you where—nowhere. If I hadn't come along, you'd still be knocking yourself out to make the Yonkers Gazette, and The Broadbelters wouldn't even be a book, much less a movie."

"Bullshit," Bonnie said icily.

Shmeer, looking stricken, put a hand over his heart. "Is that how you talk to me? Is that how you repay me?" He shook his head sorrowfully. "My God, you might think I was asking for the moon. All I want is what's coming to me."

Relenting a moment, she asked, "How much is that?"

"Two hundred thousand."

"W*haaat?* That's half!" Bonnie's eyes snapped. "You don't want a little cut—you want to amputate!"

"But I'm entitled to it," Shmeer argued. "Who made the movie deal in the first place?"

"You did," she said, adding after a long pause, "and you milked the studio out of a million dollars."

Shmeer bridled, smarting at her gibe. "Listen, sweetheart," he said caustically, "when it comes to milking, your Manny is the Dairy Queen." He pointed to himself with pride. "At least *I* was a gentleman and split the movie rights with him fifty-fifty. Now he's got a little side deal going—all because of me—and he wants to keep the whole bundle for himself."

"Why shouldn't he? It's *his.*" She sat up angrily, her color rising like a welt. "And you can stop bragging about splitting the movie rights fifty-fifty, big shot. I *know* you're the only publisher who does." She glared at him. "The rest of them all give the author the whole 100 per cent."

Shmeer snickered bitterly and pretended to address some unseen third party. "Look at the monster I created. Last year she could hardly write her name, and today she's an author and an accountant." He turned on her accusingly. "Don't tell me I wasn't generous with you. I treated you like a queen. Look at all those parties I gave you!"

"Yes, and you gave Manny the bill," she snarled.

"Only for his half. Fair is fair."

Flak shot out of her eyes as her temper flared viciously. "Don't try to con me, you old bastard. With what you made in hotel kickbacks I could buy the Plaza."

"Why, you ungrateful bitch," Shmeer sputtered. "I sent you across the country twelve times with two side-trips to Europe!"

"All at my own expense!"

"Don't poormouth me! You made a million dollars on this book!"

"But it grossed *fifty!*"

"So what?" he yelled. "What do you care how much it grossed? You got what you wanted from it!" He thumped himself boastfully on the chest, howling like a serpent-stung Lear. "And *I* gave it to you! No other publisher in the world could have taken an old dumb whore like you and turned her into a famous novelist."

She was livid. "Oh, you . . . you sonofabitch! I'd like to cut your balls off and start a pawn shop!"

"But it's *your* ass that'll still be in hock. I'm warning you, Bonnie," he roared, snatching up his copy of *Life* and waving it at her menacingly, "if you don't get back into line, you're finished! I made you what you are, and I can break you, too!"

"That's what you think!" she shouted. "I don't need you any more. I wouldn't do another book for you for a million bucks a *word!*"

"You'll do it, you stupid whore, and for a hell of a lot less! It's in your contract."

Bonnie jumped to her feet. "That does it!" she shrieked. She confronted him in a towering fury. "I'm going to break that goddam contract if it's the last thing I do! Even if I have to sue you for every cent you have!" She turned her back on him and stomped off toward the door.

From behind her came the low clucking sound of Shmeer's laughter. She wheeled around and found him leaning back in his chair, head tilted to one side, eying her derisively. His voice had taken on an ironic edge. "You're going to sue me. That's some joke. Didn't anyone ever tell you you need a case?"

His smugness undid her, the mocking expression on his face goading her into ungovernable rage. "You dirty bastard! You rotten, thieving, conniving crook! You sonofabitching, penny-pinching, skinflint *prick!*" she screamed. "You know goddam well I've got a case against you!" She glowered at him with outraged dignity. "*I'm going to sue you for calling me a whore.*"

Chapter 10 The Ultimate

MOUNDS OF newspapers and telegrams lay piled on the dining room table like drifts of snow. Flugelhorn, looking less ferrety than usual in a new sculptured haircut, was snipping an item from the *New York Post* and reading it aloud while Bonnie and Manny half-listened as they rummaged through the deluge.

" ' . . . wept when Federal Judge John J. Assumpsit delivered the favorable verdict. At her side were her husband and co-plaintiff, Emmanuel, their attorney, D. E. Deever, Jr., and Mrs. Ehrlich's personal manager, Milton Flugelhorn. The thirty-nine-year-old Mrs. Ehrlich . . .' "

"Oh, that's beautiful," Bonnie interrupted.

" ' . . . who is currently appearing in the film version of her own best-selling novel, "The Broadbelters," wore a loose-fitting camel hair suit, a leopard hat . . .' "

"Okay, skip the fashion show," Manny said, "and let's hear what they said about the decision."

"Um . . . oh, here it is," Flugelhorn said, skimming the column for the right paragraph. " 'In awarding the plaintiff release from her contract and $1,158,000 in damages, Judge Assumpsit said, "The court finds that David Shmeer did in fact employ scurrilous language against Mrs. Ehrlich for the purpose of humiliating and insulting the plaintiff and that Mr. Shmeer overstepped his rights as an employer by requiring the plaintiff to perform sexual intercourse on television and other obscene acts in public for the purpose of promoting the sale of her novel, *The Broadbelters*. It is the opinion of the court that these improper and demeaning . . ." ' "

"Say, look at this!" Manny broke in, laughing. "We got a telegram from The Swinging Nun."

"Oh, really?" Bonnie said. "What does it say?"

"It says: 'BLESSINGS STOP GOD'S WILL IS A GROOVE!'"

"That's very nice of her," Flugelhorn commented. "She's got a lot of soul." He finished with the *Post* item and picked up a copy of *Variety*. "Hey, listen to the wild headline they gave you in here: 'BONNIE BROADBELTER BELTS BLOCKBUSTER BARON!' "

"That's cute," Bonnie nodded, scanning a telegram. "Here's a wire from Sydney Crotchnick: 'CONGRATULATIONS AND KUDOS TO OUR FAVORITE NYMPH.' " She laughed. "I wonder how he meant that."

"And here's one," Manny said, picking up another wire, "from our old friend, Percy B. Hack."

Bonnie glanced up sharply. "Oh? Here, let me see it."

Manny handed it to her, and she read aloud, " 'CONGRATULATIONS ON AN INSPIRED EPILOGUE.' "

"What the hell does *that* mean?" Manny asked.

Bonnie pursed her lips. She thought of Hack—warm, tender thoughts that curled inside her like tendrils of smoke —and she smiled mysteriously. "I guess he means he's glad we screwed Shmeer," she said.

Flugelhorn looked up from the UPI wire release he was scissoring out of a newspaper. "This Hack," he asked, "is he the same one who wrote the new hit Shmeer's got out now: *TV Is a Person?*"

"Yeah, and he's the same Hack who wrote *The Broadbelters*," Manny said.

A look of enlightenment flashed across Flugelhorn's face. "Oh, so *that's* who did it. I never thought to ask." He turned to Bonnie, who was staring wistfully at Hack's telegram.

"Well, it looks like you'll have to find yourself someone else to do the sequel," he told her. "With a hit book of his own on the market, I think your boy Hack's out of the ghostwriting business."

"Oh, I don't know about that," Bonnie drawled, a cagey look on her face. "He still might do it for me if I asked him." She studied her fingernails impassively. "Percy and I had a very close relationship."

"Close, shmose," Manny said. "If we make him the right proposition, he'll do it."

"Well, then you'd better make it to him pretty fast," Flugelhorn said. "We can't wait too long to come up with a sequel if we want to capitalize on *The Broadbelters'* publicity." He thought for a moment. "I figure it'll take a year to write the book and about a year to bring it out. Now two years . . . "

"Why should it take a year to come out?" Manny asked. "Christ, Shmeer brung Bonnie's book out in three months."

"Yes, but that's *Shmeer.* We won't be using him this time, remember?" Flugelhorn sighed and shook his head regretfully. "I'm afraid there aren't too many other fully IBM publishing houses around."

"Yeah, and there ain't too many other greedy bastards like that around either," Manny said.

Bonnie looked annoyed. "Oh, what's the point in worrying about a publisher now? I'm sure we won't have any trouble finding one," she asserted. "What we need now is an author."

"You're right. First things first," Flugelhorn said. "Let me get in touch with this Hack guy, and I'll set up a meeting as soon as I can."

"The sooner the better." Bonnie picked Hack's telegram up and looked at it again. After a moment she began to smile. "Maybe the Epilogue hasn't been written yet," she said.

It was a jolt. If she hadn't been expecting him, she would never have believed that the tall, artily sideburned stranger standing in her living room in a paisley shirt, outsize tie, and trousers belted with multiple chains worn hip-hugger style, was Percy Hack.

She came toward him happily and they embraced. "Percy! It's so good to see you again."

"Oh, it is!" he said, smiling with obvious pleasure.

"You've changed a little, haven't you?" she laughed. "God, let me look at you." She stood back from him, and she could see at a glance that the difference in the "New Percy" was more than a matter of style. He had about him now a certain air of resilience—a jaunty stoicism—the kind of *weathered* look that comes of standing around in the public eye. But she thought she saw, too, some tiny telltale signs, little hints of diffidence here and there, that his old *nebbish* self was still alive and kicking inside its mod cocoon and was not dying without a struggle.

"Good to see ya, boy," Manny said, clasping an arm around him. He glanced at his watch. "But you're a half hour early. What didja do, fly?"

"No," Hack laughed. "As a matter of fact, I came by elevator."

"By elevator?" Manny looked puzzled. "Whatta you mean?"

"Didn't Mr. Flugelhorn tell you?" he asked, surprised. He grinned in an embarrassed way that was pure Early Hack. "I live in your building now. On the fifth floor."

"You're kidding!" Bonnie exclaimed in astonishment. "When did you move in?"

He looked at her contritely. "We've only been living here a week."

"You mean you've been living here a whole week and you didn't call us?" Bonnie reproached him. "That's terrible!"

"Well, I knew how busy you were with the trial," Hack apologized, "and I didn't want to bother you."

"Yeah, thanks for the telegram," Manny said. "We appreciated it."

"Oh, you're welcome." Hack smiled warmly. "I hate to sound disloyal, but I was so happy when I heard the outcome of your falling out with Shmeer."

Manny guffawed. "That was a fall-out all right—there ain't been another one like it since strontium 90."

Hack laughed. "I know. I've been following the case with avid interest, as you can imagine." He paused and added, rather self-consciously, "The newspaper is the only thing I get a chance to read these days, now that *TV Is a Person* is out."

"Oh, yes, congratulations!" Bonnie enthused. "I hear it's selling like crazy."

"Number five on the List," Hack beamed. "Of course, it'll never be another phenomenon like *The Broadbelters*," he added quickly.

"Nothin' will," Manny said, swelling with pride like a blowfish. "And the movie is gonna be an even bigger smash hit than the book. It's doing $250,000 in Chicago, $200,000 in Los Angeles, $150,000 in Philadelphia—ask Milt Flugelhorn when he gets here. He'll tell ya."

"I'm sure he will," Hack said. He looked at Bonnie and smiled shyly. "You were quite good in the movie. I saw you in it."

Bonnie was obviously pleased, but Manny cut in, laughing, "You mean you saw a *lot* of her in it. For a small part it sure covered a lot of ground."

"Oh, Manny," Bonnie said testily, "why don't you shut up for a minute and go fix us some drinks."

She led Hack over to the sofa while Manny trundled off to the bar. "I think it's wonderful that you're living here now, Percy," she said when they were seated. She gave him a close look. "How did you happen to pick this place?"

Hack paused for a moment before answering while he lit up a thin, black cigar. The TRAP course had obviously taught him a thing or two about timing. "Well, you know," he said finally, averting his eyes as he puffed on the cigar and deli-

cately blew out a whorl of bad-smelling smoke, "this building
has some very pleasurable associations for me." He turned and
faced her directly. "And then, too, it's close to my psychiatrist."

Bonnie looked abashed. "Don't tell me you're still seeing
him? My God, your money problems should be over now."

"But they're not," he frowned. "They're just of a different
degree." He shrugged helplessly. "Now I have too much."

Bonnie shook her head and laughed. He was still the same
old Hack—a sheep in a wolf's clothing. "Oh, you nut," she
said affectionately, "how can too *much* money be a problem?"

"Guilt," he said simply. "I have unresolved conflicts about
earning it . . . this way." He sighed. "But if you listen to
what Brunhild says . . ."

"Yeah, how *is* Brunhild?" Manny asked, back with the
drinks. "Wasn't she the dame you were supposed to marry?"

"I *did* marry her," Hack smiled, "and she's fine, thanks.
She's pregnant."

"Oh, congratulations," Bonnie cooed.

"That was fast work," Manny chuckled, slapping him on
the back.

Hack laughed. "Yes, I guess it was rather fast," he said.
"They'll be eleven months apart."

Manny's eyes popped. "You mean you already have a kid?"
He looked at Hack with new admiration. "Christ, you got
more on the ball than I thought."

The doorbell rang, and Flugelhorn hurried in, crestfallen
at having arrived after Hack. "Gosh, I hope I haven't kept you
people waiting," he said.

"Oh, that's all right. We had a lot of news to catch up on,"
Bonnie said. She shot a wry glance at Hack. "It seems Percy's
been pretty busy lately."

Flugelhorn slipped into a seat and turned to Manny questioningly. "Have you approached Mr. Hack about the proposition yet?"

"Uh, no," Manny said, nursing his drink. "We didn't get around to it yet."

"I see." Flugelhorn quickly took charge in his linear fashion and pointed himself at Hack, who was puffing benignly on his cigar with an air of mild expectancy. "Mr. Hack, Mr. and Mrs. Ehrlich would like to engage you as a collaborator on the sequel to *The Broadbelters*. They feel that you . . ."

Hack choked on his cigar smoke. When he had stopped coughing, he stared at Bonnie and Manny in pained disbelief. "But you know I can't accept a job like that now! How could you even ask me?" He sounded like an ex-alcoholic being offered a drink by trusted friends. "I mean, I'm sure you realize," he added defensively, "that I'm a well-known author in my own right now. I can't afford to compromise myself by writing other people's books."

"Yes, of course we're aware of your reputation," Flugelhorn said, breaching the awkward silence, "but your share in the book will be guarded with the same absolute secrecy as it was the last time."

Hack shook his head. "No, it's too risky. Look what happened with *TV Is a Person*. I wrote it under a pseudonym, and yet everyone knows I'm the author."

Bonnie looked at Hack, a puzzled expression on her face. "But your books says Percy Byshe Hack on the cover. Isn't that your real name?"

"No, it's *Bysshe*," he said. "With two s's."

"Oh, boy, it's a wonder anyone guessed it," Manny laughed. He studied Hack skeptically. "And if you was so anxious to hide, why'd you let 'em plaster that big picture of your face all over the back?"

Hack reddened and said uncomfortably, "That was Shmeer's idea. He thought no one would recognize me in sideburns." He stubbed out his cigar as though trying to eradicate it. "Look, I'd really like to help," he appealed to them, "but it's absolutely impossible. I just haven't got the time right now."

Bonnie sighed. "Well, I guess I could probably get someone else to do it"—she paused and gave Hack a meaningful look—"but you know how well we worked together, Percy."

Hack's face ripened into a tomatoey hue. "Yes, I haven't forgotten," he said. A plaintively desperate note edged into his voice. "It's a pleasure I hate to forego, but what else can I do? After I finish pushing TV, I've got my own sequel to do."

"You can always get someone else to do it," Flugelhorn said.

Hack stared at him, shocked. "What? You mean hire a ghostwriter?" He began to laugh in a disconcerted way. "No, no. I couldn't do that. It's dishonest."

"I'll pay for it," Manny said. "The same $10,000 I gave you."

Hack frowned and shook his head. "No, no. It's out of the question."

"And I'll tell you what else I'll do," Manny went on imperturbably, "I'll pay you a fee of a quarter of a million . . ."

Hack's eyebrows shot up. "Out of the question," he said again, but with less conviction.

". . . plus 10 per cent of the movie rights—another quarter of a million." Manny forgot Hack for the moment and began to chortle gleefully as he thought aloud. "With a smash like *The Broadbelters* on the books, we can hit the studio for two million and a half this time. And we won't go to no *schlock* house like Shmeer who'll want a cut. Nah, *this* time we'll find ourselves a *high class* publisher—a real educated dumbbell."

Flugelhorn cut in tersely, driving the bargain home like a jockey in the stretch. "Mr. Hack, Mr. Ehrlich is offering you a half million dollars to do his wife's book. And he's agreed to pay an additional $10,000 for a ghost . . . uh, subcontractor . . . to do your own book. You'll be getting the price of two books for the work on one." He waited a long moment. "Well, what do you say?"

Hack sighed deeply, dredging his breath up from some dark place in his soul. "Oh, why not," he said at last. "What have I got to lose besides a half million dollars' worth of integrity?"

Bonnie threw her arms around him. "Oh, Percy, I'm so happy! I knew you would!"

Manny and Flugelhorn took turns pumping his hand, and when they had all settled down again Hack asked quietly, "Do you have any idea what you want in the book?"

"Yeah," Manny laughed. "Sex."

"Oh, he knows that," Bonnie said with annoyance, "but what kind of a story should we work in?" She turned to Hack. "Shmeer wanted me to do the sequel on some famous television personalities, if that's any help."

"Hmmmmm," he said, pondering, "in *my* sequel he wanted me to enlarge upon the transvestite theme of *TV Is a Person.*"

"I've got an idea. Why don't you combine the two," Flugelhorn suggested, "and make it about some famous TV personalities who change sexes the way other people flip channels?"

Hack nodded excitedly. "That sounds good . . . very good . . . great!" He sat up and moistened his lips. "And to give it some contemporary social value," he began plotting, "we'll make the central character a beautiful Negro actress-singer who becomes the star of the first black situation-comedy on TV . . ."

"And has an unhappy love affair," Flugelhorn went on eagerly, "with the white host of the highest-rated nighttime talk show on a rival network . . ."

". . . and is so decimated by it that she has herself changed to a man," Hack concluded triumphantly, "and winds up as the star of the first black Western series!"

For a moment no one dared speak, and then all at once the

four of them were laughing and shouting simultaneously. "Fabulous! Fantastic! Sensational!" Bonnie shrieked, hugging herself and the other three in an ecstasy of enthusiasm.

Manny was the first to come down from the high. "It's terrific," he said solemnly, "but who the hell is gonna publish it?"

His question resounded in a sudden vacuum of silence. Then a long, loud groan from Bonnie rushed in and filled it. "Oh, my God, here we go again."

Hack chewed his lip, deep in thought. "The only other publisher I actually know," he said slowly, "is Augustus Bleak of Bleak House."

"Bleak . . . Bleak . . . ?" Manny repeated the name, trying to place it. Then, riding in on a whiff of distaste, it came to him. "Oh, no! Not *that* old cocker. I met him at *The Broadbelters'* opening party." He made a vinegary face. "Christ, he's one of them fancy holier-than-thou jackasses who's always comin' on with the big words and don't know the first goddam thing about makin' money."

"Perfect!" Flugelhorn exclaimed. "He sounds like just the man we want."

Manny stared at him. "Are you crazy? He's a dope."

"But we *want* a dope—you said so yourself," Flugelhorn pointed out. "Who else could we wrap around our finger?"

"Yeah, but he's such a square," Manny objected.

"He has been in the past," Hack said, "but I think he may be amenable to change at this point."

Manny looked surprised. "You mean he's ready to go commercial?"

"No, he's ready to go bankrupt," Hack said. "He needs a dirty book to put him in the black."

Bonnie pounded the sofa with her fist. "Let's try him!" she cried. "What the hell. We know all the angles. It's about time we went after someone who'll give us a little class."

"She's right," Flugelhorn said. "We need Bleak to take the

stigma off us. With our know-how and his prestige we'll have the whole market cornered—both the mass *and* the intelligentsia. Think what a coup that'll be!" He began to chuckle with delight. "Can you imagine Bonnie on the required reading list in high school some day?"

The idea appealed to Manny. "Hey, that *is* good," he said, grinning broadly. He nodded in assent. "Okay. Let's give it to Bleak."

"Good! That settles it," Flugelhorn said. He turned to Hack. "I'll make the presentation to him, but winning him over will be your job. If he balks at doing pop pornography, you'll have to talk him out of his objections with a lot of fine-sounding academic arguments."

"I'll do my best," Hack said, nodding with assurance, "and personally, I don't think I'll have any trouble." He added with a wistful little smile, "When it comes to rationalizing a sell-out. . . I'm an expert."

Bleak leaned back in his Thonet chair with the Flemish brocade cushion on it and studied the Daumier print on the wall above Flugelhorn's head. He pursed his lips meditatively as his fingers fiddled with the gold-gleaming keys on his vest chain. Finally he lowered his gaze and spoke, syllabizing his words with drastic emphasis. "Un-*think*-able, my good man. Ab-so-*lute*-ly un-*think*-able."

"But sir," Flugelhorn began . . .

Bleak cut him off with an imperious wave of the hand. "My dear fellow, did you actually believe that a house of our stature and distinction would allow itself to become a panderer of prurience for profit . . . a purveyor of perversions and profanity . . ."—he paused and gathered a few more P's on his tongue—". . . a *prophet of pornography?*"

Flugelhorn remained silent, appealing dumbly to Hack with his eyes.

"Just a moment, sir," Hack said, rising. Looking like a

barrister in his tailor-made London suit and shirt, he faced Bleak squarely and began to argue his case. "You do us a grave injustice, Mr. Bleak, by confusing pornography with erotic literature. The book we're asking you to publish may *seem* like pornography because of the plethora of sexual scenes—147 in all—but there the resemblance ends. Far from being the ordinary sex novel mechanically designed for titillation, ours is a pre-planned best-seller built like a classical nineteenth-century novel—a *Bildungsroman*, if you will—with all the erotic elements organically related to the abstract structural design of the book."

Bleak eyed him guardedly. "A '*Bildungsroman*,' eh? And do you see nothing antithetical, dear boy, in 'pre-planning' such a novel?"

"Certainly not, sir," Hack answered with calm certainty. "I find it no more contradictory to subject a book—any kind of book—to standardized production methods than any other consumer product. No one complains about his car being pre-designed—why should he object to it in a book?" He smiled archly. "Maybe what we need are novels with bucket seats."

Bleak looked shocked. "But my dear fellow, a book is a genuine creative work, not to be equated with a product manufactured for profit. Profits are the pursuit of commerce, not of the arts."

"But in a free enterprise society," Hack countered, "profit-making is a perfectly legitimate endeavor for everyone—artist and artisan alike. One might even call it the bulwark, in our competitive system, of democratic principles. As Calvin Coolidge said, 'The business of America is business.'" He paused like a marksman taking aim. "In essence, Mr. Bleak, putting out books that *sell*, as opposed to books of quality or significance, is actually the more *American* thing to do."

"You gotta sell, Bleak," Manny put in earnestly, "or the public'll think you're a Commie."

Bleak snapped his head back, as if deflecting a blow. "But we have our reputation . . ."

" 'Reputation,' " Hack quoted, " 'is an idle and most false imposition; oft got without merit, and lost without deserving.' "

". . . not to mention our responsibility to the public . . ."

"Your responsibility to the public, if I may say so, sir," Hack retorted, gathering steam, "is to *reach* them. A good book, as we both know, is seldom read by anyone except the author. But there are millions of people out there beyond the gates"—he pointed out Bleak's huge, dingy window—"who must be served. *This* is the kind of book they read, and Mrs. Ehrlich is the kind of author they acclaim."

"But we've always taken the high road . . ."

"*Damn* the high road," Hack responded fervidly. He took a step closer to Bleak and adopted a pleading, compassionate tone. "Please, sir, I have only your interests at heart. You gave me my start as a writer and now I want to repay you—to save you—if I can. In this spirit I ask you, why should you cling stubbornly to the high road, a pathetic and lonely figure, while all around you the Shmeers are dancing in fields of gold?"

A tear of self-pity glistened in Bleak's eye, and he brushed it away with his finger.

"How much better it would be," Hack went on relentlessly, "for *you* to be reaping the big money harvest and plowing the profits into, let's say, the 'Bleak Foundation for Impoverished Poets.' "

Bleak nodded, a rapt expression on his face. "Yes . . . yes . . . the Robin Hood of the book business."

"And I ask you now, sir, this one last question," Hack said, coming full circle as he entered his final plea. "How are we to know that the purely commercial book may not, at the same time, be a genuine work of art? Or may not achieve greatness with the respectability of success?" His voice rose to an impassioned pitch. "The scorn of the critics will blow away like chaff, and today's pop novelists—Harold Robbins, Irving Wallace, Irving Shulman, Bonnie Ehrlich . . . and Percy Hack—pioneers in a brave new genre that dares to portray reality without artifice or art—may yet become the Faulkners and the Steinbecks of tomorrow. And their books, once dismissed as pornographic trash, may yet stand in history as classics."

"My God," Bleak gasped, utterly beside himself, *"yours may be the first dirty book to win the Nobel Prize!"*

Slowly, as in a trance, he got to his feet and held out his hand to Hack. "My son, Bleak House is honored to have you —and Mrs. Ehrlich—with us."

When the hubbub of congratulations had died down and tranquillity had been restored, Manny could be seen seated beside Bleak's desk, earnestly explaining a brochure to him. "Now you see, this here," he was saying, "is called a 'Runaway Blockbuster.' It's first class, and that's the kind we're gonna do." He stopped for a moment and looked up from the brochure. "Oh, by the way, you'll hafta get yourself a couple of machines."

"Machines?" Bleak stared at him. "What kind of machines, my good man?"

"Computers. You know, Univacs and stuff." Manny smiled knowingly. "For this kind of book they got editors beat a mile."

Bleak began to sputter. "But I . . . I . . ."

"Don't worry," Manny laughed, "I'll underwrite 'em and you can pay me back from the profits." He turned back to the brochure. "Now with the first class you get a guaranteed minimum of forty-eight . . ."

Bonnie, sitting alongside Hack now on a small, worn settee and gazing at him with fond admiration, said softly, "Percy, you were wonderful. Really marvelous. I never heard anything like it."

"I was just wondering," Flugelhorn piped up from his over-stuffed chair, "what do you think we ought to call it?"

Hack frowned, wrinkling his forehead in thought. "I don't know. Maybe we ought to try something hip this time, something with a Now sound, like . . . uh . . . *The Sex Bag*."

Flugelhorn shook his head. "That's no good," he said. "It sounds like a douche." He thought for a moment. "Maybe we can tie in the two themes—the TV thing and the transvestite bit—in a double entendre title like . . . oh, ah . . . *The Crossed Tube.*"

"Well . . . it's not bad," Hack said, "but they might think it's about transplants." He turned to Bonnie. "What do *you* think, Bonnie?"

He stared at her. ". . . Bonnie?"

But she was not answering. Her eyes were dreamily half-closed, and her head was tilted back, and she was far, far away —in a huge auditorium in Stockholm, Sweden. The King had just presented her with the Nobel Prize, and now, as she made her way up the carpeted stairs to the center stage, the audience rose en masse and applauded thunderously. She stood at the lectern, proud and regal in her St. Laurent see-through gown, and the tears streamed down her cheeks while the ovation rolled over her in a tidal wave of sound. Then the roaring stopped, and an unearthly stillness descended as that vast, resplendent sea of guests waited for her to begin her speech.

She glanced up at the loge, at the radiant faces of Manny, Flugelhorn, and Hack, and in a voice trembling with exultation, she began:

"Your Royal Highnesses, ladies and gentlemen. Today I am the happiest woman on the face of the earth . . ."